PRAISE FOR CB SAMET

"CB Samet is a master of the craft ..."

— READERS' FAVORITE REVIEW 2017

"CB Samet has a way of bringing you into the hair-raising suspense, keeping you at the edge of your seat."

— VORACIOUS READERS REVIEWER

"There is plenty of romance, intrigue, and drama in this book to keep the page turning."

— BOOKSPROUT REVIEWER

Award-winning author

GRAY HORIZON: 2019 Readers' Favorite bronze winner in thriller category

MASTERS FILE: 2018 Readers' Favorite honorable mention in romantic suspense category

THE AVANT CHAMPION ~Rising~: 2017 2nd place in fantasy EVVY Awards

BEST-SELLING AUTHOR in *Heroes with Heat and Heart Volume 2* and *Heroes with Heat and Heart Volume 3* Charity Anthologies

MERIDIAN FILE

THE RIDER FILES, BOOK 1

CB SAMET

AVANTSTAR PUBLISHING

For my many friends and coaches
past and present who enjoy the game

FREE EBOOK WITH NEWSLETTER SIGNUP

In the bustling streets of a sprawling Atlanta metropolis, where shadows dance and danger lurks around every corner, an unlikely love story unfolds amidst the web of a gripping romantic suspense thriller.

When the notorious Chinese mafia sets its sights on tightening its grip over the city's underworld, chaos ensues. As the danger escalates, a resilient female cop, Diz Ocana, finds herself thrust into the heart of her friend's kidnapping.

Meanwhile, skilled and compassionate paramedic Rico Cabrera, has dedicated his life to saving others. Growing up in the same neighborhood as Diz, he knows firsthand the darkness that plagues their city. Fate reunites them, kindling a connection that defies the boundaries of their respective roles.

*~~~***<<<SIGN UP HERE>>>***~~~*

Avant Star Publishing, LLC

Cover Art: CirceCorp design

(circecorpdesign.com)

ISBN ebook: 978-1-54391-333-0

ISBN print: 978-1-7324525-4-1

CHAPTER 1

Tennis kept Aurora's mind from dwelling on the death threats. She sprinted forward for a low drop shot. Bending her knees, she sliced under the ball and watched it sail back over the net with a wicked spin.

Her opponent backpedaled and hit a defensive lob.

Perfect.

Stretching high, she spiked the ball hard. It whipped past her opponent after striking the back corner of the service box.

The crowd gave an enthusiastic coo.

Aurora pumped a fist as she walked to the back of the court and accepted another ball. She ran the toe of her shoe along the white service line, brushing aside red clay. The clay courts at Park Manzanares provided good preparation for her upcoming matches at Roland-Garros. Paris was the next grand slam.

Forty-love.

She tuned out the murmuring of spectators. Bouncing the ball twice, she exhaled slowly.

Jupiter has sixty-seven moons.

She leaned back, arms extended forward.

The speed of light is one hundred eighty-six thousand miles per second.

Gracefully, she bent her knees.

Hawaii, Ireland, Greenland, Antarctica, Iceland, and New Zealand have no snakes.

She paused for a second before the motions to serve.

Sync.

Aurora took her racket down and rocked back. Shifting her weight forward, she tossed the ball. Her tall, slender body fully extended as she brought the racket through in one smooth motion.

Ace.

A wide smile broke across her face as the small crowd clapped wildly. She gave a victory wave to the fans.

Game. Set. Match.

A win.

One-third into the season and she was off to good start. This was the year.

Her year.

She could feel it.

The threats in the mail had escalated because she was becoming a force with which to be reckoned. Perhaps they were a normal consequence of approaching celebrity status.

She shook hands with her opponent over the net—a Canadian who was ranked thirty spots higher than Aurora. She'd played to the other woman's backhand as strategically planned. The woman's forehand power and accuracy were deadly. Aurora's own forehand was respectable but not as powerful. Her strength resided in finesse, but she had been working on improving her power.

Ice. Need ice.

Her ankle begged for relief. What had begun early in the match as a dull ache had progressed to a stabbing pain.

While exiting the court, she signed a handful of autographs. A man in sunglasses held her gaze a beat too long. She looked away first and shook off the unease.

With deliberate effort, she avoided the appearance of limping as she made her way with her tennis bag to the women's locker room. The media didn't need fodder to start broadcasting her weakness.

Out of the shadows emerged a tall, lean figure.

Aurora caught her breath, her heart quickening. "Dr. Ruchkin. Oh my gosh. You almost gave me a heart attack."

The aging physician flicked strands of black hair intermixed with white streaks from his face. "My apologies, Miss Meridian." His low, deep voice with its rich Russian accent echoed in the small corridor. He bowed slightly. "I saw your match had concluded, and I thought I would see if you are in need of my services. How is your ankle?"

"Fine," she snapped.

She'd been edgy since receiving the death threats. He shouldn't be lurking in shadows like a predator.

"I have treatment options beyond ice and salves," he offered leisurely.

"No, thanks."

She knew he was talking about steroids or even growth hormones. He had preached the advantages of building her muscle mass for a stronger game and to prevent injury—something about lame horses and weak ankles. Some players on tour partook of enhancements, but Aurora was leery of putting anything in her body designed to alter its natural composition.

Not sure if that makes me old-fashioned or new age.

Mason Stone sipped his cup of black coffee and looked calmly at Maxine Rider.

She scrubbed a pudgy hand across her face. "I want you to keep a low profile until this blows over."

"Fine. But I'm not accepting probation. None of this goes in my file because I didn't do anything wrong."

I did my job.

His boss looked around the small coffee shop before dropping her eyes to her cappuccino. "I know, Mason."

"She was high." He tried to suppress the steam on his simmering temper.

"I already know that. I know it's bullshit, and that's why I'm not grounding you. Just moving you to a low-key case. Very dull."

"No high-profile celebrities?"

"No."

"Good," he said gruffly. He disdained working for spoiled, entitled, twenty-two-going-on-sixteen brats with daddy issues and unlimited access to illicit drugs to self-medicate into raging lunatics or comatose corpses. He'd seen enough broken edges behind glossy magazine covers to know fame didn't protect anyone, but he was at the limits of what he'd tolerate.

He had been a Navy SEAL, and babysitting was beneath him.

Maxine slid her tablet over to him. He savored another sip of coffee before thumbing through the electronic file. His eyes roamed the pages.

He grunted. "Death threats?"

"Yeah, she's a low-ranking tennis player on the circuit—WTA. Probably nothing. The FBI is investigating the letters. Her parents have hired us as security while she's on tour."

Women's tennis professional. He scanned the profile. Professional athlete or not, she could just as easily be on the party scene like the singer from his last case.

His eyes fell on her date of birth. "Old for a tennis player."

"She finished college at age twenty-two before going on the pro tour. She's been playing all her life. Apparently she was almost somebody six years ago."

"And then?"

Maxine shrugged. "And then she wasn't."

Mason swiped the page to a collage of pictures. Aurora Mercedes Meridian. A lean, fit, blond woman with piercing green eyes stared back at him. Her sun-kissed skin shone radiantly against a white tennis dress. The younger photo of her displayed sharp angles, accentuated by hair pulled severely back in a ponytail. In a more recent photo she seemed softer, more curves. Her blue gown flowed around her like liquid sapphire, while her blond hair cascaded in ringlets down bare, tan shoulders.

Must be high maintenance, especially with a middle name like Mercedes.

Skimming the file, he followed the money. The parents. They were financial giants, owning vineyards and restaurants along the West Coast.

He swiped backward to the most recent photo. There was something in her eyes—not the polished shine of a celebrity trained to pose, but a glint of ... hurt maybe? Except she didn't look fragile. She had a lot of fight left in her.

So who mailed Aurora Meridian the hate letters? Someone after her, or someone after her parents?

"Mason," Maxine warned. "I know that look. I'm not asking you to solve the client's problem. You just need to keep her safe until it blows over or the Feds solve it."

He nodded absently.

She leaned forward and put a hand on the tablet's screen, obstructing his view.

"Mason," she repeated.

"Yes, boss." He looked up, staring past her with a neutral face.

"Low profile."

"Got it."

He shifted his gaze and looked at Maxine. She was a thick, older woman, but there was nothing soft about her. As a former Marine, she had acquired a decisive and fearless nature. Maxine had the contacts to hire quality help—former SEALs, Special Forces, and Rangers. She put together good teams. It was no secret Maxine had sunk her entire savings into her security company. She prided herself on never losing a client or an employee.

Now, thanks to him, she faced the possibility of public disgrace. Instead of taking the easy road—firing him to save face—she stood by his innocence. The accusations angered him, but the guilt he felt at what he was putting Maxine through crushed him. He wouldn't resign, though. He wouldn't allow anyone to have that type of power over him.

"And, Mason?"

"Boss?"

"Get a haircut. You look like a blond puppy dog."

He ran a hand through his long hair. He'd grown it out to blend in at the rock scene. His last client had told him he looked like a hit man when it was military short.

"Aw, Max. I didn't know you cared."

"I don't," she lied.

His gaze wandered to the novel she had been reading while she waited for him to arrive. He caught a glimpse of a shirtless man wearing jeans and a cowboy hat before she flipped the book over and put a hand on top. He looked into her glaring eyes.

"Does she get the guy?" he asked with a wry grin.

Maxine was a sucker for romance novels—one of her many quirks. She had confessed one night at a company party after a few drinks that a book wouldn't cheat, lie, or steal. As such, she had decided it would be her only source of trustworthy romance.

No one on the team knew all of the details, but they had pieced together that her husband had left her when she served in Afghanistan and her son David had blamed her. They were still estranged.

"Book your flight," she said, ignoring his question. "The client's in Madrid at a tournament. You're joining Billy and Dorian. I'm swapping you and Barry."

Mason grunted. Barry's age and balding head would deter any sexual advancement. He could better handle the rock brat from Mason's last job without entangled accusations.

"I gotta book my own flight?" he asked.

"I ain't your damn secretary," Maxine scoffed. "When you earn enough money to pay part of my secretary's salary or pension or health care, then she'll book your tickets. Until such time, put on your big boy pants and book your own damn flight."

He enjoyed riling her.

"Economy class," she reminded him.

"Yes, boss." He envisioned his long legs on the overseas flight with his knees bent up to his chest in a tiny seat. International travel packed like a sardine.

———❦———

AURORA SANK into the warm bathwater and closed her eyes. She replayed points from her tennis match in her mind, critiquing her movements and strokes as she thought about how to improve her strategy. She would watch videos later, coaching herself on what she should do differently next time.

Better movement. More fluidity. "Wheels up, Aurora," her dad would tell her when she was a little girl. She imagined herself as a young girl, flying across the court. Sometimes her body felt airborne, at least prior to her injury.

Coach Jareh would tell her "fast feet, fast feet." She missed having a professional coach, but a tight budget prevented such luxuries. She'd been playing and critiquing herself long enough that she usually knew what parts of her game needed improvement and the mechanics of how to improve them. Still, an observant eye could help guide her.

Her muscles relaxed as the eucalyptus-scented salts dissolved in the water. Closing her eyes, she wanted to bask in the glory of her win today.

When she opened her eyes a few moments later, she found herself staring at her red-painted toenails. Blood red. Her pulse quickened as she recalled the threats she'd been receiving. Her stalker had said, among other horrible things, that she would die in a pool of her own blood. Death threats. Letters—old-fashioned ones with cut and pasted words. Nothing electronically traceable.

Aurora's mouth went dry as her imagination turned her bathwater red. She swallowed and blinked. Normal, clear water surrounded her.

Taking a deep breath of eucalyptus, she reminded herself that a team of bodyguards hovered one door down from her locked hotel room. They escorted her to and from every match and stood vigilant as she played. They assured her they would keep her safe.

Meanwhile, the FBI worked diligently to find the stalker.

Besides, she wasn't a helpless victim. No easy target. She embodied strength as a fit athlete with a wicked serve. She could put up a fight. Could she win? But could she win—walk away—without a career-ending injury?

When she exited the bathtub and dried off, she scrubbed the color off her toenails. The sharp scent of acetone replaced the fragrant eucalyptus.

Pinks and peaches only.

No more red. Not on her body. Not anywhere near it.

CHAPTER 2

Mason knocked three times on the hotel room door before it opened a crack.

"Billy," he greeted his coworker.

"Mason," the short woman replied. She opened the door wider and snapped her black bob cut out of her eyes with a quick motion of her neck.

He entered, pulling his luggage behind him.

"How's it been?" He took a seat in the hotel room's lounge chair. He'd walked most of the kinks out of his legs since the plane flight—flights—but still needed to do some lingering stretches. In lieu of that, he rolled his neck in circles a few times.

"Good. Quiet." Billy knew he wasn't asking about the weather; he was asking about the client. "Full three-agent team for tournaments. Two for most outings."

"Quiet. I like the sound of that."

"It'll be a nice change from the brat you've been babysitting. Don't get me wrong, this one's still a princess, but without the drugs and nightlife."

Mason nodded solemnly.

Billy spoke again as she sat on the edge of the bed, her voice dropping an octave. "I'm sorry, man. Max told me about the shit that went down."

"Yeah." He ran a hand through his now shorter hair. He still left a little more length than usual.

"It'll blow over."

"Yeah," he agreed half-heartedly.

Billy was a quality partner, and he appreciated her letting him know upfront she knew he was innocent. It freed him from feeling like he would have to talk about the incident or explain the circumstances.

Her lips quirked. "It's those baby blue eyes, you know. They'll get you into trouble every time."

He arched an eyebrow at her.

"Not with me, of course. I like brains over beauty. But flighty girls can't control themselves."

"Funny," he said flatly.

Billy snorted at her own humor before changing the subject. "The exercise routine is pretty intense."

"Oh?"

"Aurora likes to run, and despite the fact that every hotel has a perfectly functioning treadmill, she likes to run outside."

He smiled mischievously. "How'd that work out for Barry?" Mason had no doubt Billy could keep up with the client, she was a tight ball of muscle. But Barry—

"Bike."

"Huh."

"Well, technically it was an electric scooter."

"Ah. That makes more sense."

Barry was a tough brute with lightning fast reflexes, a deadly right hook, and good aim with a Smith & Wesson, but a runner he was not. His scrawny legs couldn't move his large abdomen at anything resembling a brisk walk, much less a run.

"Where's the asset now?"

"Her room. Across the hall."

"And Dorian?"

"One down from here. You're with him. We've got a door cam set up outside her room. Window is sealed, and there's no balcony. Fire exits are located at either end of the hall, keycard entry only."

"Thanks, Billy. I'll go introduce myself."

"Mason?"

"Yeah?"

"Fair warning. Whatever you do, don't call her Prime."

He frowned. "I thought Prime was her big tennis nickname." He recalled the headlines he had read during his Internet research about her.

PRIME MERIDIAN IN LINE TO CONQUER THE FRENCH OPEN.

CAN PRIME MAKE IT PRIME TIME?

AURORA MERIDIAN IS PRIMED TO WIN.

Billy grunted. "Sure. When she was almost somebody. Then, with the ankle injury, she hit bottom. Now, I think it's just a reminder of what she never was."

⁂

AURORA BLINKED at the tall bodyguard standing before her. She had been notified of the change, but was not prepared for how different Barry's replacement would be.

"Miss Meridian, I wanted to introduce myself. I'm Mason Stone. I'll be taking the place of Barry Howell."

His blue eyes and wavy blond hair made him look like something out of Norse mythology. She instantly grew annoyed at her body's response—dry mouth, flushed cheeks. She turned away from the open door and busied herself folding her clothes.

She heard the bodyguard step inside the hotel room and close the door.

"They told me Barry was being replaced. Something about a high-profile case, so I was like, 'Thanks for pointing out I'm not a high-profile case.' I'm somebody's sloppy seconds—very fitting, I think. But I'm not footing the bill, so it's not as though I can do anything about it. In fact, I'm going to be quiet about it, because I'm grateful my parents are providing Rider services. I have felt safe with all of you. I don't want to seem ungrateful." She pursed her lips.

Rambling. I'm actually rambling like an idiot.

"Miss Meridian—"

"Aurora, please." She turned and looked at him pointedly. He couldn't be much older than she. She did not want formal names. She was a tennis player, not an executive.

"Miss Meridian, I assure you that you are as important as any other client we assist."

She narrowed her eyes at him, trying to decide if he spoke honest words or patronizing ones. Somehow it sounded sincere, but it couldn't be true.

Fine. He could call her Miss Meridian. It was better than Prime. Besides, if he continued to call her Miss Meridian, then her body wouldn't do foolish things, like flushing or rambling, when she saw those blue eyes.

"Barry was cuter," she stated matter-of-factly.

... and less distracting.

Mason smiled.

Whoa. Those eyes had no business being paired with that smile. She turned back to her folding.

"I've got your daily schedule. I'll take your morning routines during your workouts, Dorian after that, and then Billy. We'll keep the same full team for matches, two-man team for other outings—meals and whatnot."

Straight to business. She liked his approach.

She nodded. Far be it for her to micromanage their security detail. She felt relieved to have them.

She looked at him sidelong. "You read the letters?"

Mason's expression turned grim. "Some of them. Nasty threats."

Death threats. Horrible, descriptive death threats. Words carved out of magazines like someone had cut them straight from their own rage.

After the first half-dozen, she stopped reading them. Billy censored her mail now and passed along the threats to the FBI. Aurora used to receive about one threat a month. As far as she knew that was still the case.

"I stopped asking about them. I guess when they capture the maniac or the threats stop coming, then your team will let me know."

Mason frowned.

"You disapprove?" She moved to the kitchenette and placed a mug of water in the microwave to heat.

"No."

For someone in security and protection, he wasn't a good liar. "Then what?"

He pursed his lips before speaking. "You may consider looking through them again."

Aurora glared at him, heat rushing up her neck and into her face.

He continued, "The notes seemed quite personal, and there may be something in the syntax or verbiage that could give you a clue to the origin."

She swallowed hard. Her hands shook with anger. "You have no idea what it's like—to read how someone wants to kill you. To feel the hate seething from them. To have every shadow and sudden movement be terrifying."

"No, ma'am, I do not," he replied, though she sensed he did know fear.

His eyes flashed a look of pain and empathy. The effect deflated the building chastisement she readied to unleash.

Very calmly she added, "I'm playing the best tennis of my life right now, and I can't do that if I'm shaking with fear every time I step onto the court."

And this is it. My time is up.

If she didn't win now, she never would.

She fumbled with a tea bag, trying to open it to put it in her cup. She also knew the letters had appeared as she improved and made her comeback. Not a coincidence. She was winning. She was a contender. But who would go so far as to threaten bodily harm and even her life?

Her whole life had been built on precision, on controlling every swing, every breath. Fear was the one opponent she couldn't outplay—yet.

"I'm sorry I upset you." He took the tea bag from her shaking hands, gently opened it, and dropped it into her mug.

When she looked up at him, his posture stiffened but his expression radiated sincerity. She hated that he stood so close, not because she feared him, but because her pulse couldn't seem to choose between panic and...something far more dangerous.

She shrugged. "Easy to do on this particular topic. Maybe after the US Open I will, but not now. I can't look at them now."

"I understand."

Did he? How could he? How could anyone?

He turned his broad shoulders and walked back toward the door, reaching for the knob. "I'll see you in the morning," he said as he left.

As the door closed, she sighed and swirled the tea bag in the cup of warm water. The scent of orange spice rose into the air. She had definitely not been staring at the backside of him as he left. She definitely did not need any more distractions.

***

MASON UNPACKED HIS CLOTHES.

Dorian Chaplin sat in the hotel room's chair reading *Inferno*, the first part of Dante's *Divine Comedy*. He was an average-built man in his fifties with chestnut skin. His relaxed demeanor never betrayed his past as a former agent. Mason knew he was a British nationalist with Indian in his genealogy.

Mason had seen a portfolio of Dorian's many disguises. The man was a human chameleon. He could mold to all preconceived American stereotypes. With a mustache and accent, witnesses would claim he was Mexican. With a trimmed beard and a prayer bead bracelet, people assumed he was Muslim. Wearing a turban and a steel kara on his wrist, suddenly he was Sikh.

The mystery was, who had Dorian been an agent for in his previous career? Only Maxine Rider knew.

"What do you think of the asset?" Dorian looked up from his reading.

Career-endingly gorgeous. "She's a paycheck," Mason replied.

He knew such a callous statement would offend Dorian's refined sensibilities. However, after his last client debacle, he wanted to reassure his colleague such a thing was neither instigated by him nor in danger of repeating itself.

Since he had already managed to provoke Miss Meridian within the first five minutes of meeting her, he had probably thwarted any potential flirtatious behavior.

He felt remorse for upsetting her, but the inadvertent glimpse it gave him into her character seemed worth it. She was no damsel in distress. She was scared because—who wouldn't be? But she didn't crumble and fall apart thinking of the threats. She wasn't immobilized by fear, which might be the difference between life and death for her if this maniac ever came after her. With celebrities, stalkers often tried to make good on their threats.

Predictably, Dorian frowned. "I think she's somewhat lost. A salmon caught between the salt water she's always known and the fresh water she must swim through."

Mason shook his head as he hung up his suit pants and coat in the small hotel room closet. "Did you just compare the client to a fish traveling to lay eggs?"

Dorian shrugged. "Well, I would compare *your* last client to a pond-dwelling amoeba, so a fish is quite better."

Mason chuckled. He took his toiletry case to the bathroom and withdrew his toothbrush. "How's Katie?"

"She's well. Enjoying her career. Writing. We're both delighting in this newfound freedom called *empty nest*. Meanwhile Dia is traipsing around Europe in her gap year before college."

Mason smiled around his toothbrush. "How very British of her."

"Yes. Not sure if it's about exploring culture or just escaping obligations."

"What teenager doesn't want to delay obligations?"

"You didn't," Dorian said. "Straight into the military, wasn't it?"

Mason shook his head. Dorian knew his background but didn't share his own. Wouldn't or couldn't?

After toweling off his face, Mason said, "Enlisting was my way of delaying obligation. Once I enlisted, somebody else determined the course of the next several years of my life."

"Point taken."

"At least a gap year is a shorter and brighter path to delay commitment than enlisting." Mason took off his shoes and started to stretch.

"Mmm. Shorter, yes. But you and I both know the darker world lurking out there."

"My dark days were in the Middle East. And yours were in . . ."

Dorian only smiled.

Mason chuckled. "I'm sure Dia will be fine."

One of the door cams blinked red. Motion. For a breath, Mason wondered if it was their threat—until Dorian's voice murmured, "Just a housekeeper."

CHAPTER 3

$\mathcal{M}$ason woke at quarter to five and dressed in his exercise clothes. He splashed cold water on his face to try to dispel the jet lag. As the new guy on the job, he had been assigned to Aurora Meridian's early morning routine. He didn't mind. Exercise had been difficult on his last job with so many late nights. His focus sharpened when he was able to work out routinely.

He slipped on his earpiece and left Dorian sleeping as he exited the hotel room.

At five in the morning when Aurora opened her hotel door, Mason stood in the hallway, waiting for her.

She blinked at him. "Timely."

He lifted his sunglasses to look at her.

"If you cut your hair shorter, you'd look like a thinner terminator in those shades," she said, slipping on her own sunglasses, which were a futuristic version of a wraparound eye shield.

An inadvertent quirk escaped his lips.

She sighed. "I know. Cat, meet kettle. Laugh it up, big guy. My sponsor requires I wear these in public."

They walked toward the elevator as he dropped his sunglasses back on his nose.

"You get paid to wear sunglasses?"

"I get paid to wear ugly sunglasses that make me look like a cyclops," she clarified, but there was amusement in her voice overlaying the irritation.

Mason suppressed a laugh but didn't dispute her statement. Her hair was pulled severely back in a ponytail and the dark wraparound bands accentuated some of the sharper angles in her face, shoulders, and arms.

More cyborg than cyclops, he thought.

As they exited the hotel, Aurora wasted no time starting her jog. He fell in beside her, matching her pace.

The air wafted with the scent of baking churros and steaming espresso. Spanish bluebells and red carnations adorned the storefronts.

Aurora picked up speed after the first half mile. Mason fell a few paces behind her. From this vantage point, he could see nothing but curves.

Focus, you moron. He picked up his chin to resume surveillance of the surroundings.

A delivery truck rumbled too close to the curb, and Mason subtly shifted his body between Aurora and the street. Reflex, not flirting — and Aurora gave him a grateful nod.

After a five-mile loop, Aurora slowed to a walk, and Mason caught his breath. She labored a bit to breathe as well, and he suspected she had pushed hard to test him.

Not a problem. He would accept a physical challenge any day. Already he liked this job. Well, he liked the moments when she wasn't smiling or trying to be friendly. Uncomfortable moments. He needed to guard against too much familiarity. Last time, a false accusation had nearly destroyed his career. He didn't intend to give anyone that chance again.

He escorted her to the gym where he inspected the room. One entrance/exit point. With keycard access only, he didn't have to worry about a non-guest gaining easy entry.

He spoke to Billy in his earpiece. "Billy?"

"What's your twenty?" she asked.

"Hotel gym. All is good."

"Copy."

Aurora began a series of stretches.

Mason watched the door.

"You should stretch after a five-mile run," Aurora commented.

He looked around the empty room and nodded. Staying near the door, he began a series of hamstring, quadriceps, and lower back stretches.

She had taken her sunglasses off, but he left his on over his eyes. Because she seemed to think the glasses made him unapproachable or intimidating, leaving them on would maintain the appropriate professional distance. Unfortunately he could tell she wasn't looking at his face as he stretched.

She finally seemed to notice she was staring at him. Her expression became one of annoyance as she selected a nearby weight machine for strength training, facing away from him.

Annoyance at him or herself? It didn't matter. If she felt any physical attraction toward him, she obviously had no intention of entertaining it.

AURORA DRESSED and dried her hair after a shower. She opened her laptop to work alone in her room when her phone rang.

She clicked it on speakerphone. "Mrs. Rider?"

"Please, just Maxine. I am checking in on you since I changed your team." Her gravelly voice came crisply through the phone.

After the first time she'd talked to Maxine Rider on the phone, Aurora had to try to find what the woman looked like. Her company website didn't have photos of her or any employees. An internet search turned up an old Marine photo, but Aurora suspected the woman, now in her fifties with a rough voice and direct speech, no longer looked like the rosy-cheeked, bright-eyed girl in her twenties.

"Yes, I met Mason Stone. He seems . . ." she struggled. "Gruff. No, stoic."

The word felt too clinical for him; she suspected the emotions were there, just buried deep,

Stony on the outside. Stormy on the inside.

"Long flight," Maxine suggested in a tone that indicated she catalogued rather than dismissed Aurora's observation.

"Of course."

"Team dynamics may change, but protocols won't. The important thing is you feel safe at all times. Stoic Mason is very good and quite analytical despite being a man of few words . . . and an occasional pain in my ass."

Aurora stifled a laugh. Was a woman of Maxine's position supposed to be so blunt? Aurora had only spoken with Maxine a few times, but she always got to the point, embellishing only with a few choice curse words.

"I feel safe," Aurora assured her. "But I don't foot the bill. Don't you want to talk to my parents?"

Maxine grunted. "Honey, you're who we're protecting, so your opinion about how safe you feel is the opinion that counts."

"I feel protected. A little caged, but safe."

"You're winning."

Aurora smiled as she shaded in the leaves of a rose she was designing on her laptop. "I am, aren't I?"

"Keep kicking ass."

"I fully intend to."

"You've got my number if you need anything."

"Yep."

"Even if you need me to adjust any members of your team."

Aurora tried to imagine how the tough, former Marine went about *adjusting* her employees. "Yes."

When she hung up the phone, a knock sounded at the door.

"It's Mason. If you're on the phone, I can come back."

Aurora opened the door. "It's okay. Maxine called."

As Mason entered the room, it seemed to shrink in size with his presence, warm and solid.

"Max called you?" his voice filled with pure astonishment.

She walked back to her computer to save her work. "She said she was checking up on you. Wanted to know if you're behaving."

His face drained of color as his Adam's apple bobbed in a nervous swallow.

"I'm kidding," Aurora said.

Wow, Maxine ran a tight ship. The former Navy SEAL quaked in his boots.

"She called to ask how *I* am," Aurora explained.

His stiff posture relaxed only slightly. "Max called you," he repeated himself.

"Is that so strange?" She lifted her tea mug up and took a sip.

Ugh. Cold.

She set it back down on the table.

"She doesn't usually call clients beyond the initial interview and team installation." He picked up her mug and carried it to the kitchenette where he stuck it in the microwave.

Aurora could see Mason's mind churning. He seemed worried their conversation had been about him. Was he in some kind of trouble?

"She told me once she has a son my age. Maybe she likes me."

"She must," he agreed, his tone still baffling her.

"You're so surprised she would chat with me?"

"Chat and Max have never been used in the same sentence before this moment. I am surprised she would chat with anyone."

"Tough women need friends, too."

Mason gave her a considerate look as though contemplating if she referred to Maxine or herself.

Probably both.

He brought her warmed mug of tea out of the microwave and handed it to her.

She accepted and sipped.

"Did you design that? It's beautiful."

She glanced back at the unfinished digital rose. More shading would create the appearance of light shining from the side.

"Post-professional tennis career plan. We can't all make a hundred million in prize money like Djokovic."

"I guess the rest of the world doesn't reflect much on second careers of professional athletes."

"Well, if you're a Williams, Sharapova, Clijsters, Graf, or Davenport, then you'd make enough prize money that your second career can be an afterthought. The rest of us have to make plans."

"Your plans are graphic design?"

Although he asked, she suspected he already knew.

"I want to run my own design company someday." She sipped her tea.

"You have your parents' ambition," he observed with a twinkle in his eye.

"Some tennis professionals go on to coach, others become commentators, and others model. Some extend their tennis careers to the senior tour. Others are entrepreneurs."

"It seems you would be able to do any of those."

Surely he didn't know her well enough to know the expansiveness of her capabilities. However, he made the statement with such authority that she wondered how much information resided in a Rider SI client profile. She recalled signing a waiver about them invading her personal privacy. Anything electronically stored would be explored. Basically, that was her whole life.

Mason seemed to appraise her, as though considering each of those career choices for her.

Heat crept into her cheeks, thinking of him imagining her as a model.

He straightened as though he suddenly realized he had been too freely conversing. The tone of the conversation had been casual, but his body language now conveyed they were finished.

She set down her tea cup. "I assume you didn't come to warm me up—to warm up my tea."

Ugh. Freudian slip.

His ears reddened as he cleared his throat. "I want to review your schedule tomorrow. You've got tennis practice. Billy suggested you might want to grab a nice lunch after practice."

"Oh! Cafe Melo's. They have this huge sandwich called a *zapatilla*. It feeds two people, and it's so good. And it's in my budget." She hesitated. "There is usually a long wait, though."

"I'll stay for practice, and Billy can pick up takeout. We don't want to take you into a crowd."

She nodded, curbing her disappointment. The atmosphere of quaint and popular local spots was part of the allure, but she would have to trust the experts.

Safety trumps fresh zapatillas.

WITH THE SCHEDULE REVIEWED, Aurora watched Mason leave. This time she didn't stare at his backside... for quite as long. The small hotel room inflated large and too quiet without his presence.

She called her friend, Monique Johnson.

"Mercedes, it's the middle of the night over here."

"And you work the ER night shift, so suck it up, MoJo."

Her friend sighed. Aurora wasn't sure if the exasperated noise stemmed from her comment or the nickname MoJo, which she didn't love. She'd used Aurora's middle name, though, so she'd ask for it.

"Slow night?"

"Yeah."

She knew the nurse practitioner liked to stay busy. Slow nights were agonizing for her.

The women had met at the Mid-Atlantic Women's Tennis Championship in D.C. several years ago. At the time, Mo was attending school to become a nurse practitioner and had been doing volunteer work as a medic at the tennis matches. Aurora had needed a rewrap on her ankle. They struck up a friendship. Mo was the first friend she had made after her fall from near success. She was the only person who had never known the blonde, brat tennis queen—*Prime Meridian*.

Aurora had explained to Mo that after her ankle injury she

applied for protected leave for her injury. She came back the following year, which had probably been too soon. Her ranking in the Women's Tennis Association plummeted. Mo had faith Aurora would fight her way back to the top.

Unfortunately, Mo's current career had her confined to the bowels of a New York emergency room, so they mostly kept in touch by phone and text.

"How's life with bodyguards?"

"Confining."

Mo let out a chirrup.

"What about that one guy, Baldy? Is he still on a motorized bike to keep up with your run?" She chuckled as though envisioning the scene.

"I got an upgrade."

"Mysterious much? Do go on."

"He can keep up."

"Your tone implies he can keep up with more than just a run."

Aurora sighed. "I bet he could."

"Oh, really?"

Had she said that aloud?

She swallowed and tried to keep her voice neutral. "Well, he's former Navy SEAL. He makes me feel...protected," she admitted softly. "Which is ridiculous, because that's literally his job."

"Playing with fire to have a crush on your SEAL bodyguard," Monique observed.

"It's not a crush, and I would never—"

"I know you wouldn't." Her interruption conveyed disappointment rather than admiration of character.

"What is that supposed to mean?"

"It means you're a sexy woman in her prime who has closed herself off from men and hasn't dated since the Fisk fiasco. So, I know you wouldn't do something as carefree and reckless and cathartic as date your bodyguard."

Aurora bit her lip to remain silent. Compliments and insults were so woven into her friend's words that she didn't know how to respond.

"How is your night going?" Aurora asked, hearing the sound of fingers on keyboards and hospital machines beeping in the background.

"I'm staring at an x-ray of woman who inhaled a pushpin."

"That sounds awful."

"She was tacking up a poster in her daughter's room with the pushpin between her teeth. She laughed at something her daughter did and whoosh—down the trachea and into the right lower lobe it went."

Aurora's mouth gaped open. "Oh my gosh. I put bobby-pins between my teeth all the time when I'm fixing my hair."

"The dangers we never consider," Mo said sagely.

Aurora gasped. "What are you going to do about it?"

"I need to arrange transport to Beth Israel. They have interventional pulmonologists who can fish it out of her lungs."

"What if they can't get it out?"

Mo's tone turned grim. "Lobectomy. That means surgically removing a lobe of her lung."

"Surgery for a pushpin?"

"Hold on a sec, let me take this call from the ICU intensivist."

A pause was followed by Monique talking to someone else on another line. "Fifty-four-year-old with pneumonia and ARDS. Hemodynamically stable. I'm having trouble with oxygen despite generous amounts of sedatives and analgesics. You okay with paralytics — cisatracurium?"

Another pause.

"Of course. Sedatives with cisatricurium. Okay. Bye."

Mo gave a tsk of irritation. "Sorry. I'm back," she told Aurora.

"What's ARDS?" Aurora had no interest in joining the medical workforce, but she loved listening to Mo's stories.

"Adult respiratory distress syndrome—ARDS—is a severe form of acute lung disease. It has a high mortality rate—especially if I can't adequately oxygenate him. Regardless of the many causes of ARDS, when it's so severe that the patient has low oxygen levels despite life support on a breathing machine, I have to use heavy sedation to keep the patient's body and the ventilator synchronous. If those efforts don't improve oxygenation, I have to paralyze the patient eliminate all voluntary muscle movement, thus reducing extraneous oxygen consumption to conserve it for vital organs."

"So, why did you sound irritated with the doctor?"

"He told me to be sure to keep the sedatives going when I start the paralytics. Of course I'll keep the sedatives going. No self-respecting medical professional would infuse paralytics without sedatives. Such an oversight could mentally traumatize someone."

"Yikes." Aurora shuddered as she thought of being rendered immobile and subjected to life support with no medication to blunt the discomfort and intrusiveness of the procedure.

"Anyway. You found my hot tennis toy yet?" Monique said.

"Um ..."

"Honey, my future husband may be out there on your tour. I'm counting on you to set something up."

"Right. When I'm not up at 5:00 a.m. running or doing yoga, when I'm not playing tennis, and when I'm not hiding out in my hotel from death threats, I will work on finding your future husband."

They joked about it, but Monique had lamented to her on more than one occasion the difficulty in finding a romantic match as a professional black woman who also worked the night shift.

Monique gave a tsk. "I know you're sightseeing and lounging in cafes. You can make time for me."

"I promise to hone my matchmaking skills."

"That's more like it. Now, I gotta go. I've got a couple of critical patients to check on."

After the call ended, the room felt too quiet again. Too still. She checked the deadbolt twice before focusing back on her digital artwork.

CHAPTER 4

The woman cursed as she sat hunched over a desk. The damn glue kept sticking to her gloves. She had to wear gloves because any *pridurok* knew crime detectives would test the letters for DNA. She knew that from American TV shows. What she hadn't known was that some gloves were filled with talc powder, which made a mess of her manicured hands. Also, the gloves stuck to the glue, making the process of adhering the letters to the paper more cumbersome.

Nevertheless, designing and creating the letters gave her a sense of accomplishment. She felt like she was playing in art class. Instead of painting or sewing, she forged letters.

Lovely little notes for lovely little Aurora. California girl with her California tan. Hadn't those American Beach Boys wished we could all be California girls?

She rolled her eyes.

Smeshnoy. Ridiculous.

She gazed at her latest composition. She grinned with satisfaction, imagining a frightened Aurora, shaking with the letter in her hand. The little brat just needed a nudge—a reason to lose. The threats were hollow, of course, but Aurora wouldn't know that. Once she quit tennis, the letters would stop. Then, the wine heiress could go back to her boring, simple life.

Alone.

The threats were hollow, of course. She wasn't *actually* going to hurt Aurora.

Not yet.

A shiver of excitement ran down her spine, and she forced it away.

Lights out, Aurora Borealis.

MASON ACCOMPANIED Aurora on a lighter routine. After sunrise yoga in the park, they went back to the hotel gym for lower body weights.

The morning yoga had been peaceful as the sun slowly crept over the horizon. There were so few people out at that hour, keeping the perimeter clear was easy. He mostly walked in circles around the park, scanning for threats and occasionally glancing back at Aurora.

Now they were confined to the gym, alone together again. He busied himself with weights as well, but thought casual conversation would break the silent tension he felt after watching her bend and lean and stretch all morning.

"How young were you when you started tennis?" he asked.

"I'm told I picked up my first racquet at three. Lessons started at five."

"Did you always know it would be a career?"

She adjusted weights on the machine and started new repetitions. "Early on my parents pushed pretty hard. I think they saw talent and latched on without thinking of the consequences."

"Consequences?" He frowned.

Her green eyes saddened. "A little girl training all day and not having normal playtime and normal playdates." She looked at Mason and then smiled mischievously. "By the time they'd realized what they'd done—the monster they created—I craved the win. I had to have it. I had to mow down the competition. They stopped pushing me, but it didn't matter because I kept pushing myself."

Mason swallowed hard, as memories of driving himself to be physically harder and intellectually better flooded his mind. He'd been consumed with self-driven egomania in his twenties. He'd been indifferent to who he knocked down—or killed—on his mission to be a super-soldier.

Aurora continued, "I was a self-centered brat for a long time."

Mason's eyes crinkled in amusement.

"That's funny to you?" Her voice became tight.

He turned toward her unapologetically. "Only because I can relate. I spent most of my twenties trying to be better, faster, and smarter than all of the other soldiers."

"Makes for good medals, but not many friends."

He blinked at her. "Yes, exactly." For a moment, he saw the same ruthless ambition he'd once wielded reflected back at him.

She walked to a wall and started a low squat.

Mason backed up next to her. He slid down to her level, his back flush against the wall. He lowered himself another inch.

She cracked a smile and brought her back even with his.

His eyes sparkled with enjoyment.

"Still competitive much, soldier?" she asked.

"No more than you."

The minutes ticked by until their knees shook and the burning spread up and down the muscles in their legs.

"Truce?" Aurora grunted.

Mason nodded. He pushed himself off the wall and offered Aurora a hand to stand. She accepted and stood.

He watched her legs wobble unsteadily, so he held both her hands until she gave him a nod. Her fingers were smaller than his, but her grip was strong. Too easy to imagine what those hands felt like wrapped around his shoulders, pulling him closer—

Releasing her, he shut down his thoughts. He was a professional dammit. Taking a step back way from her took more effort than it should have.

They left the exercise room.

"Billy tells me you're a former Navy SEAL."

"Yes, ma'am."

"Did you like it?"

He pushed the elevator button. "I liked the challenge. I like knowing the things I did saved lives."

"And when your term ended, you went to work for Maxine?"

"Yes. I was a SEAL for six years. Total military time served was twelve years."

"Is that a standard service?"

"Service is variable. Some guys make a career from it after leaving, and others retire at the twenty- or thirty-year mark." Images of his friends filled his memories—brothers by bond, not blood. Some never had the chance to decide to stay military or go civilian. The ultimate sacrifice.

When his eyes focused back on Aurora, she shrunk into the elevator looking stricken.

Her voice flowed like a whisper on the wind. "I didn't mean to stir memories."

"It's okay." After he left the SEALs, the next year of his life was plagued with guilt. He'd finally relinquished his demons. He had ensured his stability was in check before returning to meaningful employment. Aurora needed to know a competent soldier protected her, not a wreck at the mercy of his past.

He eased his expression into a smile. "It's important to remember those who sacrificed themselves. Just because memories can be unpleasant for the living doesn't mean we eliminate them."

She appeared to relax at his words.

"Do you have friends who are in or out?"

"Both."

When the elevator doors opened, they walked down the hall to her room.

"Are others in private security?" She fidgeted with her key card.

"Some. Others contract with the government. A good friend of mine owns a gun range."

Too soon they returned to her room, and the conversation halted for him to perform his inspection.

He finished and dismissed himself.

AURORA FLOPPED onto her bed after her shower, thinking of Mason's friendly behavior and the way his warm, calloused hands had wrapped around hers when he'd steadied her trembling legs after the wall squats.

He was her bodyguard, not a friend. Not...anything else.

Her mind shifted to tomorrow's game. Quarterfinals. She hadn't gotten this far since her injury. For years she hadn't reached a major. She'd played in small-town America, sleeping in motels and gagging on what passed as a continental breakfast.

The international games were particularly costly with arduous travel, confusing airports, and languages she didn't know. Back at her career prime when she had big sponsors and money, a first-class plane flight followed by rented car ride to a first-class hotel passed seamlessly. Now, sometimes funds were so tight, she shared taxis and rooms with other tennis players, women united and struggling to rise to the next tier. Her pride prevented her from asking her parents for travel money.

She'd descended from arenas with thousands of spectators and internationally known sponsors to small, half-filled bleachers in events sponsored by the local bank or used car dealership.

Obscurity. Swallow that porcupine of a pill.

Initially life had been a lot of lonely nights, a lot of self-soothing. At least until she dispensed with the self-pity. Amidst those lonely nights, when she stopped moping long enough to perform detailed self-examination, she gained a new clarity.

She remembered what she'd been like during near stardom. She'd felt the unequivocal sensation she deserved to win. She'd worked, slaved day after day, and sacrificed everything when girls her age frolicked to movies, pursued advanced college degrees, or started families.

She deserved victory.

The reality, she understood later, was she was no different than the hundreds of young women tennis professionals killing themselves for the same prize. The brutal sport taxed the body to the extent most players were finished by age thirty—finished with their entire life's work and they still had two-thirds of their life left.

Everyone had to consider a backup plan—some had clothing lines, perfumes, or ties to acting. Others were ready to be full-time moms. Future plan development required a brave disposition because one had to admit one's entire identity was going to be scrapped, or at least relegated to a few plaques and trophies on a display case.

All of these women had to start from scratch—start anew. An inevitable new beginning to an inevitable ending. Everyone had to plan for the new beginning without ever knowing if the preceding end would be marked with glory or failure.

Aurora had a post-tennis plan now. Well, her graphic design business entailed a work in progress.

Her phone rang.

"Hi, Mom."

"Aurora, how is practice going?"

"Going well."

She sat up in bed and idly flipped through a stack of magazines Billy had brought her. "I've been working on your new wine label. Should be done this week."

The wine was a fruity zinfandel, and her mom had wanted a feminine label. Aurora experimented with a pink high heel, adding sparkling rhinestones.

Who doesn't drink fruity wine in six-inch pink heels?

Her mom launched into details of the marketing platform. Basically, she targeted lonely, thirty-year-old women. Did she stop to consider she was referring to her own daughter?

Aurora listened as she flipped through a fashion magazine. Her eyes froze on one of the clothing models.

Natasha Bodrov.

Lean and catlike, her long legs filled most of the page as she wore a skimpy black dress. Her full, red lips were pouting and unsmiling. She never smiled in any of the photos Aurora had seen. Because she didn't know how or because she lost all appearance of sensuality with a smile? Aurora liked to imagine Natasha's smile emerged more like a sneer, so the woman had to keep it contained.

A sneer would fit her personality. Aurora had learned through friends—reassuring her about her breakup with Jimmy Fisk—that Natasha behaved like an entitled tsarina, terrorizing everyone on the photo shoots. She treated her own agent like garbage. Surely, she would be no different toward Jimmy—a thought that made Aurora smile.

A match made in cold Siberian hell.

Seeing Natasha reminded her of the relationship she had once thought she needed but had since been freed of. It also reminded her that freedom was lonely. The tour was lonely. Mix in the extra isolation of limited public exposure due to death threats and the desolation crushed her relentlessly.

"Aurora?"

"Yes?" She snapped back to the present phone conversation with her mom and closed the magazine.

"I said, do you like your security team? Maxine told me they made some changes." Her mom's tone was casual, but Aurora heard the unspoken anxiety beneath it. *We paid enough, are they good enough?*

"Mason."

She thought of him watching her. Those blue eyes missed nothing. He was like a vault—rarely did she glimpse the interior. Through those glimpses, she could imagine what he would be like off the job.

"Mason?"

"Mason Stone," she added quickly. "He was a Navy SEAL. Very organized."

What had her mom picked up on in her use of his first name so casually? Simultaneously he made her feel safe and want to throw caution to the wind.

"They're a great team. You picked a good security service. Rider SI seems to know what they're doing."

Rambling again, Aurora.

She tried to dampen the images flipping through her mind—Mason's mouth in a quirk, his intoxicating eyes. She'd seen a deep and distant sadness when he thought of his teammates, as though standing alone on an iceberg staring into an azure ocean of memories. She had wanted to extend a hand of comfort, which would have been completely inappropriate. He was her bodyguard, and they hardly knew each other. Instead, she had retreated into the corner of the elevator.

"Okay. Well, good luck tomorrow."

"Thanks, Mom."

AURORA FINISHED her usual pre-game routine—warm-up, stretch, and review of fast facts. Handy fast facts during the game kept her focused. Without them, she would start analyzing the game even as she played it. Her mind would subsequently interfere with her shots.

She headed to the court, ready and sharp.

Her Spanish opponent, Ana Sierra, would not be an easy conquest. She skittered across the court with ease and unwavering stamina.

Ana's black hair streaked up and away from high cheekbones. She wore a power red outfit, the same one she had worn during her last commercial for her sponsor—a luxury watch company. They made classy, expensive watches, not cheap, clunky sunglasses.

Ana won the coin toss and took first serve.

Aurora walked to the baseline, turning her racquet in her palm.

Ostriches can run faster than horses.

She took a wide stance at the baseline as she watched her opponent bounce the ball.

Elephants can smell water up to three miles away from them.

The first serve came hard and fast, just wide. When it did land in the service box, returns would be tricky.

The second serve kicked high, but Aurora managed to push it back over the net deep into the other side of the court.

As the points played out, Aurora found she had more power than the small woman, but Ana possessed phenomenal accuracy. She got her racquet on every ball Aurora drove at her. The return shots landed on the white boundary tape at every angle imaginable.

Aurora conquered the first set, but lost in the second.

At the break between sets, she did a mental assessment of her body. She was not too fatigued going into the third set. She flexed her arm and leg muscles—still loose. Mercifully, her ankle barely throbbed with discomfort.

They battled far into a third set and tied. Aurora felt her focus slipping. She reached for her fast facts, but only found the ones she had learned about stalking.

Half of stalkers commit acts of violence.

Celebrity stalkers are the most unstable.

Was she a celebrity?

The sun shrank behind the stands, and half of the crowd watched the match in shadows. She couldn't see their faces. She couldn't read their expressions. Could her stalker be among them, plotting her demise?

Glancing back at the entryway to the court, she saw Mason standing in his navy suit and sunglasses. Billy would be somewhere in the crowd.

I'm safe, she reminded herself.

After a grueling three hours, her concentration shattered. She lost the tiebreaker. She shook hands with Ana Sierra, walked to the side of the court, and packed up her bag.

Aurora signed a few autographs and then left with Mason at her side.

In the depths of the locker rooms, she stretched, showered, and emerged to go back to the hotel.

"You played well," Mason commented.

"Thanks. Maybe I should be upset after having been up a set, but I feel like I'll do well in Paris if I play that good. Surprisingly, I'm not mad about it. She played the best game of her life and deserved the win. I lost focus in the end."

Rambling again.

This annoying behavior seemed to manifest only with Mason or while thinking about him.

"Any reason?" he asked.

"I started thinking about those damn death threats and wondering if my stalker was in the stadium."

He fell quiet again. She wondered if he thought she blamed him since he brought it up the first day they met.

"If you want to confront the letters, you don't have to do it alone," he said.

She glanced sidelong at him as he led her to the car where Billy would be waiting. The quiet conviction in his voice warmed something in her chest, and she had to remember that, despite his reassuring tone, what he was proposing wouldn't be a pleasant experience.

She sighed heavily. "Talk to me about it after Paris. Let me get through the major first."

CHAPTER 5

Madrid. May 8th. Aurora Meridian is a name almost long forgotten in tennis. After an ankle injury wiped out an entire season, she spent two years clawing her way through entry-level tournaments, unable to reach a single major.

Die-hard fans have been tracking her slow, stubborn rise in rank. Last year she finally fought her way through the qualifying rounds of all four majors. This year, her game is sharper, but she has an uphill battle to even rank in the top fifty women's players.

Will Aurora rise from the depths of primordial soup and transform once again into Prime Meridian?

⁂

Mason packed his bag in the hotel room with Dorian.

"She made it to the quarterfinals. Respectable," Dorian said.

This job marked Mason's first with Dorian, but he enjoyed the man's relaxed demeanor even if his British accent took some acclimation.

"Yeah. She works hard enough for it, too."

"I'm glad you're running with her. I couldn't run five miles a day if my bloody life depended on it."

Mason curled his lips. "Not like your MI6 days?"

Dorian grinned.

Mason wondered if he could pry any details from Maxine about Dorian's mysterious past. Probably not. He was lethal by reputation and spoke French and Russian fluently, but for whom had he worked before Rider SI? Everyone knew Mason had been Navy SEAL, Barry had been Special Forces, Ryan and Reece had been Rangers, and Billy had been a Marine like Max. Dorian was the enigma.

Mason added, "Of course that was before Scotland Yard."

Dorian gave a crooked smile, betraying nothing.

Mason shrugged as he carefully rolled his clothes into his bag—undergarments and casual attire on the bottom, heavy toiletries in spill-proof bags in the middle, and dress shirts and suits flat on top. He noted Dorian packed with similar efficiency.

As long as Dorian exceeded expectations at his job and oozed professionalism, perhaps his origins didn't matter too much.

Dorian had a daughter and wife he seemed to care about deeply. Mason wondered how he had managed to have a family while being whatever covert agent he'd once been.

Because Dia was soon to be in college, Dorian would have to have started a family while he worked as an agent. Notably, the one time Mason had met Katie at a company Christmas party, the couple had seemed enamored with each other. He had a long-lasting love and a daughter who had grown to be well-adjusted.

How had Dorian managed a career as an agent and maintained the love of the mother of his child?

Mason had seen quite a few failed military marriages. Sometimes even the ones that didn't divorce were still dysfunctional. Night after night alone and wondering if their husbands or wives still lived left spouses feeling neglected or worse—as in Max's case. The bitterness grew to resentment. A loving relationship turned as violent as war. When the end came, the best-case scenario was a simple divorce. The worst case was financial ruin and shredded families.

Like poor Max.

Dorian had been one of the few to beat the odds. Luck or strategy?

Mason pulled his phone out of his pocket as he walked out of his hotel room.

He called Claire.

"Stone Mason, to what do I owe the pleasure?" she said melodramatically.

"The list."

"Of course, the list. No, 'Hi, Claire, how are you today? How's the weather in Atlanta? Did you know you're my favorite tech gal?'"

He smiled. "It's May so it's warming up there. And you already know you're my favorite techie."

"It's nice to hear it once in a while. All of you get to gallivant across the globe and call me up demanding information. Meanwhile, I'm the computer geek. Locked up in a cubicle, chained to a desk, no adventure."

He walked to one end of the hallway and stared out the hotel window. "You're our most valuable asset, Claire. We can't afford to let you gallivant. Besides, I seem to remember last year you got trapped in an elevator and declared it the most adventure you wanted for the next decade."

He thought about her panic attack in the work elevator. Never had he seen her blue hair look so contrasted to the pale white of her ghostly skin as when he and Barry pried open the doors. To this day she still only took the stairs up to Rider SI offices.

"Fine," she retorted.

He could tell from her tone he'd provided the compliments she craved and deserved. Every word held truth. She was their source of all information. Every employee at Rider SI was more expendable than Claire. The young introvert was one of Maxine's prize possessions.

She began her summary, "I'm about halfway through the list. Aurora's parents have no bad debt and a thriving winery. They're taking over another winery before it's bankrupt so it's a win-win for both sides. Heir to the other winery is a USC brat, but he fares better with the buyout—if his dad doesn't spend his inheritance on another failed entrepreneurial adventure."

Mason looked at the Cybele Palace in the distance—a beautiful palace turned municipal building. The constant congested traffic surrounding it squelched any interest he may have had in touring it.

"Jimmy Fisk, ex-boyfriend, no dirt in his background. His girlfriend, Natasha Bodrov—ridiculously beautiful by the way—is the niece of Russian crime lord Vladimir Pronin."

"Niece of a Russian crime lord" was never a phrase Mason liked in a background report.

"Other than being an unfortunate connection, it doesn't reek of psycho death threat origination. Next, Aurora's doubles partner—adorable Irishman, Alex Rory—completely benign. Dr. Ruchkin is a Russian physician who covers the tennis circuit, mediocre by his scores. He bets on horses, not tennis, so he doesn't stand to win or lose by sending death threats. Aurora's friends—based on online social media and who she texts the most—are Monique Johnson and Elizabeth Morgan. Both appear clean. Monique is an emergency room nurse practitioner. Elizabeth is also a professional tennis player, but on the ITF circuit."

"ITF?" Mason asked.

"International Tennis Federation. Second-tier tour for women's professional tennis. Apparently when Aurora came back to the circuit after her injury, she couldn't maintain her higher rank. She dropped a few notches. I learn so much when we take on cool clients. ITF even has a neat logo."

"Is there anyone from the ITF who could have it in for Miss Meridian? Maybe jealous she went from second tier to first?" Mason asked.

"I haven't delved into that group's Web chatter yet, but it's on my To Do list."

"Okay. Anything else?"

"Other contacts from her mobile phone are Ralph Hutch, a former agent—"

"Former?"

Ex-agent dropping off after Aurora's fall from glory could hint at wounded pride or financial motive.

"They haven't had much contact since Aurora's fall from celebrity status."

Mason scowled.

Parasite.

"And a reporter—Marco Gold. Divorced. Two kids. He's written nothing but nice articles about her—again, when she was worthy of reporting."

Mason ran a hand through his hair as he listened.

"That's the group most closely linked. I also sent you an email on the top two hundred women's tennis players. Lastly and painstakingly, I'm combing through twitter accounts and texts for death threats or animosity."

"Okay. Good work. Negatives are helpful."

"Mason," her voice grew serious.

"Claire."

"Those were some messed-up accusations. We're all behind you, you know."

He leaned his head against the window momentarily, distant car lights twinkling like stars around the palace. He felt lucky to have a team of friends who stood by him even when the accusations could destroy the company employing them.

"Thanks, Claire."

"Someone may have sent the spoiled, lying rock star a virus and destroyed her computer."

"I'll be sure to not tell Max."

"Unlike you, I have a petty, spiteful streak, despite my happy-go-lucky exterior." She dropped her voice to a sinister tone. "Woe to anyone who crosses me, or my friends."

WHEN THE CALL ENDED, Mason pocketed his phone, walked down the hall, and knocked on Aurora's door.

She swung the door open and waved him in but didn't stop talking on the phone. As she walked over to her computer in her faded blue jeans and a rose-colored top, he closed the door.

She stepped in front of the laptop and put a hand on her hip. "Sage, it's a star. They asked for a star."

She paused.

"Well, it's not the devil's star. The satanic star is an upside-down, five-pointed star. To be technical, since mine has six points, it would be the Creator's star or the Star of David—if it were religious at all."

Peering at her computer screen, he saw an elegant star beside script letters reading "Starlight Industries."

Her graphic design work, he surmised.

"Waves?" Aurora snapped the screen shut and glared at Mason momentarily.

He turned away and strode over to the kitchenette and poured himself a glass of water.

"So they want a sun? I'm confused because their company name has a star in it."

She started stuffing things into the suitcase on top of her bed.

"Okay. They want an *estoile*."

When his gaze drifted down at her bare feet, he paused to admire pink painted toenails. Several toes were wrapped in white tape. He wondered what sort of beating they took from all of those long hours on the tennis court.

"Yes, an estoile. It's a star with wavy edges. No, it won't be mistaken for anything cultish, but some people may confuse it with a sun."

She paced again.

"I'll change it. I'll have it to you tomorrow."

She clicked her phone off and tossed it on the bed.

"They asked for a star. I gave them a star. If they wanted an estoile, they only had to say a star with wavy edges."

After walking into the kitchen, she blinked at Mason as if noticing him for the first time. She pulled out one of her premade protein concoctions and drank.

"Is this an okay time to review the travel plans?" he asked.

"As long as it doesn't involve stars. I've been working on this design for a week. Now I have to design an entirely new one."

"Keep it," he suggested. "It's beautiful, and maybe a church will come to you looking for a logo."

She seemed to consider his suggestion. Her green eyes glowed bright in a face framed by blonde hair casually pinned back with loose strands that had freed themselves.

"This discussion is star free," he promised. "I just want to cover security and travel details from Madrid to Strasbourg—plane to car to hotel."

"I'm all yours."

Mason turned his face impassive, trying not to betray the thoughts such a statement from Aurora provoked in him. For one reckless heartbeat, he let himself imagine what it would mean if she weren't talking about schedules.

Lovely Aurora.

Who was completely off limits.

———

AT THE AIRPORT terminal prior to boarding, Aurora's phone rang. As she reached for it, her gaze snagged on a man across the walkway who seemed to stare a beat too long. Her heart rate doubled but before she could mention it to her bodyguards, the man turned and walked away, rolling luggage in tow.

"Alex, I'm on my way to Strasbourg." She shook off her paranoia.

"Right, *a stor*. How's the form? You did good making it to the quarterfinals." His quick Irish accent required deciphering, but she had learned to do so.

Her coach had introduced them over two years ago. They each needed a mixed doubles partner.

"Alex Rory. How's the form?" he'd introduced himself. She learned later his phrase was the Irish equivalent of "How are you?"

"You're Irish."

"Aw, dash it all. I hoped if I didn't wear my shamrock shirt, you wouldn't notice." He'd flashed a brilliant smile.

She'd rolled her eyes at his comment and looked to her coach.

"Coach Jareh?" She'd turned to him in disbelief.

The aging Polish man had grinned. "Da. It's good. You two will be good together. Make many wins."

He had been right, of course. They had made many wins. Two years they had played together. Two years she'd suffered through Alex's incessant cheer. But somehow they worked, and they climbed the ladder of mixed doubles success, hopefully toward a grand slam this season.

"I'm excited to have gotten far in Madrid," she said to Alex.

Her success had not been as lucrative as the Miami Open prize money, but it would cover her Strasbourg expenses and her entire stay in Paris.

"You should've been more aggressive with your serve and volley."

"Oh. Thanks, coach," she sassed with no malicious in her voice.

She made a sour face even though Mason, Billy, and Dorian were the only ones who could see her. None of them looked in her direction. Billy thumbed her phone, Dorian read a book, and Mason's eyes roamed the airport. It wasn't as though someone could get through security with anything more deadly than a toothbrush. Could she be killed with a toothbrush? Was Mason capable of killing someone with a toothbrush?

She shook off the images and continued the phone conversation. "I emailed you a training schedule for Paris so we can coordinate."

"Right. Is it color-coded like the last one?" he teased.

"I try to be helpful."

"It was lovely," he said.

She wanted to reach through the phone and smack the patronizing tone out of him.

"How's having a team of bodyguards?" he inquired.

"Never alone and always lonely," she replied.

She'd meant it jokingly, but the truth hit home. Silence crackled on the line. Even Alex, the eternal optimist, had no snarky reply for that.

Mason's gaze fell on her. She ignored his curious stare.

"Sounds dismal," Alex said.

"Not more dismal than death threats."

"Right you are. But it'll pass, *a stor.*"

She looked back at Mason until he averted his eyes.

"I'll see you in Paris," she told Alex.

After she hung up the phone, she picked up her tennis magazine. The lead article featured Slavica Stefanovic—the Serbian tennis princess. Not only did she possess a tall, blond, Nordic beauty, but she maintained rank in the top five in the world. She was also eight years younger than Aurora.

Aurora stared at the page, feeling a sense of loss as she gazed upon what she might have been had it not been for her injury. A photograph of Slavica on the court occupied an entire page. Her interview talked about the difficulties in growing up in a nation making the transition from communism to democracy.

Aurora had no such tale of hardship. She came from a wealthy, functional family. A difficult day for her was when rain ruined tennis or when her parents traveled to promote their wines and couldn't make it to a game.

So much had changed. Now death threats loomed over her. This was not an experience she wanted to share with the media regardless of any support it may garner from fans. She wanted no one's sympathy. Except perhaps Mo. Mo would give her just the right dose and promptly tell her to suck-it-up and get her head back in the game.

She continued to skim the article on Slavica. An entire page blossomed with a full-length photo of her in a trendy tennis dress. She stood beside the sleek sports car of her sponsor. Slavica may have grown up deprived, but she wasn't deprived now with her large contract. If she invested the money well, she could be set for retirement in ten years.

Aurora chuckled at herself.

What a thirty-something thing to think.

Funny how her priorities drastically varied from what they had once been.

Slavica, at twenty-two, burned through her funds like many celebrities. Aurora heard about the parties in almost every city following a tennis tournament—win or lose. Five years ago, she would've been at every party, chasing sponsorships and photos. Now she couldn't name a single friend from those nights worth calling. She hadn't missed them either.

As the boarding call echoed through the terminal, her gaze drifted to Mason, standing and scanning for danger.

What she missed, she realized, was something she'd never really had: someone to provide quiet company outside of the stadium lights and flashing cameras.

CHAPTER 6

axine drove to the gun range. After a long, stressful day, she needed to shoot something.

All of her agents had checked in, and all of their jobs were going well—Barry, Reece, and Ryan were protecting the singer, while Mason, Dorian, and Billy were protecting the tennis player.

Her business covered expenses, but barely. Now there were bottom-feeding lawyers involved with the rock star. The fiasco would be over soon when they all met and reviewed the surveillance video. Unfortunately, they would still have to pay for the lawyer.

Maxine was ready to be done with the millionaire brat. She mistakenly had thought protecting a young girl would have some intrinsic value. The job had been nothing but a headache.

After arriving at the gun range, she checked in and picked her spot. She slipped on her ear and eye protection and set the target range.

Maxine had other jobs waiting. More worthy jobs. She needed to hire more operatives. Quality ex-military scooped up the more lucrative security gigs, making Maxine's search for employees more difficult. She couldn't offer large paychecks, first-class flights, or even top-of-the-line technology. Maybe someday.

She assembled the cartridge into her SIG, slipped on her shooting earmuffs, took aim, and squeezed the trigger.

What Rider Security and Investigation offered beyond standard private security jobs was a solid career, a family of operatives, and loyalty. She vetted everyone she hired and had to examine thirty resumes for every one hire. Prospective employees needed to have genuine military training, US or otherwise, and a college degree.

Next, Claire had to work her background computer magic to make sure they lived and worked on the right side of the law.

Lastly, Maxine did the interview. Few applicants ever made it that far. She needed to observe them to see if they could stay cool under pressure. Despite military training and seeing the atrocities of war, they still had to have a conscience. She needed to see if they had done their own background check on Rider SI and knew they were meeting the boss. More importantly, she needed to know if they could take orders from a woman.

Today she had dealt with lawyers, crap for applicants, and bills. She continued to fire her handgun and continued to hit the target. The paper targets didn't talk back, didn't accuse, and didn't lie. If only clients and lawyers could be so obliging.

Stress relief came from shooting her gun or working in her garden. Needing a double-dose of stress relief, she would finish here and then go toil in the dirt.

Damn cutworms were destroying her tomato plants.

⁂

Aurora led the second set four to two. The young girl she played embodied all power and no consistency. Aurora had been able to shake her confidence early in the first game. Age and experience were conquering youth and agility. The strategy worked this time, though Aurora knew it wouldn't always.

When she started solid, she could shake up the confidence of younger players and then hit cruise control to keep the winning pace. When she faltered early, she didn't do well coming back for a win.

Some players thrived on the comeback, but Aurora struggled when the score fell out of her favor.

Her other advantage in tennis was her strong foundation in finesse from her younger game. Only after her injury did she take the time to build more strength and power. She always had her finesse as backup when strength faltered.

Frances Cardinal's short blond hair was slicked back and held in place with her visor, which proudly displayed her sponsor's logo. She had come to court with fiery determination.

Aurora found the woman's grunting sounds with her every swing annoying. The noises made her want to conquer Fran that much more.

Now, well into the second set, the grunts lessened and the remaining noises more resembled cries of desperation than assertions of power. Fancy Frances with her fuchsia skirt floundered. Aurora was ruthlessly on the hunt, and she smelled victory.

Aurora whipped a powerful first serve, pulling her opponent out wide. Fran dove and tipped the ball with her racket for a short lob. Aurora smashed it cross-court.

When she turned to look back smugly at her opponent, she saw Fran down on the court, writhing in pain.

The crowd went silent.

Fran clutched her knee. Aurora wondered at the possibilities—meniscal tear, ACL tear, lateral or medial cruciate ligament tear.

Aurora saw herself on the ground, a devastating ankle injury. She remembered the sensation of the world expanding out from her, suddenly vast and strange and eerily empty. Everyone distanced themselves from her—sponsors, coaches, friends (or those she had mistaken for friends), and fans. The few who tried to offer comfort, she'd pushed away. She didn't want their sympathy, and they couldn't empathize with the sudden void in her life.

She could empathize with Frances. She knew the despair of wrecked hopes and dreams. Medics would arrive soon, but the seconds would feel much longer for Frances. Aurora also knew no one wanted the vulnerability of being aided off court by medical personnel.

Aurora walked to the other side of the court, depositing her racquet against the bench. She knelt next to Fran.

A tear escaped the young woman's eyes. Aurora knew those tears. They represented dashed career dreams, not pain.

"Don't you let them see you cry," Aurora whispered softly. She slipped an arm around the woman's waist. She thought of what words she would have wanted to hear if someone, anyone, had come to help her off the court so many years ago. "You are a tennis goddess, and this is only a setback. It's not the end." She helped Frances stand. "Hold your head high as we walk together, and when you return to defeat your next opponents—stronger than ever—they will remember your resolve and fear you because of it."

Fran did as Aurora instructed, and they walked to the bench. Frances gave her resignation to the umpire as Aurora helped ease her onto the bench.

The medics arrived, and Aurora packed her bag.

"Aurora?"

She turned to Fran as she hoisted her tennis bag on her shoulder. Fran extended her hand.

Aurora leaned over the medic tending to Fran's knee and shook her hand.

◆

Aurora stared out her hotel room window. She loved Alsace. Nestled in northern France on the border of the Rhine River and Germany, it had traded ownership between the two countries, and thus gained the charismatic architecture of an old German town and leisurely ambience of France.

Her gaze snagged on a dark figure turning down an alley before disappearing. For one irrational moment, the back of her neck prickled.

"You okay?" Mason handed her a protein shake he'd prepared

from the mix she carried with her on tour. He was such a strong, calming presence.

Turning toward him, she accepted the drink and gave him a grateful smile. "Yeah."

"You played well," he said.

"Thank you."

She wanted to play strong after losing in the quarterfinals in Madrid. Her best performance so far had been making it to the finals in the Miami Open.

The prize money had been crucial. She dug her way out of some debt that had piled up from her previous year on tour. If she kept this pace, she could maybe buy some of her coach's time again. Playing better also meant the possibility of better sponsors.

The Internationaux de Strasbourg constituted a women's only event, and the tournament didn't have much prize money, especially considering the travel and hotel costs for the beautiful little city. The mental and physical success of getting near to the finals was the important objective before Paris.

"I hate that Fran got hurt." She sipped her drink.

"That was some remarkable sportsmanship. The crowd gave a robust applause."

"Walking with her?" Had they clapped so ferociously? Had she been so absorbed in the moment she hadn't noticed? "I've thought a lot about my own injury—what I wished either I had done differently or other people had done differently. Hopefully her moment of defeat won't be as bad for her."

"What did you say to her?" He sat on one of the barstools by the kitchenette.

"'Chin up princess or the crown slips.'"

Mason gave her a quizzical look until she finally cracked a smile.

She shrugged. "Close enough, anyway."

He chuckled, a pleasant rumble that caused warmth to spread through her. The sound chased away all the shadows and worry bearing down on her from the strain of competition to the mysterious stalker.

"Are you a princess?" he asked.

"We all are in our own narrative. Even the handmaiden sees herself as the heroine."

He looked thoughtful for a moment. "Some people see themselves as victims."

"Winners don't. Everyone on the WTA had to win to get that far. We're all winners, even if we don't win every match."

He regarded her carefully. "Well said." He stood. "I'll see you in the morning for a run?"

"Indeed you shall."

"Will that be with or without your tiara?" he asked.

"Why, dear sir, my tiara is always upon my head."

Mason turned toward the door grinning and left with another chuckle.

⁂

Two days later, Aurora returned to her hotel room in dismal spirits after losing the second round in Strasbourg. Her focus had faltered. Her backhand seemed to desert her. She had fought hard and took the game to a third set but ultimately lost.

Mason escorted her to her hotel room quietly. At least when Billy accompanied her after a loss, she would acknowledge it. "That sucked," she would say and mercifully avoid anything as patronizing as, "You'll get 'em next time."

Stony Mason. Not a word of comfort. He had done his job, kept her safe. A win or loss made no difference to him.

After his usual room inspection, he poured her a protein shake and a glass of water. He didn't need to wait on her, but she wondered if he went through the motions as a way of showing his sympathy even if he couldn't express it with words.

"Thank you," she said.

"Ma'am." Somehow his tone in that single word conveyed "You're welcome" and his shared disappointment at her loss.

When he left her hotel room, the room felt too quiet. She drank the protein shake and then reached for her phone, needing her MoJo.

"Hey, honey," Monique answered the phone.

"Hey, Mo."

"I know that tone. You lose?"

"Yes."

"Good. You can stop wasting all of your time and energy on tennis and find me a husband."

Aurora smiled. She put the phone on speaker and leaned over to stretch her hamstring.

"You're not injured?"

"No."

"Okay. Scrub it off then. You love Alsace, so walk off the gloom. Take in some eye candy. Eye Candy is still there?"

"His name is Mason," Aurora said.

"Ah. That's a yes."

Aurora bent one leg up and twisted to stretch her back. "How's your work?"

"The usual. Drug addicts. Alcoholics. Motor vehicle crashes." Mo switched the conversation back to tennis. "Was she better, or did you lose focus?"

"Some of both."

"Are you losing focus because of Eye Candy?"

"No."

Surprisingly, no.

In fact, when Aurora started to think of the threats on the court, she found reassurance in Mason's presence and was able to re-focus.

"The letters?"

"Yes. The letters, the fear of injury, and the overwhelming pressure I'm putting on myself at this being my last season."

"Is it your last season?"

"I'm thirty. It likely is."

"But you don't know for certain, so that's one distraction you should take off your plate."

"Right," she lied.

"What about Jimmy?" Mo asked.

Jimmy Fisk was playing his usual A-game, steamrolling the competition and flashing his pearly white teeth while doing so. He oozed confidence on the court and schmoozed the media off the court.

Their past remained buried.

"Not a concern." This time Aurora told the truth.

Mo snickered. "Every social media picture captures him and beanpole Natasha arm in arm. They're so connected they need a combo name. Natammy? Jimmasha?"

Aurora laughed. "They can have each other."

"Um. Hang on."

"Trauma's here," a voice in the background told Mo.

Footsteps sounded followed by a male voice. "Hold still. You're in the emergency room. We're trying to help you."

"Smell's like alcohol and vomit," Mo said. "Is he belligerent from the alcohol or a head injury?"

A male voice answered, "Your guess is as good as mine. Pupils are equal and reactive though."

"Do you need to go?" Aurora asked.

"Not yet. They have to get him on the monitors before I can go in the room." Her voice moved away from the phone. "Debbie, can you fetch propofol, fentanyl, and rocuronium? I need him paralyzed and intubated if we're going to assess him safely. If the he has internal injuries, he could be harming himself with all that thrashing."

"Sure thing, Mo."

Aurora listened to the controlled chaos in the background, suddenly aware that her lost match, aching pride, and even her death threats existed in some strange parallel universe where people were literally fighting for their life.

"Hey, Deb?"

"Yeah?"

"Double dose of everything. I have a feeling he'll need enough to put down an elephant."

"I'm on it."

Mo's voice came back to the phone. "Lord, Jesus. Is it a full moon? This and a GSW coming in on the chopper."

"Wow," Aurora marveled.

"Anyway. How is the graphic design business?"

"Slow. But slow is all I have time for right now. I haven't built up my online profile. Also, there are all sorts of online bidding and competitions to drum up more business. For now, I've usually got one little project per week, and it gives me something to occupy my thoughts. Keep them off death threats."

"I wish I could be there for you. And why is your case not solved yet? Why hasn't this creep been caught yet? This is the age of technological advancement. Can't they trace the ink to the exact manufacturer and the paper to the forest and the tree that had yielded it?"

"I think it's more complicated than that," Aurora said, but appreciated her friend's annoyance.

"I don't like. I don't like such a small security team. I don't want this psychopath to find his way through their defenses."

"They're really good. I trust my team."

"Fine. Fine. Tell me more about Eye Candy. We both need a distraction."

"No, Mo."

"Give me something," Mo implored.

"He's attractive, but he's also cold as ice." Except when he was doing little thoughtful things like making her protein shake or warming her tea.

"Oh. Maybe he's one of those hard candies, soft on the inside. Sweet raspberry candies."

"He's no raspberry."

"Huckleberry?"

"Great. Now next time I see him, I'll be picturing him with a cowboy hat and a six shooter."

"And shirtless."

"Mo." The word escaped as a groan, but the image was clear— glistening shirtless torso with a holster low on his hip and his face partially hid by the shade of his hat. There was no unseeing that visual.

"Now the mental image will be worthwhile. You'll thank me later."

"Hanging up now," Aurora said.

"Have fun."

When she ended the call, she tossed her phone on the bed and stared up at the ceiling. Her season threatened to slip through her fingers while stalker letters piled up somewhere—and all she could see, thanks to Mo, was her half-naked bodyguard in a cowboy hat. No helpful.

But that huckleberry might be the only thing standing between her and the stalker promising to harm.

CHAPTER 7

urora and Billy walked down the Rue de Beaux-Arts. A pleasant May breeze blew, and Aurora wished it would carry away the knot of disappointment in her chest. Every laugh from a café table they passed felt like it belonged to someone whose life was going right.

"Thanks for the walk," she told Billy.

Billy had been thoughtful enough to declare that Aurora needed to get out of her confined hotel room. Mason followed them somewhere in the shadows, no doubt listening to their conversation through the little earpiece devices they used.

We're all winners, Aurora had told Mason. She scoffed at her own words. Easy to say such a thing after a win. All of her previous wins seemed to shrink away in the wake of a loss.

"I'm a recluse," Billy stated. "Lock me in solitary confinement and that's fewer people I have to interact with. You're a social creature, more normal that way," she said it as though it were actually abnormal. "You flourish on crowds and social events and human connection. I might not understand it, but I've begun to recognize when you start to wilt, we need to sprinkle some human interaction on you."

"You say normal like it's a bad thing," Aurora said.

"Meh."

"Well, thank you for your powers of perception." Was she read so easily? No one, other than Mo, offered this type of insight.

Billy scowled. "You don't complain much. A lot of the divas we protect start getting belligerent, and that's how we pick up on the need for a change of scenery."

"Hah. You didn't know me ten years ago. I used to be a belligerent diva."

"What changed?" Billy stuck her hands in her jean pockets. Despite the casual move and the leisurely pace of her step, her eyes roamed their surroundings.

Aurora considered her answer. "I became a nobody. With my injury, I lost my tennis game, my sponsors, and my boyfriend. Suddenly, when I had legitimate issues to complain about, I lost the desire to do so."

"Perspective," Billy summarized.

"Yes. I gained perspective."

"Not everyone gets that opportunity."

"Yeah. Thanks, Mom."

Billy snorted. "Not everyone stops feeling sorry for themselves long enough to pull their shit together and become competitive again."

"True."

Aurora guessed Billy didn't dispense compliments often.

Mason followed the women at a distance, listening to their conversation and feeling oddly like he was eavesdropping rather than providing surveillance because of the personal nature of the topic. He took in the quaint shops and the sounds of boats on the nearby river as they walked.

They stopped inside the *Bistrot et Chocolat* and picked up two *dome de chocolat noir*, which, based on their conversation, consisted of some type of mousse within a hard chocolate exterior. He would have gone for the waffle with chocolate dipping sauce, but nobody asked him if he wanted anything. He didn't eat while doing surveillance anyway.

A man on a bicycle slowed as he passed them, eyes lingering on Aurora a beat too long. Mason's shoulders tensed until the cyclist moved on.

"So, Mason was a SEAL?" he heard Aurora ask.

His eyes briskly looked at the women, walking and eating their domes.

"That's pretty elite, right?"

In the distance, he couldn't tell if Billy nodded or shrugged.

"And you've both been to war?" Aurora asked.

"Afghanistan."

"Talk about perspective."

He heard Billy grunt.

Mason's perspective had changed. First, he wanted to be the best—best at hand-to-hand combat, best at obstacles, best with a gun. In battle, survival became paramount. All of those skills were important, but there had also been an element of sheer luck in not getting killed when bullets flew and bombs detonated. After the dust settled and the body count was finalized, the living bore survivors' guilt.

He'd faced the families of those lost—the anguish and the accusatory looks. What had he done that he'd survived but their husband or son had not? They wanted to blame someone. Even if accusations remained unspoken, their eyes revealed a measure of betrayal. Before the battles, he'd been one of the cockiest and most self-centered soldiers. The jump for mourning families to imagine he was to blame was less of a laborious leap and more like a hopscotch skip.

Aurora and Billy entered the *Musée des Beaux-Arts*. Mason stared at the baroque palace-turned-museum. He could hear Aurora telling Billy the ornate building had belonged to French nobility. Its walls barricaded a large, paved courtyard. Two columns connected by an arch framed a central gate. Christian statues adorned the front facade.

Perhaps he could come back to beautiful Alsace someday. Take a moonlight stroll hand-in-hand with—

With whom, you moron? Aurora Mercedes Meridian? Your client?

Good thing Billy was the one walking with Aurora. He paced three hundred feet away, wondering what it would be like to hold her hand. He liked being in her space, and on more than one occasion had to restrain himself from offering a shoulder to lean on. He'd never experienced romantic ideas about a client. And since when did river walks with a beautiful woman occupy his thoughts at all?

I will beat this.

The tennis season would run through until October. Five months. He had survived tours in hostile territory three times as long as this assignment.

If the death threats ceased, then his time with her could be shorter. Bittersweet. He needed to comb through her file again. He also needed her to scrutinize all of the letters. Facing the letters would be hard on her, but they might discover the identity of the sociopath if Aurora focused on helping.

His stomach churned at the idea of making her suffer through it, but protecting her mean asking her to face the fear those threats invoked. He hated that , but he could coax her through the fear and provide moral support.

Brilliant idea. Because that will make it easier to say goodbye when it's time.

WHEN THEY HAD FINISHED TOURING the museum, Aurora led Billy to a church in Alsace—the Strasbourg Cathedral, a stunning and prodigious gothic architectural behemoth. It was one of the tallest churches in the world, and strikingly beautiful despite the asymmetry in having only one tower—the north tower—as the south remained incomplete.

Aurora thought about how it had survived two world wars. Billy and Mason had survived wars, too. Like the cathedral, one couldn't tell by appearance alone that scars and internal damage lurked beneath the surface.

Mason was an attractive man, and if not for the depths of his eyes, a person could look upon the facade admiringly, like the church, without knowing the history that had marred it. A man like him lived alone because he chose to. She understood resurrecting walls, and she wouldn't try to dismantle his, despite the intermittent temptation. Besides, she felt certain his barriers took the form of a puzzle box or maybe a minefield, neither of which she had any interest in navigating.

As they walked back toward the hotel, she tried to absorb the surrounding German architecture mixed with brightly painted colors. They paused on a bridge over one of the many city canals connected to the Rhine.

The gentle flowing water was surrounded by beautiful old buildings dotted with vibrant flowers in window boxes. The imagery was too picturesque and romantic to be fully enjoyed in solitude.

A commotion sounded on the other side of the river along the Quai des Bateliers. Aurora turned to see a conglomeration of people and reporters. As pictures were frantically shot, a young woman dashed away from the crowd.

Slavica Stefanovic had emerged from Restaurant 1741 to be bombarded by fans and paparazzi. She dove into a car before it sped away from the curb.

Aurora had been walking around town for over an hour and had traveled unrecognized.

Life in obscurity.

Then again, her anonymity allowed her to take a casual walk, converse with an acquaintance, and enjoy a beautiful day. She wasn't dashing out of restaurants and diving into vehicles. Even with a stalker, she had more freedom than a top-ranked tennis professional.

Aurora packed for Paris in mechanical motions, automatic after a lifetime of packing and unpacking.

Her phone buzzed. "Lizzy! I'm so glad you called."

"Hi, Aurora."

Elizabeth Morgan had been one of the women on the International Tennis Federation pro circuit to befriend Aurora. They had shared taxis and motel rooms, even meals sometimes, as they struggled for enough winnings to pay for the next plane flight.

"You're playing great, Aurora. You're on a comeback."

"Thanks. How's your game?" Aurora felt ashamed to realize she hadn't been following any of her friends on the ITF. She had been too busy studying her competition for her next match and working on her graphic design business.

"Not bad. Semifinals of Båstad."

Båstad possessed beauty and elegance as a little town on the coast of Sweden. It was pricey to travel there for the small amount of prize money.

"Well done!"

"I'm calling about a favor, Aurora." Lizzy's tone had become somber.

"Absolutely. What can I do?"

"It's a big favor."

"Okay."

"I want to play Marseille. The prize money is good, and I'm playing so well. I'm also broke. I can't make the travel expenses—unless I backpack from Sweden to France—and I can't pay the lodging."

She zipped her suitcase shut. "Lizzy, of course I'll help you."

"No, not like that. I don't take handouts. Pay me to be your rally partner and pseudo-coach. You know I give good advice. I'll get you ready for the French Open."

Her heart warmed. "Sounds great. Do you need a place to stay in Paris?"

"I have a friend I can stay with in Paris. I know you'll offer, but I don't want to stay with you. You need to focus on the major."

A knock sounded at the door—Mason's familiar three knocks.

"One sec," she called to him.

"We're heading out to Paris today," she told Elizabeth. "I'll transfer money to you for your travel expenses. We'll meet up and work out a schedule. Okay?"

"Thanks, Aurora."

She said goodbye to her friend and answered the door.

"Ready, Miss Meridian?"

She nodded. "I just got a call from a friend of mine, Elizabeth Morgan. She's going to be coming to Paris to help me train."

"Shouldn't be a problem," he assured her.

His words made her wonder if Rider SI had already looked into her friend as a threat. They had said they would check anyone who contacted her for security purposes. The thought of a background check on her friends sickened her. Her friends' privacies would be invaded because of this stalker.

Crap. Lizzy entering her orbit meant her entering into the blast radius of the stalker, too.

So much for sticks and stones but words will never hurt me.

Words had driven her to near solitary confinement. Guilt simmered under the relief of knowing she'd have a friend in Paris.

MASON WATCHED Aurora work on her computer from his peripheral vision. He'd heard the last remnants of Aurora's conversation with Elizabeth Morgan from outside her room's door. Aurora planned to help a friend and fellow tennis player in need.

He saw the way Aurora watched every dime and kept track of her spending on her phone. She didn't have much to spare, but she didn't turn away her friend. She hadn't even hinted at the fact that, unless she did well at Roland-Garros, paying a rally partner would strain a strained budget.

He leaned over and looked at Aurora's computer screen, careful to keep his shoulder from brushing hers. She had been working intently as Dorian drove them from Strasbourg to Paris. Billy sat up front, navigating.

"Did Max hire you?" Mason asked Aurora.

Her screen displayed a gold-embellished graphic design of "Rider Security and Investigation" on a business card.

"No. But your business cards are plain. I'm giving her an upgrade."

"Looks extravagant."

"Good. That's the idea. You're charged with protecting people. They want you to ooze professionalism and money. If you have money, you have the resources to provide protection."

Mason knew Max ran a tight margin. Gold business cards were not necessarily representative of the company's financial status.

"Makes sense," Billy said from the front passenger seat.

Aurora moved the text around on the card, appraising the best location.

As Mason stared, he glimpsed her lovely bone structure in profile framed in blonde hair that probably felt as soft as he looked. He detected a hint of honey on her breath from her morning tea. He wondered if her lips would taste as sweet.

Knock it off, you moron.

Aurora settled on a location for the company name. "Not sure about a logo, though. Any thoughts?"

"Can you frame that as a multiple choice question?" Mason asked.

Aurora smiled. "Depends on what Maxine wants to convey to clients. If it's strength, something like Atlas holding the globe is good. It also implies the company international. If she wants to convey justice, you might want scales. Those could make you look like a law firm, though."

Billy snorted. "Max hates lawyers. No frilly symbols, either."

Aurora opened another screen. "These are all symbols of courage and strength."

Mason scrutinized the small forty or so icons, glad to have a task to focus on other than this woman's dizzying proximity. His gaze landed on a trident, reminding him of the Navy SEAL eagle and trident symbol. Many others symbols appeared to be hieroglyphic or Chinese characters. One consisted of overlapping diamonds.

He pointed. "This looks like a chess piece. I like that one."

"The drum or *dono*. It represents goodwill and diplomacy." She enlarged the image.

"You should use a chess piece," he said.

"Okay. Which one?"

"Rook. It represents the castle walls, which protect the valuable players—king, queen, bishops, and knights."

Billy shot him a look over her shoulder as though shocked he had some sense of creativity.

He stared back, daring her to comment.

Dorian chimed in. "In the ancient Persian form of the game—*shatranj*—the rook was actually a chariot, more of an aggressor than defender. Perhaps Maxine's rook could represent the company's ability to protect through both defense and offense."

Mason stared at the back of Dorian's head as he drove. He again wondered at Dorian's background. The man was entirely too well read to be a bodyguard.

"Perfect," said Aurora. "Rook it is." She switched over to her design software and began creating a rook logo for Maxine's surprise business card.

Rook, Mason thought. Understated and dangerous when overlooked. Just like Max.

CHAPTER 8

*A*urora dragged a towel across her damp face and sucked in a deep breath.

"You're tacklin' the birdie a bit hard for practice," Alex Rory commented. They'd been rallying for a grueling hour.

"Yeah, well. We've got a match tomorrow. I want to win."

The tall, dark-haired Irishman stuffed his racquet into his tennis bag. "Aye, and the fact your new bodyguard is watchin' is entirely unrelated."

Aurora glanced at Mason—the statue in his suit and dark sunglasses. She had introduced Mason and Alex when they met at the courts for practice. Fortunately, her bodyguard stood too far away to hear Alex's insinuation.

"Unrelated," she snapped, narrowing her eyes at Alex. She took a long drink of water from her bottle.

He held up a hand in surrender. "I'm not passing judgment. I understand he's hired help, and that makes it a bit . . . complicated. But, hey, life's messy anyway."

"I'm not going to sleep with my bodyguard," she replied in a harsh whisper.

Ugh! First Mo, then Alex.

Alex smiled, his full set of charmingly crooked white teeth twinkling at her. "I diddunt say anything about sleeping with him. But now I know where your head's at. You know, you can have a meaningful relationship without jumpin' his bones."

Aurora jammed her racquet into her bag before slinging it over her shoulder. "Yes, I know that, thank you."

"I'm merely suggestin' you might benefit from a meaningful relationship," he kept his tone light as he leaned in closer, "with a man."

Aurora felt her cheeks burn. Although she needed the tennis practice, their interaction came with a price. Alex always found a way to aggravate her about something. Admittedly, if she wasn't so damn lonely and so damn attracted to Mason, she wouldn't be aggravated by Alex's comments.

She spun and walked off, though Alex's long legs kept pace casually with her quick, irritated steps.

"You are unbelievably annoying," she murmured.

TEN MINUTES later Aurora's irritation at Alex finally dissipated as Billy drove her and Mason back to the hotel.

"You and Alex okay?" Mason asked without looking at her.

She looked sidelong at him, recalling what Alex had said. What would a relationship with Mason look like? Long runs together. Breakfast discussions over acai blueberry smoothies. Would he take her cold teacup and wordlessly heat it up for her?

Maybe he would sit at the table wearing just his boxers and divulge the dark past lurking behind those baby blues.

Great.

Now she envisioned him in just his boxers.

Thanks, Alex.

Mason spoke again, "Seemed like he said something that upset you."

Only because it was true.

"Yes, he did."

"About what?"

Aurora felt her voice grow hoarse as she said, "Meaningful relationships."

She hoped he didn't probe further because she didn't think herself capable of lying to Mason.

He turned slightly as though appraising her. "Is that going to interfere with your mixed doubles tomorrow?"

Hah! He thinks Alex and I are a couple.

She shrugged. Better for Mason to think that than suspect the truth.

His tone and subtle frown suggested he wanted to offer support but perhaps didn't want to get inundated with details of a lovers' quarrel.

"We'll be just fine," she replied with a fiendish smile.

Before matches, Alex always rubbed her buttons with a brittle pad followed by jabbing them. With their current winning streak, she would let him continue.

Scratch and jab away, my Irish lucky charm.

PARIS. Roland-Garros, Aurora marveled.

One of the four annual Grand Slam tournaments. How many phenomenal tennis heroes had stormed this red clay? Djokovic. Muguruza. Borg. Nadal. Federer. Evert. Seles. Navratilova. Henin. Williams. Sharapova. And on and on.

Aurora had made it through qualifying and won the first and second rounds in singles. If she could make third round in women's singles, she could afford the hotels and plane flights. Last year she'd lost in the first round, and the draw hadn't been bad. She pushed that dismal thought from her mind.

Clay was good. Clay slowed balls and gave them a little more bounce. While she had been building her power for the last year, it wasn't of the caliber of some of the women who were heavy hitters. But her topspin was formidable, so the extra kick of clay would take the ball a little higher and offset some of her opponents' power.

"Alex," Aurora greeted the tall Irishman with brief disinterest as they walked down the corridor.

"Aurora," he replied courteously.

She found his wide smile annoying. It seemed to expand over the time they played together—as if he knew it annoyed her, so he intentionally made it larger.

She had asked him one time if his boyish smile represented his game face.

"You dunnot like it, *a stor*?" he had asked in his thick Irish accent, calling her his treasure.

"It's too friendly," she retorted.

"No worries. I'll be smiling just the same when I spike the winnin' overhead."

And he had. He somehow managed to smile and play competitively. He also lobbied steady, encouraging words toward her throughout the entire game.

"You know what this match is?" he asked as they continued through the corridor.

She adjusted her tennis bag on her shoulder. "Our ticket to the semifinals?"

My next paycheck, she thought hopefully.

"Aye, but it's our twenty-fifth match together."

She narrowed her eyes at him. "You're referring to our deal."

"You remember, *a stor*," he said, entirely too pleased.

She shrugged. "I promised a celebratory dinner if we survived twenty-five matches."

"Well, I had to twist your arm, but yeah, you agreed."

She arched an eyebrow. "I think that may have been when I was still learning to decipher your quick Irish accent."

He winked at her.

"Dinner," she agreed. "And if we win, it'll be my treat."

"Fantastic. I've just the place then." He beamed.

There goes my paycheck.

The winnings from doubles comprised a fraction of the winnings from singles, but she needed the points. Her and Alex needed to take mixed doubles by storm.

They walked the hall together, mounting anxiety about the match sparking between them.

Mason took flank, while Billy would be somewhere monitoring the crowd from the stands.

The sun shone ahead as they neared the courts. Red clay stretched before them—a red sea of opportunity. Together she and Alex—

Thwack!

Just before they entered the courts, Alex smacked Aurora on one butt cheek. In open-mouthed dismay, she turned to gape at him. Instead of looking at her, he waggled his eyebrows at Mason who shook his head before looking to Aurora with a question in his eyes as if assessing if she was okay.

She rolled her eyes in Alex's direction to convey. This was a battle she didn't need Mason fighting for her ... he could do real damage.

Before Aurora could give Alex a verbal chastisement, they appeared in front of the crowd, Alex waving and smiling. She'd let him get away with it on court because that's where their rituals lived, but outside of that white rectangle, he'd lose a hand.

"Are you kidding me?" she demanded through clenched teeth in a forced smile.

"Nah, it's alright. I seen them do it in American football all the time. It's good luck."

She pursed her lips and soon realized people all around snapped photos and could be catching some unsightly facial expressions. The pictures would be circulated on somebody's social media page ad nauseam.

"I've a good feelin' about Paris, Aurora."

She looked at Alex and smiled genuinely.

Yeah. Me, too.

Her eyes scanned the crowd. A hundred unfamiliar faces. Was *he* here? Even if her stalker lurked about the stands, he would have had to pass inspections at the gate. It wasn't as though he could be armed. Could he?

A man in a dark cap sat motionless in the stands, watching. She couldn't see his face from this distance, and that made it worse.

Alex must have read her worry because he gave her a quick squeeze on the shoulder.

She arched her neck back around to see Mason, stoic behind dark sunglasses. He gave her a two finger I-got-your-back salute. She smiled at the odd way she actually found the gesture reassuring.

Setting her bag down, she pulled out her racquet.

Game time.

⁂

THAT EVENING AURORA slipped on her silver earrings.

"Everything set on your end, Mason?" Of course it was, but the constant silence squeezed her nerves.

He was even more quiet than usual. How did he stand it? Protecting someone without speaking with her seemed drone-like. Laborious.

He had congratulated her on the mixed doubles win, but that was the extent of their conversation in the last four hours.

"Yes, Miss Meridian."

She looked away from his piercing angel eyes to step into her silver sandals.

"Are you ever unprepared, sir?"

He didn't reply.

"How many... how many more letters?"

He blinked, and that granite exterior cracked slightly. "A few."

Her blood chilled. She was nearing the time when she would have to face those harsh death threats.

"Not tonight, okay?" he said gently. "Let's focus on your celebratory dinner."

The genuine concern in his earnest gaze had her wanting to hug him. Fearing rejection if she acted so recklessly emotional in the face of his tight control, she nodded brusquely and turned away.

"Well, it's a restaurant so you can't stand in a corner while we eat."

"Billy and I will get a nearby table," he said.

"Nonsense, just join us," she said.

"I can't monitor the surrounding traffic if I join your table," he explained.

She frowned. "Mr. Stone, have you read the FBI summary?"

He nodded.

"Whatever this creep is planning, it's evidently private. So a dinner group is fine. You and Billy can join us."

She took a step closer to him. A flash of something like alarm crossed his face, and he took a step back.

A flush of anger spread across her chest. She wasn't making a move on him. She was having a conversation. He hardly needed to treat her like a leper. Turning away again, she rubbed at her arms.

When she looked back, he held out her black shawl. She stepped into it, suddenly close, almost touching, but with her back to him.

"Won't that be ... odd ... for Alex?" Mason asked.

She turned around and looked up at his troubled face. She backed away laughing.

Mason's brow furrowed in confusion.

"You should have better files on all of us. Alex isn't having dinner with me to sleep with me."

His cheeks flushed, which she found intriguing. It also further accentuated his blue eyes.

"He's gay," she explained.

"Oh."

A long pause settled between them as though he contemplated how his company's background check hadn't unearthed that little nugget.

"How do you know?"

"First, he's my tennis partner. Second, he stole my crush."

Mason looked perplexed again. "Jimmy Fisk?"

"Ugh. No. Your file didn't miss that mistake, I guess." She sighed and wrung her hands.

"I'm sorry. I didn't mean to make you uncomfortable." His voice sounded distraught.

Aurora released a nervous laugh. "It's my own fault. I was lusting after Hans like a silly schoolgirl when Alex came in and swept him off his feet. I guess I've been a little angry with him about it ever since." She hadn't been broken-hearted over Hans, but it was another failed human connection.

Mason didn't respond. The man listened well, she'd give him that much.

"I realize it's absurd to let such a thing upset me, but I had fairly low self-esteem after Jimmy and after my injury."

Mason's blue eyes looked genuinely troubled.

"Now my rambling has made you uncomfortable. Guess we're even." She picked up her clutch and continued, "I'm not so fragile I crumble at the memory of silly crushes. Nor am I so severe I can't laugh at my own idiocy."

His lips curled in a grin, but he didn't comment.

She pursed her lips. Conversation with him would continue to be dully one-sided if he insisted on maintaining this closemouthed professional barrier. Perhaps his contract read somewhere: *They are clients, not friends.* Something like a zoo sign except instead of "Don't Feed the Animals" it read "Don't Converse with the Assets."

Yet, at a time in her life when death threats lurked in every shadow and her life dwelled in isolation, she needed personal bonds. She would feel better under the protection of a friend instead of a stranger, even if it violated some weird code of conduct for him.

MASON OPENED the car door for Aurora. She sat in the back seat without looking at him. A vise squeezed his throat. He'd obviously hurt her feelings by not engaging more in conversation. She had opened up and shared a weakness. All he'd done in return was make faces. He understood she was unaccustomed to sharing personal secrets. Given his callous handling of her raw emotion, she wasn't likely to make that mistake again.

Good. She shouldn't.

Intimacy could dissolve into unemployment for him. But did it have to be so extreme? She obviously tried to be friendly. Why couldn't he be friendly? Surely, that little effort would be okay.

Aurora was lonely, but by her own design. She followed a rigorous workout schedule and ate her meals alone. She only talked to her parents every few weeks. Monique's friendship was maintained over the phone, never in person. All of this made keeping her safe easier, but her commitment to tennis created a fortress of isolation.

"I'll join you for dinner," he said.

She stared out of the car window as Billy pulled away from the curb. "Splendid. Don't strain yourself too much with being overly chatty."

Her bitter tone drove into him like a knife. He clenched his teeth before letting out a sigh.

"I'm under a sort of probation," he blurted out, "at my job."

Aurora jerked her head toward him but said nothing.

He continued, "My last assignment involved protecting a pop singer. More often than not I protected her from herself—late nights, drugs." He licked his lips and swallowed. "After a concert one night, she was completely stoned. Fans got wild, and we had a rough extraction. Reece was cut with a broken beer bottle, and I landed a cracked rib. I got her back to her hotel room in one piece. She came on to me. I left, and she was pissed." He felt nauseated just retelling the story. "She is threatening a sexual assault charge."

"Against you?" Aurora gasped.

Something about her sweet voice of shock and disbelief felt like a healing proclamation of his innocence. A wave of relief washed over him.

"The hotel security will show me in and out of there quickly, but the thought of being accused of something so abominable is—"

"Horrific," she finished, looking outraged on his behalf.

She held his hand in hers. Her soft, warm skin spread heat up his arm and into his chest.

""If this sticks, my career's over. Maybe Max's company with it. That is the reason I keep my distance."

"I would never—"

"I know you wouldn't. But I'm dealing with these accusations right now."

Crap. The conversation had just dwindled to an "It's not you, it's me" talk.

"Let's make a deal," she offered. "I promise I will in no way cross any professional boundaries if you promise to be just a little bit friendlier."

Trust. She was offering him trust, even after he'd pushed her away. He wasn't sure he deserved it, but he wanted it anyway.

She squeezed his hand and released it. The warmth of her touch lingered. His eyes wandered down to one bare leg, up her hips, and over her perfectly situated breasts before he forced his gaze upward.

He smiled weakly and nodded. Although her words brought some measure of reassurance and he believed she meant to maintain a professional relationship, he worried about how he would prevent himself from crossing boundaries with her when it became increasingly difficult to think of her as merely a client.

Professional lines were enforced to keep clients safe. Crossing them put her at risk.

CHAPTER 9

When they arrived at Arpège, Mason opened the door for Aurora. She waited on the sidewalk for him as he leaned toward the driver's side window. Billy pressed the button, and the glass slid down halfway.

Billy spoke first. "You take the table. I'll park and take the outside perimeter. Com check when you're in the door."

Mason nodded and gave her a small smile.

She wriggled her eyebrows.

Damn, he felt lucky to have good partners. Despite his backseat confession to a client, Billy wasn't giving him the evil eye. The woman was blissfully nonjudgmental.

Mason escorted Aurora into the restaurant with one hand on the small of her back. It was an unusually possessive gesture, but he felt a jolt of unusual possessiveness. His fingers touching her back were intended to be tactical, but the physical contact felt more intimate than simple protection.

His protective instincts flared on high alert, cataloging exits, staff positions, and anyone whose gaze lingered a little too long on Aurora. While she was correct that her stalker was unlikely to make a public appearance, he didn't operate under assumptions his client's safety was guaranteed at any time.

Aside from the threatening letters, Aurora increasingly became more of a high-profile security risk the more games she won in tennis. Furthermore, her parents' money raised the possibility of Aurora being kidnapped for ransom.

He hadn't pointed out to Aurora the many reasons she needed protection all of the time from more threats than just the obvious one. She didn't need another worry.

Alex had already arrived, snagged a table, and ordered wine. He waved them over to the table.

Mason's eyes scanned the room. The restaurant appeared uncrowded. A few couples and groups occupied tables. No lone diners.

Alex dressed casually fashionable in a pressed white dress shirt and blue jeans.

"Mason!" He greeted him warmly as they shook hands. "You're joining us? Excellent. We'll get a third menu and wine glass."

Mason noticed Alex shooting an inquisitive look at Aurora. She proceeded to give him a leering, challenging glare.

They're like brother and sister, Mason realized.

He pretended not to notice as he pulled out a chair for Aurora. She seemed to stifle a surprised hesitation and accept the seat.

"Just the menu," Mason replied to Alex. "No wine for me."

Alex shrugged. "Your loss, Stone. But I understand. You're on the job."

The waiter arrived, poured the wine, and filled water glasses. He set the open bottle on the table before leaving.

Mason spoke. "I understand this is a celebratory dinner."

Alex raised his wine glass with a nod.

"To a winning combination," Aurora said as she raised her glass to him.

"To a partnership, *a stor*," Alex countered.

She seemed to consider the words briefly. Evidently finding them satisfactory, she gently connected her glass to his.

Mason watched as they drank. He felt like he was witnessing a real milestone in their relationship—tennis partnership.

Yet, he noticed something devious in the way Alex intently watched Aurora drink her wine.

As she sipped, her smile faded. She set down the wine glass with some force. The red liquid sloshed in the glass, nearly cresting the rim. Her face reddened as her eyes flashed angrily at Alex. Slowly, deliberately, she turned the bottle of wine until the label faced her.

Very pointedly she said, "You unbelievable ass."

Alex unleashed a wolfish grin and set down his own glass of wine.

Mason felt an unease as though he might have to intervene in an unsightly scene at any moment.

Inexplicably, Aurora's eyes changed from murderous outrage to admiring amusement. Despite her apparent efforts not to, a slight smile stretched her lips.

Without taking her eyes off Alex, she turned the wine bottle so Mason could read the label. He leaned forward, studying it in hopes of finding an explanation for their bizarre behavior.

Aurora Borealis

Meridian Vineyards

Mason looked at Aurora. "Your parents' vineyard. This is one of theirs. Did they name the wine after you?"

Aurora's eyes flickered over to him. "Well, is it named after me, or am I named after it? That's the big question—the big joke." Her words sharpened again, but her irritation didn't stop her from taking another sip of the wine.

"Joke?" Mason asked.

She flashed him a pair of narrowed green eyes, and once again he felt the background information Maxine had on her was woefully inadequate for the complexity that was Aurora Mercedes Meridian.

Aurora bit her lip, and her haughty defiance seemed to deflate. "I've never gotten a straight answer as to what came first—the wine or me. Maybe they occurred simultaneously. It's not even one of their better wines. The reviews called it a 'mediocre blend of flavors that do little to satisfy the palate.' After my injury, I returned to the circuit a less formidable adversary and one critic called me 'a mediocre blend of talent insufficient to satisfy the audience.'"

Mason sipped his water. "Seems harsh." In truth, he thought it was outrageous, and a flash of something like protective anger coursed through him. For the first time, he wanted to track down a critic instead of a criminal and introduce their face to a wall.

Alex said, "The press either love you, hate you, or are bored by you. The latter of which is the career breaker."

"Press coverage helps sponsors recognize you or avoid you," Aurora added.

The waiter returned, and they ordered dinner—steaks all around the table.

"So now you understand the chip on her shoulder. Well, one of 'em." Alex drank another sip of wine.

Aurora glared at Alex, though with less than her usual malice.

"I've almost broken down the wall twixt us, though," Alex boasted.

Aurora countered, "Have you now?"

"Sure. In no time at all you'll forget you blame me that Hans is gay."

Mason watched as Aurora paled.

"You knew about that?" She looked mortified.

"'Course I did. Though who could blame you after what Jimmy-the-arse did?" Alex sipped his wine, but didn't stop talking. "Yeah, those long sideways glances and puppy-dog eyes at Hans. Not unlike the way you look at your Norse god bodyguard."

Aurora sputtered and choked on her wine. She put a napkin to her mouth as her pale face turned crimson.

Mason spoke, hoping to direct the conversation away from him. "What did Jimmy do to you?" He knew Alex referred to Jimmy Fisk, all-American tennis athlete.

Aurora leaned back in her seat, composed once again, and flicked a wrist at Alex. "By all means, Alex, enlighten the Norse god since you seem to know everything about me."

Mason took a deep breath, hoping he wasn't turning as red as Aurora had.

"Aye. He dated Aurora durin' her rise. When she injured herself, he dumped her for a supermodel."

Mason glanced at Aurora who sat stiffly silent, the way an innocent person might listen to her acquittal. He knew some of the details, but it generated more empathy hearing it rather than reading it in a file.

Alex, who had drained his wine glass, poured himself another and topped off Aurora's glass.

"'Course the press printed some rubbish about Aurora becoming temperamental and breakin' Jimmy's heart. Don't get me wrong," he winked at Mason, "she's always been temperamental, but you can't break a heart if there isn't one there to begin with."

Aurora fidgeted with the wine glass in quiet contemplation.

"So they printed absolute garbage?" Mason asked.

"Yeah. Everybody on circuit knew the truth. 'Cause we all know Jimmy's true nature. 'Course the public ate up a heartbroken all-American who ran into the arms of a Russian supermodel. Woe is Jimmy."

Aurora finally spoke, her voice filled with calm redemption. "Everyone knew the truth?"

Alex shrugged.

Mason drank his water, suddenly wishing he had wine. Perhaps wine would blunt the mix of emotions swirling through him. He felt sympathetic toward Aurora's love loss, but not sorry she was single. He felt a rising urge to clobber Jimmy with his own tennis racquet the next time he saw him. As for Alex, Mason admired his nonchalant insightfulness.

The salads arrived and conversation lightened, as the two bantered about tennis points and strategized their next match.

Mason enjoyed watching the conversation flow and learning about tennis strategy. He mostly listened as they talked and ate their way through the main course. Aurora and Alex kept to just the one bottle of wine, reminding him how vastly different this job was from his last job.

"Billy, we're wrapping up dinner. Can I get an all clear on the exit route?"

"Copy. Give me two minutes to finish the perimeter sweep ... Thor."

Shit. She'd heard the Norse god comment. He wasn't going to hear the end of that.

⁂

AURORA LOOKED to the sunny sky, trying to summon the strength and resolve to continue her match. She had pulled her hamstring. It had been just a twinge in the fourth round, but today the muscle clenched and refused to cooperate.

Sprints to and from the net made her feel as though someone wrung the muscle like a dishrag. The pain inhibited her ability to cover the entirety of the court efficiently for her singles match.

Wheels up, Aurora.

Her wheels hardly rolled, much less lifted. She couldn't cover the court in this singles game.

Her opponent had recognized her weakness. She'd stopped trying to overpower Aurora and now ran her relentlessly—the cat playing with the mouse before sinking in her claws.

Aurora wanted the quarterfinals win, but she was already down four to two in the second set.

The Panama Canal is a forty-eight-mile-long man-made waterway. Construction began in 1881.

The inevitability of a loss crushed her. A single tear snuck down her cheek as she brought her focus back to the court.

It opened in 1914. Almost one million boats have passed through the canal since then.

She bounced the ball and rocked back on her right leg.

Sync.

She took the racquet back for her serve and bent her knees. Her leg protested, taking her off balance just enough to cause the ball to smack the tape on the net and drop on her side of the court.

On her second serve, her opponent strategically dropped the ball short. No problem. Momentum carried Aurora forward.

She reached the ball, but her injured leg made it difficult to get low and under it. Without the maneuver, she couldn't get the power she needed to put the ball past the other player. She hit the ball, trying to force topspin on it. Her opponent struck it back—a beautifully placed lob.

On a good day, Aurora could have backpedaled to get it. On a great day, she could have overhead smashed it back to the other player. Today, with her muscle feeling like it slid down a cheese grater with every flexion and extension, she could do nothing more than watch the ball sail past her.

The next several points went much the same. Aurora accepted the loss with a handshake over the net.

The roar of the cheering crowd blurred into one relentless noise. Somewhere up there, in all that faceless cheering, her stalker could be smiling.

Goodbye, French Open.

She would never play singles on these red clay courts again.

After packing up her bag, she held her head high and walked off the court. She didn't stick around to watch her Swiss opponent revel in her earned victory. Every step pained her, but she refused to show either the crowd or the media weakness. She did not limp; she did not cry.

Once off the court, Mason escorted her, taking the heavy tennis bag from her shoulder.

He leaned in and spoke softly. "You're injured. What can I do to help?"

"Put one hand under my elbow and let me offload some weight, but make it appear as though you're just escorting me."

He followed her request perfectly, leading her away from prying eyes and to the infirmary.

Once inside with the doors closed, he helped her ease into a recliner. He set her bag next to her and tucked his sunglasses into his coat pocket.

"Ice pack or heat pack?"

She breathed out slowly as she settled in the chair. "Ice."

He rummaged around until he found a plastic bag and filled it from the ice machine.

The cold sent a dull ache through her leg muscle and to the bone as she positioned the bag. "Thank you."

She closed her eyes, biting back bitter tears of defeat. She had wanted to win so badly.

"Is it bad?" Mason asked.

She opened her eyes and met his stormy blue gaze of concern.

"No. It will heal. I'll be better in time for the Birmingham Classic."

But the French Open singles title was gone forever.

"Can I get Dr. Ruchkin? Do you need something for the pain?"

"I don't take pain medication. I don't take steroid injections. I limit caffeine and wine. Zero artificial sugar. This body stays drug free."

Mason arched an eyebrow. "Except for those chalky protein shakes. What's in those? Probably medical grade talc or something."

Aurora glared at him.

Mason's expression eased, seemingly relieved to see her distracted from the pain. Except, he didn't understand that her pain was as much emotional from her defeat as it was physical from her leg.

"It's protein and vitamins. No drugs."

"Smells like there's an entire bottle of vitamins in those things. It has to be ten thousand times the FDA recommended daily allowance."

"Three times," she corrected him.

He grinned.

And there it was again, another rare moment when he let his guard down and she witnessed the real Mason Stone.

Dr. Ruchkin entered and took in the two of them with a surprised look. "My apologies, I didn't know I had a patient."

He smoothed his black cotton pants and straightened his button-down shirt.

"I'm okay. I just needed a place to recuperate," she said.

Dr. Ruchkin's gaze traveled from Mason to Aurora. His eyes roamed her body, seeming to assess it for injuries. "Hamstring," he surmised. His gaze lingered a second too long on her leg, his expression calculating in a way that had nothing to do with compassion.

"It's just a strain."

He walked toward his medical cabinet. "I can give you—"

"Just ice," both Aurora and Mason said in synchrony.

She smiled at Mason, appreciating his attentiveness.

"Da. Da," Sasha Ruchkin said in surrender.

"Five more minutes and I'll be okay to leave," she told them.

Back to her hotel room to lick her wounds.

Alone.

Her French Open singles run was over even though stalker's game wasn't.

CHAPTER 10

Paris. May 25th. Aurora Meridian crashed and burned on the red clay yesterday. Now halfway through this year's tennis season, fans hold out little hope of seeing more competitive play from this once-favored American player. There is speculation she may have suffered an injury on the court, which has raised concern about her upcoming doubles matches.

In a brief comment this morning she assured us, "Alex and I are a strong team, and you will certainly see us on the court tomorrow." Can Rory and Prime rally to the finish line at Roland-Garros?

———

urora and Alex battled the French couple in mixed doubles. Their competition floated on the clay as if born from it. Aurora and Alex couldn't force a ball past them. She and Alex weren't making many mistakes, but it felt like they played four opponents instead of two.

"Chin up. Serve us a win, *a stor*." Alex smiled at her, but she couldn't summon one in return.

Aurora smoothed dirt from the baseline.

A solar flare releases ten million times more energy than a volcano.

She bounced the ball, watching it disrupt the spot of clay where it landed.

Solar flares are nearly as hot as the sun.

She shifted her weight to her right leg and brought her hands with her racquet and ball down to her thighs. Pain flickered down her hamstring, but she forced her leg to cooperate.

Sync.

She served an ace.

Alex jogged back to her and gave her a fist bump. "That's my girl."

He returned to the net.

She wanted to absorb his enthusiasm and radiate just as he did. Forget prize money. She wanted to win for the win, but also for Alex. He deserved it. He called her his treasure, but, in truth, he was her treasure. He could have chosen a better, stronger, younger partner, but he'd stuck with her.

Her next first serve banked just wide. She gritted her teeth and irritably wiped red clay from the backcourt line. Her second serve kicked high with spin. The woman returned it short. Aurora sprinted forward. As she neared the ball, she took her feet into a slide. Her racquet caught the ball just before the second bounce.

The man crowded the net. Aurora had no place to go with the ball but at him, and she was too rushed to put any pace on it. With lightning speed he smashed the ball right back at her. It whizzed past her knee, and she couldn't get her racquet on it.

They lost the match on her serve. Despite the loss, Alex gave her a brief embrace.

She frowned. "I'm sorry."

"Don't be sorry. They fanned like little pixies all over the court. We couldn't get the birdie past them. You still played great."

Somewhere up in the stands, someone whistled sharply, and her heart stuttered before she realized it was nothing. Just noise. Just an enthusiastic fan.

Aurora and Alex shook hands with their opponents.

As they left, they signed autographs. Before entering the corridors, they knocked the red clay off their shoes. She had the strange urge to keep the clay on her shoes and scrape it off later. She could put it in a tiny porcelain vase—her little keepsake of Roland-Garros.

"We'll get them at Wimbledon, *a stor*." He winked at her.

I don't deserve you, Alex Rory.

AURORA SAT AT A LOVELY CAFE, Le Cardinal, sipping tea and reading a crime novel. From her outdoor seat she could watch cars drive in circles on the Place de la Porte de Saint-Cloud.

She could relax here in Paris and forget she'd lost at Roland-Garros. She had made it so far. The hamstring pull had been her doom. It would be better in a few short days, but Paris singles and mixed doubles were lost. A few more days in Paris relaxing would soothe her bruised ego.

"Hello, Aurora."

Her world grew several shades darker as a shadow of past and present descended. She raised her sunglasses but already knew Jimmy Fisk intruded on her moment of tranquility. She knew his voice too well. She knew all of its many inflections from sweet to sour to unfeeling.

Unfeeling had been his last tone. Unfeeling and unapologetic. He had to leave because of her—her mood swings, her unpredictable outbursts, her sudden injury, and fall into obscurity. He hadn't listed the last one, but she had known it was a reason.

The reason.

Admittedly she'd had some outbursts and mood swings, but only because she knew he'd already left her. Physically he'd still been there, keeping appearances so the breakup wasn't so obviously timed after her injury, but emotionally he'd already vanished. She felt certain he'd been dating supermodel Natasha Bodrov before he'd ended things with her, though it wouldn't become public knowledge for another month.

"Jimmy," she said calmly, "how's Natalie?"

He looked like he might correct her but stopped himself.

"She's good," he replied, a touch of sadness in his voice.

For a brief moment, the old part of her who'd once wanted his approval was tempted to offer her a seat. The new, wiser version felt no such inclination.

She resisted the urge to look over her shoulder for Mason. He'd been across the street a few minutes ago. He had to be close. Didn't ex-boyfriends qualify as threats they needed to neutralize?

Jimmy's sandy brown hair was perfectly styled, matching his straight, white teeth. He wore blue jeans and a gray T-shirt. He looked like a movie star, and he played the role of doleful ex-boyfriend.

Is that remorse?

Surely, it wasn't so simple that as her fame returned so would he. They had been apart for years. He must know she would see through such a ploy. Even here. Even in Paris.

Loneliness may have been her main companion, but flashing his brown, puppy-dog eyes failed to make her forget he'd left her at the lowest point in her career and in her life.

She wasn't angry with him anymore. If anything, she recognized the value of his absence. If she'd had someone to lean on—a crutch —then she wouldn't have relied on herself and learned the strength of her own independence.

"I saw your first round match. You're playing great. Very strong."

She forbade herself from gushing at his compliment.

"Thanks, Jimmy. That means a lot coming from the eighth ranked male player."

Jimmy's eyes fell to the empty chair beside her.

Her heart galloped. She could not allow him to sit. Whatever his agenda was, it would serve only to distract her from the game.

Mason appeared. His robotic sunglasses had vanished, and his hair was attractively tussled. He had removed his suit coat and unbuttoned the top two buttons of his dress shirt. He held his square jaw and shoulders in a relaxed pose. He looked good enough to eat.

"Aurora," he said, picking up a hand and kissing the back of it, "sorry I'm late." He arranged his suit coat on the chair, took a seat, and snapped open a napkin.

As zing of delight licked through her from his touch. She stared at him like he walked out of a dream, but she couldn't help it.

As he poured himself hot water from the teapot into an empty cup, he added, "Who's your friend?"

She felt her mouth quirk. Like he didn't know.

"Mason, Jimmy Fisk. Jimmy, Mason Stone." Her eyes never left Mason's face.

Mason stuck out a friendly hand, and Jimmy shook it. Nothing in the appearance of Mason's grip suggested a show of force. He could undoubtedly tell by the hungry way Aurora stared at him that Jimmy didn't need a show of force to feel second string.

Mason smiled at Jimmy as he dipped a fresh tea bag into his steaming cup. "Of course, Jimmy Fisk, the tennis player. I've seen you on TV. The car commercial." His voice stayed casual, and his demeanor was vastly different from any behavior Aurora had seen him previously display.

Thus far he'd mostly waffled awkwardly between formal and frigid. His act at this moment was so convincing she thought Mason was the real movie star in this scene.

She finally tore her gaze away from Mason to look at Jimmy who seemed to perk up at Mason's feigned delayed recognition of him.

Mason took Aurora's hand in his as he continued speaking. "You're married to that model, Nisha, right? Quite a catch."

Heat climbed through Aurora's arm.

"Natasha," Jimmy corrected him, his voice falling an octave. "We're just dating."

"Oh," Mason said, his brow furrowing as though he felt genuinely disappointed. He took a sip of the tea, then replaced the cup in the saucer.

"What do you do, Mason?"

"Weapons specialist."

Jimmy raised his eyebrows.

"Handguns, rifles, semi-automatics, automatics, bazookas, tanks, surface-to-air missiles. Basically anything that goes boom."

Jimmy gave a dry swallow.

Aurora sucked in her cheeks to suppress a smile.

"I'm sorry. Where are my manners? Would you like to join us?" Mason offered as he squeezed Aurora's hand.

The table only held two chairs, and those were occupied. Mason made no effort to get a third.

Jimmy's eyes flickered around the tables. "No, uh, thanks. I was just passing by."

"Have a good day," Mason dismissed him, adding another smile.

Jimmy nodded slowly. "Goodbye, Aurora."

"Bye, Jimmy."

He slunk away with a downtrodden spirit that incurred feelings of irritation in Aurora rather than pity.

She turned to Mason in disbelief.

He watched Jimmy go, already covering his gorgeous eyes with his unflattering sunglasses.

"Thank you for that." She seemed to break some type of spell with her words.

Mason retracted his hand—a pity because it felt like it belonged in hers. He stood, straightening his starched white shirt.

"You're not going to finish your tea?" she asked.

"No, ma'am. I needed to have a face-to-face interaction with Jimmy. I wanted to know if he was capable of writing those letters."

She turned her attention to the closed novel on the table and flicked at the edges of the pages irritably. Her cheeks burned with the humiliation of having thought for a moment he had come to her side because of her. To save her. To support her. And yet, she had to be grateful also with the way Billy has slunk away from them because of Mason.

But the charade had just been an information-gathering session for him. Nothing more. And she wanted to keep the fantasy going.

"I could have told you that," she said. "He's narcissistic but not psychotic."

Mason nodded in agreement, his calculating demeanor seemingly oblivious to the emotions surging through her.

She rubbed at the spot on her hand, annoyed by the way the warmth of his touch seemed to linger there.

Despite feeling like her cafe respite had been ruined, possibly by both men, she remained seated as Mason left, determined to finish her tea.

MASON TOOK his position back across the street. He'd given Aurora an out and gotten his read on Jimmy. So why did she look like he'd just yanked the chair out from under her?

Dorian spoke into his earpiece. "Weapons specialist? Nice touch."

"Thanks."

"I think you scared him off for good."

"That was the intention."

"You also robbed her of any chance to confront her past and face her ex-boyfriend."

Mason looked in Dorian's direction across the street and scowled. Aurora hadn't looked like she braced herself to unleash pent-up animosity toward Jimmy. She had appeared in search of an exit, trying to find an escape route away from Jimmy.

"She's done with him. Any interaction would have served only to interrupt her relaxation. She needs to de-stress after tennis, not deal with that asshole."

If he'd wanted to completely spare her distraction, he could have stopped Jimmy from reaching Aurora's table. Curiosity had prompted him to let the interaction run its course for a few minutes. Once he was sure Aurora remained stoutly uninterested in Jimmy romantically, he introduced himself to discern Jimmy's character.

"Sure you weren't saving her from making another bad choice?"

Mason grunted. Aurora wasn't in danger of reconnecting with Jimmy *Fiasco*. "Did you see her expression? She wants nothing to do with him."

He thought about the hurt in her eyes just before he'd left. Maybe he *had* stepped in too fast. Maybe he'd protected her from a conversation she was finally strong enough to have. The thought sat wrong in his gut.

"I saw her expression when she looked at you," Dorian said mildly.

Mason watched Aurora from a distance as she sipped her tea and read her book. She had stared at him hungrily, and it had felt thrilling. As thrilling as holding her hand.

"She was surprised to see me in a different character, that's all."

"Keep telling yourself that, Thor."

Dammit, Billy.

She must have told Dorian the story. He had apparently been waiting to unleash it at the opportune time.

"Guess that makes you Loki."

"I've been known to be a bit of a trickster. More of a chameleon than a shape shifter, though."

Billy spoke into their earpieces. "I'm here to relieve Mason. What's all the com chatter?"

"Nothing," Mason answered.

As soon as he made eye contact with Billy, he waved as he left the sidewalk.

Across the street, Aurora lingered over her tea and book, unaware that two men in her life had just been weighed and measured. Jimmy Fisk, discarded.

Her stalker, still unaccounted for.

CHAPTER 11

The woman pulled at her long, auburn hair.

Infuriating Prime Meridian.

She wasn't quitting. She was supposed to cower in fear at the death threats. She was supposed to lose and quit.

She was winning too many matches.

Nevozmozhno. Impossible.

Although she'd failed in Paris, the media started to support her again. The tennis player would weasel her way back into magazines and on television—probably wearing those idiotic sunglasses. Before long, she would be famous. The letters were failing.

At this pace, Aurora would be in a position to take things that no longer belonged to her.

The woman clawed angrily at her scalp. She couldn't let that happen. Aurora could not rise to power. But how to stop her? Threats with words hadn't worked. Something more tangible.

She paced her hotel room suite from the king-sized bed to the Jacuzzi in the bathroom.

Delivering a stronger threat wouldn't be easy. Aurora had bodyguards.

Bodyguards. What a joke.

As if Aurora was someone worth protecting. Between the tennis player's relentless protection and the way she avoided all major social events, making a more substantial threat would be challenging.

Yet, ways of reaching her existed.

And I have the resources at my disposal.

MASON LINGERED in Aurora's hotel room. He fixed her a protein shake and water, not because he was expected to but because the motions prolonged his stay.

"Good practice," he commented.

"Thanks." She took the shake and drank, then began to stretch. "I was in a nice groove. I think practicing with Lizzy is helping. She's got a different pace on the ball compared to Alex. When she's not under pressure in a match, she plays great angle shots."

He diverted his gaze out the window, politely listening. He enjoyed the sound of her voice, and was always amused when she would reach the end of her thought and then speed up talking, as though suddenly self-conscious she was rambling.

He'd known women whose ramblings skipped along with their thought process, instantly losing him. Alternatively, some had more of bickering-ramble about random observations—someone's hair color made her look too pale, or so-and-so was wearing sandals without moisturizing her heels first, or some lady was drinking a Bloody Mary before noon. Mason had no tolerance for judgmental rambling.

Aurora's was pleasant rambling and always in context.

When she stopped speaking, he turned back to her as she arched her back in a yoga backbend. "You have a week before the Birmingham Classic."

"Yes."

"It would be a good time to go through the FBI files." He had kept mostly silent about the files, especially through the French Open. If she went through them this week, she would have several weeks to let the poisonous words wash out of her system before Wimbledon.

She looked up at him and blinked. Malice stewed in her eyes, but also consideration and a hint of resignation, probably because she knew he would approach the subject again.

Before she answered, her phone rang. She came out of her pose to answer the phone. "Hi, Mo."

She likely intended accepting the phone call to signify his queue to leave, but he decided to remain and push for a verbal answer.

"Yes. Thanks. I am enjoying Paris."

Aurora shot Mason a look, but he wasn't leaving.

"Nothing bad, just the usual aches."

He watched her fidget with the zipper on her tennis bag.

"You know I don't take medication."

"No, not even ibuprofen."

"I know the side effects are low. I know it's not habit forming. I don't like medications."

Mason wondered if Monique knew the real reason. He'd learned through Billy, because blunt Billy had just asked Aurora straightforwardly. A week before Aurora's career-devastating ankle injury she had taken an antibiotic for bronchitis. She learned later that a side effect of the antibiotic was weakening tendons. She attributed the injury to the medication and had since sworn a vow to never take drugs.

"Mo, I have a large, grumpy man in my hotel room. I should go."

Mason watched Aurora's face flush pink. He stared at her curiously, wondering what Monique had said.

His reaction deepened her flush. He felt a grin growing and quickly suppressed it.

Aurora turned away from him. "Okay. Bye, Mo."

She whirled around back to Mason. "Fine. You win. FBI files."

He crossed his arms. "It's for your benefit, not mine. The only person who wins if we don't examine those letters is your stalker."

She cocked her head toward him, the gears of her mind churning.

Damn.

"You want to see them."

If you *don't examine the letters,* he should have said.

"They're in the FBI's possession," Aurora continued, "so you can't see them unless it's with me."

"True." He'd seen some of them and photocopies of others, but wanted to see all of them. "But what I said about you needing to see them is also true."

He waited for her to unleash an angry outburst about him trying to manipulate her in order to look at the letters.

She wrapped her arms around her torso in a gesture that made her appear small and vulnerable. Softly she asked, "Why do you want to look at the letters?"

He stepped forward and put his hands on her arms. "It's my job to protect you. I need to understand everything I can about who is threatening you in order to do my job well."

He looked into her emerald eyes, surprised he didn't see an ounce of anger or fear in them.

"Okay. I'll talk to Agent Coble and set it up."

Relief plowed through him like the passing of a storm at sea. Was that all he had needed to say?

Help me help you.

She was willing to go through the misery of looking at those letters because it would help him, whereas she had rejected the offer previously when he had explained she would be helping herself. She'd walk through hell if it meant making his job easier.

He realized he stood entirely too close. The gravitational pull of her lean body and full lips made him want to embrace her. He released his hands from her arms abruptly and stepped away, severing the connection before any damage could be done.

"Thank you," he said dryly.

Confusion clouded her expression before it hardened into irritation, and he realized his mistake in touching her at all.

So much for not doing damage.

"I'll let you get back to stretching." He turned and left.

MASON HUNG up the phone when he finished another fact-delivery conversation with Claire. He drank a sip of water from the bottle on the hotel room desk.

He noticed Dorian staring at him. The man had exited the bathroom at some point during his phone conversation, but Dorian had been quiet. His graying hair clung wet to his scalp and a towel encircled his waist.

Mason wasn't sure how much his partner had overheard. Mason had been discussing all of the suspects Claire had ruled out as possible stalkers. No debts, no grudges, and no clear motives. A whole list of people who wouldn't write those letters, and not a single one who would.

Mason and Dorian stared at each other a moment. Mason waited for the man to chide him for investigating.

Instead, Dorian turned and pulled pants and a shirt from his suitcase. "Alex and Aurora got far in Paris."

"Yeah." Mason felt relief at Dorian ignoring his investigative work.

Dorian slipped on his shirt. "Think they'll win Wimbledon?"

"I think they have it in them."

Dorian walked back to the bathroom to finish dressing but left the door open. "I've been on her protection detail for months now. I find myself fervently wanting her to win. I shouldn't. She'd be less of a target if she'd stop playing so well."

A mechanical click emitted from the door followed by Billy entering the room. She stuffed the hotel keycard back in her pocket.

Dorian was still speaking. "I don't think I'd watched a tennis match a day in my life until this job. Now, I'm so enthralled, I keep hoping we'll get hired by another one after Miss Meridian. Probably a terrible thing to think because that would mean another one is in trouble."

Billy snorted, which felt like the equivalent of a child saying, 'liar, liar, pants on fire.' "Is that because you enjoy the game or the short skirts?"

Dorian emerged from the bathroom dressed and shook his head at her. "You might knock, Billy."

She gave him a bored look.

"I also have a college-age daughter and a wife. I am neither a pervert nor an adulterer. I like the competition. I like the intensity of seeing who will keep her wits about her and win."

Billy nodded at Mason. "What about you?"

"What about me?"

"You and the skirts."

Mason scowled. "We're here to provide protection, Billy. Give our maturity a little credit."

Besides, he only cared about one skirt—from a purely protective standpoint. Yeah, he'd just keep that lie going because Aurora was off limits.

Billy looked back and forth between the two men. "Since we have a few days in Paris and the matches are done, I'd like to take two days off and sightsee. You both okay with that?"

"Yep," Mason replied.

Relaxation. Sure. Except he wasn't giving any to the client. He was soon to drag Aurora through the worst reading session of her life.

"'The mind should be allowed some relaxation, that it may return to its work all the better for the rest.'"

Billy blinked at Dorian.

"Seneca. Roman philosopher," he explained.

She rolled her eyes. "Those quotes of yours work on women?"

"I don't know." He rubbed a hand along his smoothly shaven jaw. "I use them for guidance in life, not as pickup lines."

The tall, lean, British man would hardly need pickup lines to secure a date. He also had a reputation for being loyal to his family. Mason kept his mouth shut as he knew Billy was attempting humorous antagonism.

Billy laughed as she left the room. "Thanks. Call me if I'm needed."

———— ❧ ————

MASON SAT at a table adjacent to Aurora's and close to the entrance of the hotel lobby. She conversed casually with an American black man in his forties, wearing plain khaki slacks and a short-sleeved, button-down shirt. His reporter's notebook rested on the table, but he hadn't taken any notes yet.

Aurora appeared relaxed in the company of the reporter. Her guard wasn't walling her off as it normally did when she left the tennis court as reporters hurled questions.

"How are the kids, Marco?" she asked.

Marco's expression beamed. "Zack, you know he's ten now, plays the piano and the violin. His mom says he's going to make first string next year. Zanetta is still doing ballet, but she's at an age where she's distracted by boys."

Aurora smiled.

Mason wondered if Aurora had ever been distracted by boys or if her tennis game had always been unwavering.

With the beauty she possessed, he suspected finding an interested partner wouldn't pose a problem. Her file had no boyfriends in several years—nothing since Jimmy Fisk. A dejected ex-boyfriend would have been an easy go-to for the origin of the death threats. None existed. Tennis consumed Aurora.

Although now with the threats, a relationship could put her partner in danger. *Not if it was me.* Dang. Where had that thought come from? He squashed it and turned his attention back to the conversation.

"You're playing great," Marco said.

"Thanks."

"I appreciate the interview."

"You're one of the few reporters who didn't crucify me after every loss. It's nice just to be interview-worthy again," Aurora said.

Mason had hounded Claire for additional background on Marco Gold before Aurora's meeting. As an average reporter, he had produced nothing sensational. He mostly wrote articles but occasionally did radio interviews. He only had one or two video interviews.

"What do you think is making the difference this season?" Marco asked.

Aurora ran a hand along the big leather chair. "The first few years after my injury I focused on strength building and the mental game. This year the strength, finesse, and mental toughness are coalescing better."

Marco commenced taking notes.

"What will be your biggest obstacle in the weeks and months ahead?"

Death threats, Mason thought.

"My competition is younger and better funded."

"Do you feel your experience is an advantage?"

Aurora laughed, a rich and wonderful sound that made Mason wish he'd been the one to instigate it.

"It certainly helps not being the brat I was. Don't write that down." She sobered. "Yes, my experience will hopefully help me keep my focus through the tough matches."

"There are rumors of death threats. How are they affecting your play?"

Aurora's eyes revealed a sadness. "I'm sorry, Marco, but that discussion is off the table. It's personal, and it doesn't need to be publicized."

His pen stopped moving. "You're the boss." He closed his notebook.

Mason understood why Aurora liked this reporter. He was willing to exclude a sensitive topic even though writing about it would garner him a larger audience.

Mason leaned back in his chair and took a swig of his black coffee.

"Yes, I'm getting death threats. Death letters. The FBI is involved."

Marco's expression turned grim. "I'm sorry to hear that. Are you safe?"

"I have a protection team."

Yes, Aurora, you are safe.

Why hadn't she said yes? It bothered Mason to think she didn't reflexively say yes. Did they not make her feel safe?

The reporter's eyes roamed the room. "Are they here now?"

Aurora's mouth quirked. "They're always present. It's some comfort," she added meekly.

Marco frowned. He seemed to be genuinely troubled to have discussed a difficult topic for her. He forced cheer into his voice. "Well, we all know America's sweetheart tennis couple—Fisk and Meridian—is a thing of years past. While he's moved on to the Russian supermodel, no one seems to know what is churning in Aurora's heart."

For a fleeting moment, Mason thought Aurora's eyes flickered to him. Perhaps she wanted him to rescue her from an awkward conversation, but that wasn't going to happen. He inwardly cringed. If Marco thought having her talk about her latest relationship would veer the conversation toward a happier topic, he was mistaken.

Aurora pushed a strand of hair out of her face. "Tennis is my only love right now, Marco." She smiled. "You can quote me."

A server in the kitchen dropped a plate. The distant shatter had Aurora flinching slightly. When she glanced at Mason, he tried to radiate reasurrance. *I have your back, Aurora.*

She leaned back in her chair. "What about you? You've been single for over five years now. No persons of interest to fill the void?"

Marco chuckled at Aurora turning the attention to him. "A divorced male with children working as a reporter covering the tennis circuit does not embody a desirable bachelor."

"Come on. You're like a young Morgan Freeman."

His eyes crinkled at the compliment. "I'm happy to date would that there be an interested, eligible woman accepting of my travel and my family responsibilities."

"I'm sure there will be."

He grunted. "Back to tennis. With Wimbledon coming up, what's your strategy?"

From his table, Mason watched her straighten, shoulders squaring as she slipped fully into "Prime Meridian" for the press and conveyed confidence in herself and passion for the sport.

Wimbledon.

The next battlefields for her career... and for whoever wanted it destroyed.

CHAPTER 12

urora sat down at her hotel room desk and opened her laptop. Mason stood behind her. The sun beamed through the window and over neutral colored furniture.

The next tournament was the Aegon Birmingham Classic followed by Wimbledon. Subsequently, she would travel back to the United States for the Citi Open, followed by Montreal for the Rogers Cup, and then New York for the US Open. For now, she had five more days in Paris.

She had agreed to review what the FBI file had amassed on the death threats at the behest of Mason. The mature adult in her wanted to be helpful, but the wounded, petty part of her wanted a reason to be angry with Mason for coercing her. Perhaps resentment toward him would wash out the attraction she felt for him.

Was she being truthful to herself? He had claimed he needed to see the files to help her. For him, she could do this.

She had arranged a video conference call with Agent Coble who had been working on her case from the beginning. She leaned forward on the desk as the call connected, fighting the fluttering anxiety in her chest. Mason's presence brought comfort, she reluctantly admitted to herself.

Agent Coble flickered onto the screen, looking seasoned with his thin hair and receding hairline.

"Miss Meridian," he greeted her with a strained smile and Boston accent.

She guessed by the many deep wrinkles about his eyes and mouth that he didn't smile much. Not surprising in his line of work.

"I've sent you an encrypted file of scans of the letters and my notes—interviews and our team's analysis. Just take your time, peruse everything, talk about anything that jostles a memory or even just gives you goose bumps. I'll be right here if you have questions. When you're not asking me questions, I'm going to keep my end muted and wrap up some other paperwork."

Aurora nodded. "Okay. Thank you."

She moved the video screen to the lower left-hand corner and opened her email. She entered the password Agent Coble had given her for the encrypted file. With a deep breath she steeled herself against the insults and threats to come. She opened the file and began viewing the images.

Mason silently moved closer and leaned over. He radiated heat as the light wisp of his breath danced on her neck.

The angry words on the letters felt like a belt tightly cinching around her waist. She had to remind herself that whoever had issues with her had larger psychological problems, which were the predominant reason for the letters.

```
YOU  MISERABLE  BITCH.  I  WILL  CARVE  YOU  TO
PIECES  FOR  YOUR  ARROGANCE.  I  WILL  BLEED  YOU
DRY LIKE THE PIG YOU ARE.
```

```
AMERICAN  WHORE.  THERE  WILL  BE  NO  RISE  TO
FAME FOR YOU. I WILL WATCH YOU BURN.
```

And on they went.

"He or she seems to have fantasized many different ways to kill me," she said hoarsely.

Mason squeezed a hand on her shoulder. Agent Coble looked up from his screen and noticed, but Mason didn't withdraw his hand.

Aurora opened the file of analytical notes and skimmed through them.

"So you think it's a woman?" she asked.

"The syntax suggests so," Coble responded.

"And not American?"

"There are several instances where she refers to you as American. Not something one American typically conveys to another in a negative context. American to American references would be more specific—regional, like Red Neck or Yankee or Carpetbagger, or something political."

They settled into silence as Aurora continued to read.

"Anything?" Coble asked, sipping on an oversized cup of coffee.

"They definitely raise my hackles, but I can't think of anyone matching your profile. I play tennis internationally so that seems to open up any number of women's tennis fans ... assuming this is tennis related, which the threats seem to indicate."

Coble nodded. "We've already interviewed every professional you've played dating back six months before the letters began."

Aurora sighed. "So we're stuck with maybe a female fan who isn't from the States."

That seemed dauntingly, impossibly broad. A foreign fan gone rogue? Who would make it personal?

If someone wanted to target her because of tennis, wouldn't have been more appropriately timed? Perhaps years ago. Back then she had been cocky and abrasive. Hate mail during those years would have made more sense.

A cold tentacle of fear wrapped around her spine.

Time to pay for past behavior?

"Think on it," Coble advised. "If you generate any new names, we'll look into them."

"Okay. Thanks, Agent Coble."

He nodded and disconnected the videoconference.

Aurora sat there, staring at the screen and the last letter. The icy chill spread from her spine through every nerve ending in her body.

YOU WILL DIE SCREAMING.

Her throat tightened as if an invisible hand closed over her windpipe. Blinking, she realized she'd placed a hand on top of Mason's where it rested on her shoulder. Instead of keeping the contact, he recoiled from her every so slightly.

Ugh. Infuriating cyborg.

She had been drawing on his strength and comfort, not trying to seduce him.

Releasing his hand, she shrugged it off her shoulder. His spine stiffened as he stood motionless behind her.

Standing, she snapped her laptop shut.

"I'm going to get some rest." She knew the irritability she felt with him sliced into her words and was a clear dismissal.

"Of course," he said. Bland. Neutral.

Blah.

He left the hotel room and left her alone with nothing but death threats spiraling through her head. He had said he would help her through it. But, once again, she was alone.

MASON WALKED the perimeter as Aurora and Lizzy trained with grueling intensity.

Aurora had said she needed to get out of the room and escape her thoughts after looking at the death threats the day prior. If her rigorous training session didn't qualify as stress release, surely nothing else would. The brutal exercises had the two tennis players drenched.

Instead of a who-can-hit-the-ball-hardest during their unspoken competitive rallies, they worked through a series of drills without racquets. They tossed and chased down the ball, focusing on leg work, but with uncharacteristic delicacy handling the ball—as though it was the little chick Aurora liked to curse during her more aggressive practice sessions.

Next, they honed volley reflexes by having one person stand at the net while the other served, generally at a half to two-thirds speed, but still blindingly fast. Missing a ball like that could leave a welt or black eye. Neither Aurora nor Lizzy missed.

The last exercise forced finesse in the game where they had to rally within the service box, always letting the ball bounce once. Many of the balls skimmed low, forcing them to bend their knees severely, nearly touching the court to scoop up their next shot. Aurora's injured leg was fully healed.

Mason didn't keep track of who had won each game. When he'd found himself distracted by Aurora bending and the way her quick motions made her skirt flare, he decided to walk the perimeter.

The two women bid each other farewell, wishing wins. They made plans for Lizzy to meet up with Aurora after the Birmingham Classic to train prior to Wimbledon.

"Feel better?" he asked Aurora as Billy drove them back to the hotel.

She hadn't made lasting eye contact with him since he'd left the hotel room yesterday. Understandably, the threats had shaken her, but he sensed real smoldering anger toward him as well.

Aurora nodded, looking out the window. "I've been tense since looking at the letters. I needed to exercise it out of my system."

His jaw twitched under the weight of guilt. She'd needed a friend, and he had denied her that small comfort. Fearing that small comforts could lead to more, he'd resisted the urge to reach for her. He was hired to protect her, nothing more.

Mason glanced sidelong through his sunglasses. Her tense and stiff shoulders stoked the flames of unprofessional thoughts about how he wanted to erase her worries. With a touch, an embrace, he could make her forget the letters, the fear, and the worry.

And lose my job.

Except he'd sufficiently pissed her off to the extent she likely wouldn't let him touch her even if he wanted to—which he didn't.

He turned his focus entirely out the window where he couldn't see her glistening thighs and delicate fingers from the corner of his eyes.

***

MASON ENTERED BILLY'S room as she packed to leave for England. He had the schematics for the hotel in Birmingham on his tablet to review with her.

"What'd you do to Aurora?" Her tone sounded more curious than accusatory, but it still stung.

"Did she say something?" A painful lump formed in his throat.

"She asked me to make sure you're not sitting next to her on the plane."

He felt like someone punched him in the gut. He leaned over slightly and put his hand on the back of the desk chair. "I had her look at the FBI files and read through the letters."

Billy shot him a disparaging look.

"She needed to look at them and see if anything triggered a memory or a feeling of who could be behind the letters."

"And?"

"Nothing so far."

Billy grunted.

"When the fear of the letters wears off, she may think more clearly about them," he added defensively.

Billy zipped up her suitcase. "Seems you asking her to look at the letters and her degree of being pissed at you are a little discordant."

Mason swallowed. "I may not have been the supportive influence she needed at the time."

She frowned as she gruffly sighed. "You're such a jerk."

"Does she want me off her case?" The thought sickened him.

"Stop being melodramatic, you big stony baby," Billy chided. "She needs a day of space. Try being more of a friend and less of a . . . you, next time."

"I'll keep that in mind," he grumbled.

"It's not who you are anyway. Ever since the rock star incident, you keep acting like you don't know how to act. Sure, the security detail is ingrained, but you seem to have misplaced some of your human skills. Coming from me, that's saying a lot."

Billy was right ... mostly. He acted differently because he wanted to maintain his distance both to ensure no repetition of prior events and also because he felt attracted to Aurora. If he wasn't attracted to Aurora, the interaction would be less awkward.

"I'll fix it. Let me sit by her. It's a short flight and—"

"You need to give her space, Mason. Fix it later."

He clenched his jaw, but yielded.

"Did you learn anything from the files?" Billy asked.

He perked and stood straighter. "Yes. Female and foreign. The sense I get from the letters—"

"Hah!" Billy's outburst silenced him. "Max knew you would find a way to investigate." She narrowed her eyes at him. "You probably have Claire doing your dirty work, too." Billy laughed. Her short, dark bob danced around her amused face.

Mason restrained his mounting irritation. "What's funny?"

"If Claire is helping you, Maxine knows. You are not as clandestine as you are inclined to believe."

Mason felt the color drain from his face.

"Don't fret, big guy. She obviously wants you to go digging."

"She does?"

She ran a brush through her short hair and dropped it into her travel bag. "Sure. She's allowing you to access the resources, but if you overstep your boundaries, she has deniability that she ever told you to perform your own investigation."

Mason found no fault with Billy's logic.

"I'll tread carefully." He had already been walking on eggshells but felt the need to express it aloud.

"I'm sensing a trend here of you and thin ice and women." She sounded amused.

"Are you and I good, Billy?"

Her lips quirked, but her chocolate eyes held soft, warm solidarity. "Yeah, we're good."

Max could watching him from a distance. No problem. He could even manage a faceless stalker. Another day on the job. What he couldn't live with was Aurora looking at him like he'd abandoned her on purpose.

CHAPTER 13

While sitting beside Billy on the plane to Birmingham, Aurora couldn't close her eyes or she would see the death threats—angry block letters on white paper dripping with venomous hate.

Her rational mind emphasized the letters originated from an unstable psychopath. She hadn't treated anyone so egregiously as to warrant being on the receiving end of those letters. Irrationally, she tried to think of someone she had wronged ... no one to the extent that violence was a logical next step.

Everything was illogical, including how she felt about Mason. Which was what exactly? Maddeningly, thinking of him wiped away images of hostility and death and replaced them with a sensation of tranquility. She saw his face, warmed by a smile or the brief, hungry look in his eyes she had surely only imagined.

She could almost feel his touch, as though the few times he had touched her—his hands on her arm or on her back or shoulder—left a lingering warmth.

After so many stiff-lipped, tense moments, and abrupt withdrawals of anything resembling compassion, she wanted to be angry with him. She wanted the rejection to poison her feelings for him. Eradicate them. Make them wilt. She wanted to extinguish the irrational attraction and crackling electricity she felt when he sat or stood close to her.

Why desire something you can't have?

Because she was programmed to desire the impossible. Competitive sports trained her to push the limits of mind and body and prove the object of desire was attainable.

Mason's desires were clear—no client relationship. Given the misery he had been through on his last case, she had no intentions of doing anything remotely coercive or manipulative. She would never seduce him.

Despite the Rubicon divide he etched between them, she still felt safer with his stony presence than without it. Amidst the chaos of the circuit and the hideous threats, letting her useless heart dribble into a puddle seemed a small price to pay for feeling safe.

She cracked open her laptop to work on her latest design: a label for a sugar-free, vitamin-enhanced flavored water. She moved the little cluster of strawberries around the words.

Strawberries. What a lie.

As if the stuff had anything healthy in it—certainly nothing resembling actual fruit. She read the ingredients list on the wrap-around label she created. It contained a dizzying array of artificial flavors and sweeteners.

Yuck.

Aurora only craved natural ingredients.

⁂

Several days later, Mason paced the small hotel room as Billy adjusted their surveillance equipment. The soft lighting and view of Park Street and beautiful Birmingham did little to ease his angst.

"Speak, oh silent, brooding one," Billy said.

"It's wrong. It's all wrong."

Billy raised her eyebrows.

"Aurora lost today," Mason continued.

After Aurora hadn't wanted to sit on the plane with Mason, Billy had decided to try the tennis match with her close to Aurora and Mason in the crowd. And she'd lost her match.

"Aurora?"

"Miss Meridian," he corrected himself, annoyed that Billy missed the point.

"She's a professional tennis player." Billy's voice flattened. "She lost. She will lose again."

"Not in the first round. Not against a player like that."

Billy cleaned a camera lens with a soft cloth. "Are we here to help her win? I was under the impression our job is to keep her safe. Mission accomplished."

He shook his head. Aurora should have won her match today—and in in straight sets. Instead, she had been distracted and worried, constantly looking into the crowd as though someone conspired to lunge from the stands at her.

"Our responsibility extends to making her *feel* safe. She didn't feel safe out there." He continued to pace. "Her routine is wrong. I didn't travel with her, and I wasn't on the ground."

"That's mighty presumptuous of you," Billy chided with an odd chip in her voice.

"You have a better explanation?"

"Players lose. It happens."

Mason shook his head again. Aurora had been distracted. Billy didn't understand the significance. Because of this loss, she hadn't gotten enough court time on grass. This devastating defeat could negatively affect her performance at Wimbledon.

"We need to switch the team back."

Billy scowled, but her tone remained non-confrontational. "For Aurora or for you?"

Mason felt his ears burn hot like poker sticks. "No matter what you think this looks like, I want it reversed for Aurora."

Billy set down her camera and stared at him.

Miss Meridian, dammit.

Close proximity to Aurora actually made his feelings harder to bury. He'd be doing himself a favor if he kept his distance.

Escorting her to and from the court every time—win or lose—seemed to escalate his desire to stay longer with her. After every match, he fought the urge to linger and converse. If he drove and parked instead of walking with her, he could skip the temptation entirely.

"She can win with or without you," Billy said.

"Under different circumstances, I'd agree with you. But right now, with the threats, she needs a stable team."

Billy grunted.

Mason sat down and stared at her. "Look me in the eye, Billy. Believe me when I tell you the easy road for me here is to keep my distance. I'm saying this for Aurora, not for me."

He kept firm eye contact as Billy's eyes scrutinized his face. She wheezed out an exhalation as she nestled the camera back in its cushioned case. "Fine. I'll talk to her. No guarantees."

⁓

AURORA PACED HER HOTEL ROOM. The walls seemed to close around her. She couldn't concentrate long enough to read a book or work on her graphic design project.

Yesterday's loss had been so fast and so final. As quick as a ball toss, she logged another loss. She knew grass would be tough, but hadn't expected to lose so early.

She couldn't blame it on an injury. Her game was simply dysfunctional. Not only were her wheels not up, but the brakes had been locked in place.

Wimbledon would be an uphill battle. First the qualifier, then the matches.

A knock broke her rampaging thoughts. Billy's knock. Aurora opened the door.

"Grab a raincoat. I need to get out of this confinement and go to lunch," Billy said.

Aurora arched an eyebrow. "So says the woman who prefers confinement."

"I'm complex," Billy blatantly lied. She stared at Aurora as though daring her to argue.

Leaving the door open, Aurora grabbed her purse, coat, and room key. She slipped on her shoes quickly, not wanting to miss the chance to leave the room.

Following Billy to the elevator, she asked, "What about the rest of the team?"

"Dorian is on coms. He'll tail us. Mason is on break."

Break?

He portrayed such a formidable man that Aurora hadn't considered his need for breaks.

She walked with Billy three blocks to the *Mojo Pub*. Aurora shot Billy a suspicious look when she saw the black awning with the restaurant name.

Billy shrugged. "Well, I'm sure it doesn't substitute for the company of your friend, but it's all I could find."

Aurora smiled. Beneath the short woman's casual, nonchalant demeanor lurked a highly observant, intuitive woman who cared about the people around her.

After being seated at a table inside, they ordered two Young's Double Chocolate Stouts and beef stew.

Aurora drank the bitter malt beer. "Ugh. This stuff is so thick I practically have to chew it."

"I know. So good," Billy mused, staring lovingly at her beer the way Aurora stared at crème brûlée.

They ate their stew as Aurora waited for Billy's true intentions for the impromptu getaway-lunch to emerge.

When she nearly finished her tall glass of stout, Billy spoke. "First- round loss sucked."

"Yes, it did."

"You looked a little shaken up out there."

"Small detail of death threats."

Billy guzzled the last couple ounces of beer. She flung her bob cut out of her eyes. "You've actually been handling the fear pretty remarkably. What was different yesterday?"

"I don't know," Aurora said truthfully. She swirled her half-eaten stew with her fork. Yesterday, everything felt off balance. Shadows moved deviously. Faces seemed unfriendly. Was it something to do with overcast, drizzling England?

"I do," Billy said.

Aurora blinked at her.

"It's our fault. We altered your security detail. Mason needs to be on the court, myself in the crowd, Dorian on wheels."

She considered Billy's explanation. "Maybe. You're sure that's different than saying I just left my lucky rabbit's foot in the wrong tennis bag?"

Billy swallowed a bite of potato. "Yes, it's different. We had a formula you felt most secure with, and we tampered with it. The equivalent would be if we had reorganized your warm-up routine— your game would have been affected."

"So ... we change it back?"

If Billy felt offended in any way at the implication that Aurora felt more secure with Mason on point, she didn't project any sense of annoyance or dejection.

"Yes."

"Sounds simple."

"It is."

Aurora rode the train from Birmingham to London with Mason by her side. She wore her unflattering sunglasses as she stared out the window. She tried to assess her inner fear factor. Was it different with him closer? Maybe she would have to be on the court to discern a difference.

She ignored a series of text messages.

Alex: *What time are you arriving?*

Mom: *I know you don't like to talk after losses, but I'm here for you.*

MoJo: *Need some Mojo?*

Mason said little on the trip.

Big surprise.

She expected something—a comment about the loss or the changing of the guard.

Silence.

She blew a loose strand of hair out of her face and opened her laptop to critique her game. She watched a video replay of her serve.

Dropping your shoulder, Aurora.

She lost power when she dropped her shoulder.

Outside the window England rushed past at two hundred fifty miles per hour.

As they neared the train station, Aurora tucked her laptop into her shoulder bag. When the train came to a halt, she stood in the aisle, waiting to de-board. She shouldered her bag and drew out her carry-on as Mason stayed in front and Billy behind her. Dorian had been several rows somewhere behind them.

"Com check," Mason said.

Aurora followed obediently behind him as they walked toward the exit.

Mason's head turned left and right. His rigid torso held tense shoulders. He was on high alert.

As they continued to advance down the aisle, Aurora looked out the window. Throngs of people moved along the platform. Any other time before the threats, she would have moved among the crowd as another busy traveler. She pushed her sunglasses on top of her head to more clearly see the shuffling pedestrians.

Mason perceived danger, which was reason enough for her to feel scared.

Her heartbeat quickened as her mouth grew dry.

Mason's large, warm hand reached back and grabbed hers.

"Billy," he said.

"I see it."

"It's too crowded. Stay on flank. Dorian, luggage."

Billy took Aurora's carry-on bag out of her hand. From her peripheral vision, she saw Billy pass it back to Dorian.

When they stepped onto the platform, the crowd swept them into the current. Mason kept her tucked in close, using himself as a shield, as he maneuvered through the crowd.

She was breathing hard, disproportionate to the pace of their walk. Clutching him with one hand, she gripped her shoulder bag with the other.

The terminal felt hot and almost suffocating. Men and women shuffled toward and away from them at a dizzying pace. Her glasses fell off, but she didn't care. She left them to be trampled in the crowd.

Mason moved in a flash. His hand was a blur as he struck someone, maybe more than once. The man withdrew into the crowd as blood spewed from his nose.

Aurora bit back a scream.

Mason's hand was back in hers, and he never slowed as he continued to lead her out of the terminal. The sound of surprised gasps erupted behind them.

Aurora's legs moved beneath her even though she felt stiff and cold with fear. She kept her eyes on Mason and tried to focus on staying close, moving quickly.

Mason talked through his mike to the other team members, but the words sounded jumbled through the loud, thumping heartbeat roaring in her ears.

He'd just broken a stranger's nose? Was that man the threat, or just in the wrong place?

CHAPTER 14

Mason continued to hold Aurora's hand even after they cleared the crowded train station. Her pulse beat rapidly near where he held her hand as she gripped him tightly. Her panting breath and the faint chatter of her teeth resonated in his ear.

He knew London was busy, but he hadn't expected such an onslaught of people. Although part of him wanted to chase after the assailant and finish the fight, he didn't know if there were more attackers and his top priority was getting Aurora to safety. He didn't want to get ambushed by other attackers while restraining one of them.

Several blocks from the train station Mason found a pub, scarcely occupied at this hour of the day. Pulling Aurora closer, he let go of her hand and put an arm around her shoulder. He led her to the back of the pub and helped her into a chair. A waiter came, and Mason ordered a beer and a glass of water.

Aurora stared at the table with eyes wide and hands resting on the surface, palms down and fingers spread. Even pressed into against the tabletop, they trembled slightly.

"It's okay, Aurora. You're safe," he assured her.

She looked around the pub and blinked as though noticing her different surroundings for the first time. Scooping her hands up in his, he held them gently, trying to ease her stress and give her silent reassurance.

"We'll just be here for a bit, until Dorian gets to the hotel and secures the room."

She looked up into his eyes. "What happened back there?"

Her fear mixed with anger. He preferred the anger even if it seemed misdirected at him.

"Aurora."

"What happed back there? One second we were walking, and the next there was blood. Scared the hell out of me." She pulled her hands out of his.

"Aurora."

"You broke that man's nose."

Her look of anger staggered back into fear, but fear toward him—this he could not allow. Reaching into his pocket, Mason pulled out a small switchblade and set it down on the tabletop. He'd palmed it off the man's hand in the same motion he'd broken his nose; now it lay harmless and small between them.

"He was coming at you with this knife."

He had hoped to not emphasize the danger she'd been in, but he would not have her thinking he overreacted and assaulted someone without provocation.

She sucked in a breath. "Mason—"

"You have to trust me."

She nodded as her emerald eyes filled with remorse. "I do. I trust you. I'm sorry."

He took her hands again, and she didn't resist. He was simultaneously annoyed by the table separating them and grateful it prevented him from pulling her into his lap.

When the waiter returned with the beer and water, Mason was forced to relinquish Aurora's hands.

Sitting back, he appraised her expression. The darting eyes around the room had stopped. The shaking dulled to a slight tremor. Her terror had subsided to lingering anxiety.

She reached for the water and drank. He wasn't sure which

beverage she would prefer after a harrowing experience so he'd ordered her both.

"Are you okay for a moment while I check in with Max?"

Aurora sniffed, wiped at her eyes, and nodded.

After withdrawing his phone, he speed-dialed Maxine's number. "Max, I've got an incident to report."

"Hold on. Let me record."

He glanced at Aurora who'd transitioned from the water to the beer.

"Okay," Maxine said.

"We're in London. The train station was crowded. We did a rapid extraction. I disabled a man with a switchblade. As crowded as it was, I can't be certain Aurora specifically was the target."

A chair grated across the floor, and Aurora flinched. Mason extended a hand and gripped hers.

Max remained silent for a moment. "Injuries?"

"Only the assailant."

"Assessment."

"Lone attacker on a crowded platform. We're safe now. Dorian is securing the hotel. Billy's arranging transportation."

"Did anyone have a conversation with the attacker?"

Meaning, did anyone interrogate him?

"No." Mason had thought of having Billy follow after the man, but without knowing if more attackers prowled the terminal, he couldn't risk leaving Aurora's back unguarded.

"How is *Miss Meridian?*"

Agh!

He'd called her Aurora, and Maxine noticed. It explained her moment of silence after his slip. Glancing at Aurora, he was surprised to see her gaze had cleared. She watched him intently, calm trust completely replaced fear.

"She's okay. Uninjured. Just alarmed."

"Okay, Mason. Good work. Keep me posted."

"Yes, boss."

"Mason?"

"Boss?"

"You trade off with Billy when you get to the hotel."

"Yes, boss." He knew what Max insinuated.

He'd just saved Aurora from danger. Maxine wanted to distance Mason from her. She wanted to make sure a repeat of the prior client disaster didn't happen. Aurora would never pull a stunt like that, but Max was right to caution him.

He also knew the real reason he needed to not be alone with her—to avoid temptation to do what consenting adults did when alone together. He thought Aurora would willingly give herself to him, but he suspected she sought to smother her loneliness. His availability made him desirable. It was easier to believe she wanted a warm body beside her than to believe she might actually want *him* specifically. When he took the next plunge into a relationship with a woman, it would be because she wanted him specifically.

He still held the phone to his ear when he realized Maxine had disconnected.

Aurora's mouth held a lopsided grin.

He slid the phone back into his pocket.

Could she want him and not just anyone with whom to share a relationship?

"You look like you're feeling better," he said cautiously.

She nodded. "I feel better listening to you—straightforward, no-nonsense Mason Stone. Not an ounce of fear."

"Good. I didn't know if talking like that in front of you would upset you."

Even if it had, anger was more useful than fear right now.

"If you're not afraid, why should I be?" she asked.

Trust reestablished.

He admired the way she had quickly composed herself and reined in her fear.

"Do you need anything? Do you want to talk to your parents or Monique?"

She patted her hand, withdrew hers, and took another sip of beer. "I need you sitting here with me expecting me to keep my shit together and not treating me like a porcelain doll or gushing sympathetic looks."

He blinked at her, a swell of admiration and adoration practically lifted him off his chair.

"Basically, I need you just like this, being you," she added.

He grinned. "Done."

Aurora ran on the treadmill. Moisture trickled down the back of her neck and along her spine. Beads of sweat ran down her skin the same way rain ran down the window in front of her. The weather confined her workout routine indoors.

Most days she would have been disappointed. The day after being attacked while crossing a crowded train terminal, however, she found contentment in exercising in isolation.

She stared out the window, focusing on her breathing. Images of her attacker stumbling backward, clutching his face as blood erupted from his nose, flashed before her. She tried to recall his face. Pockmarked skin. Dark eyes. In his thirties, she thought, but he looked older as the result of a hard life. No one she knew.

Was the attack related to the letters? Was this the man who had been writing them? The letters, in all their horrific glory, were just words. Yesterday's attack made the threat terrifyingly real. Someone had every intention of hurting her.

She had played down the attack to her parents, saying only that the train station had been crowded and Mason and Billy rushed her out of the terminal. What could she definitively tell them? A man with a knife impeded their path. They didn't know if he'd targeted Aurora specifically.

Mason knew. Even as he told Maxine he couldn't be sure, something in his expression conveyed that he, too, perceived the threat as more tangible now.

If Aurora expressed her fears to her parents, what could they do about it? Nothing. The same damn thing she could do about the impending doom of another attack—nothing.

She gritted her teeth and sped up the treadmill. The heart monitor climbed from one hundred thirty beats per minute to one hundred fifty beats per minute.

The attack didn't fit the profile. Stalkers weren't supposed to make their move in crowded terminals. And her attacker hadn't been female. Did that mean the FBI had it wrong, or that more than one person stalked her? Oh, god. Could she have multiple people intending to harm her?

All she could do was wait—wait for the next tennis match, wait for Agent Coble to find a clue, wait for the next assault. She simultaneously feared another attack and wished for one. She didn't want the danger of being assaulted, but an attack carried the hope of Mason catching the assailant.

She snatched her towel, raked it across her brow before the sweat dripped into her eyes, and tossed it irritably back on the edge of the treadmill display. Her feet pounded along the conveyor belt as she ran in a steady stride.

She hated being helpless bait.

In the window, she caught a glimpse of Mason's reflection. Her eyes focused harder on the image of him behind her. He pulled himself up on bars, his biceps bulging under the strain. As he moved up and down, his focus wasn't on his exercise routine. He watched her intently, concern etched in his expression.

She looked down at the machine. Her heart rate raced at one hundred eighty beats per minute. She panted for air. In her anger, she had pushed herself too hard. She slowed to a jog, catching her breath.

Mason eased himself down, landing with silent stealth on the matted floor. He walked onto the machine beside her and joined her in a jog. His face morphed back to his usual neutral blandness.

"Anything you want to talk about?" he asked.

Sure. Let's talk about how much I want you to pull me into your arms when you look at me like you give a damn about my feelings. Let's talk about how I sleep alone every night imagining what you would feel like next to me. Let's talk about how I don't know if my next tennis match will be my last.

The words lined up on her tongue, too sharp and vulnerable to share. "No," she replied instead.

Aurora hugged her friend Lizzy as they arrived on the court to practice. "It's such a relief to see a friendly face. Great job in Marseille and at Ilkley."

"Thanks." Lizzy returned the hug. She tucked a strand of brown hair behind one ear before turning and grabbing her racquet and balls. "You didn't get much grass time, so I was thinking on how to help you prepare. I'm going to keep the balls low and fast, not much topspin to mimic grass. You okay?"

Aurora simultaneously wanted to share the train attack and forget about it. "Yeah. I'm good."

Mostly forget about it.

"Jimmy is winning a lot."

"Is he?"

"And he and Natasha seem closer than ever," Lizzy added.

"I assure you, any distraction you perceive has nothing to do with him and his prima donna sidekick."

Different man, different danger.

Lizzy shrugged. "Fine. You don't want to tell me. Let's play for it. I win, then you tell me what's ruffled your feathers. I lose, and you keep your secret."

"Fine."

After two hours, Aurora beat her friend six-four, six-four. They sat on the bench drinking water.

"Doesn't he get hot standing and pacing, pacing and standing?"

Aurora followed her friend's gaze to Mason. "I imagine so, but he never complains about it."

"He must be a terrible bore."

Life would be easier if he was. "He saved my life."

Lizzy turned to stare at Aurora.

"You want to know what's bothering me? Someone came after me with a knife at the London station."

"What? Who? The death threats?"

Aurora shook her head. "We don't know who. And the attack doesn't fit the profile of my stalker. The threats promise something intimate and personal, not a hired thug at a train station. It doesn't make any sense."

"Jeez. I thought maybe the bodyguards were overkill. I'm glad you have them."

"Me, too," Aurora said.

"Are they okay? Did anyone on your team get hurt?"

"No. They were flawless. Neutralized the threat without any harm to themselves or me. Heck, I didn't even know what happened until it was over." Neutralized the threat? Who was she saying words like that? She was a tennis player, not a military analyst.

"Wow." Lizzy gave a nervous glance around her. "If I get shanked because I gave you a lesson, I'm haunting your ass."

Aurora stiffened. Did her friend suddenly feel as if she were in danger by proximity? Could Aurora have put her in danger? She just wanted to train with a friend, to be with a friend. She had so few of them these days. But she didn't want put her friend in danger. She could push her away, perhaps not see her again until everything resolved.

Lizzy grinned as she changed the subject. "You remember Laine Brown?"

"Do I? She's the most annoyingly impatient tennis player." Aurora recalled how the lanky Australian would serve just as her opponent got set at the baseline or barely take a break while switching sides. Her rushed methods could unnerve players.

"Yeah. So we were playing the first round at Marseille, and she was rushing me the entire game. I'm getting annoyed even though we're tied. Then, she mishits, and the ball flies over the next court divider. We've got other balls, right? Instead, I wave my hand and call to her, 'No, problem. I got it!' and I walk—a casual, relaxed saunter—

two courts down to get the ball." Lizzy laughed. "I thought she was going to pop her strings she was so infuriated by the delay in play."

Lizzy and Aurora laughed together.

Aurora wiped the tears of laughter out of her eyes. "Can we do some concentrated training again before the US Open?" She would have weeks between the Rogers Cup and the US Open to train hard.

"Yeah. I'll have to fly back from Germany, but I can swing it."

"Fabulous."

Aurora packed her bag, wrapped up the conversation with Lizzy, thanking her for the lesson. She was ready for a cool shower and evening of relaxation.

Mason walked with her back to the car.

"Good training session?" he asked.

"I think so."

"But?"

"But, I'm wondering if my friends could become targets. The letters existed in a sphere less hostile than the new escalation to violence. What if my interactions with friends put them in danger?"

Mason took the tennis bag from her shoulder. "I think it unlikely."

"Why?"

"The answer isn't as reassuring as you might like."

"I'm a big girl, Mason."

"The tone of the letters centers on harm to you. Physical harm more than emotional suffering. For that reason, I don't think the attacker is interested in targeting people you care about."

He was right; she didn't feel better knowing his assessment of the situation.

CHAPTER 15

*A*urora had reached Wimbledon. She had achieved this feat only twice before. The draw was good. She wasn't playing any of the top ten in the first through third rounds. Three of those top ten were favored on grass courts. To get further in Wimbledon, she needed to play those women later... or not at all if someone else beat them.

Grass was not her friend. The ball sped faster on grass, rewarding power players and penalizing finesse players. The lower bounce on grass meant players had to get to the ball earlier. Worn-down areas of grass played inconsistently with the lusher regions. The baseline became bald and slick after several matches. Moisture and rain only made it more slippery.

But the smell of lawn tennis and the way the scent of grass clung to the yellow birdie made the struggle of play worth it. She always breathed deeply just before a serve, taking in the fresh, earthy aroma.

Four days flew in a blur. She would play in the second round of singles tomorrow, and she and Alex would play mixed doubles the day after that. She was poised to do well for her next match because she hadn't worn herself down with long games.

Her security team worked flawlessly. She even started to have doubts about the train station attack. According to Billy, no new threatening letters had arrived since arriving in London. Maybe the assailant hadn't been after Aurora specifically. Maybe the switchblade was to cut purse straps. He could have just been a desperate thief.

While her brain tried to rationalize the danger away, her gut knew better.

THE NIGHT before her quarterfinal match, Alex, Aurora, Mason, and Billy went for dinner at a local pub known for their fish and chips.

Alex ordered lager, which Aurora mimicked, telling herself she would need the carbs on the court tomorrow. Mason and Billy drank water.

Alex gulped his beer voraciously. Following a burp, he said to Mason, "Did you see the backcourt overhead smash Aurora made?" He grinned like a proud papa.

Mason nodded.

"Brilliant. I keep telling her she ought to stay. Play another year. Keep shinin' like the Aurora Borealis she is."

Aurora munched on a potato chip and swallowed. "Original." Although she tried to sound irritated, she couldn't conceal her smile. She blamed Alex's infectious enthusiasm. "Besides, I'm at my *prime*, remember? It's only downhill after this."

"Shame," Alex said with a shake of his head.

"It might be fun to keep playing doubles," she thought aloud.

"There it is!" he exclaimed, beaming.

He threw a rough arm around Aurora's shoulder. She suddenly wished she'd been sitting closer to Mason—no danger of any sudden outburst with him. His programming prevented outbursts and rambunctiousness.

"I knew she loved me." Alex squeezed her close before releasing her.

"I'm not making promises," she said.

"Understood. Don't crush a boy's dreams though." He finished his beer in a long guzzle and set the mug down on the wooden table with a thud. The only thing missing was Alex dressed in furs and a kilt, yelling, "More wine, wench!"

Aurora smiled at the image.

Alex stood and stretched.

"Where are you going?" she asked.

"Hot date with Hans. Don't worry, Mum, I'll get enough rest for the game." He bent down and gave Aurora a peck on the cheek. "Wouldn't hurt your game if you had your own hot date." His eyes flickered playfully toward Mason.

Aurora felt a flush creep up her neck. She scowled at the backside of Alex as he disappeared out the front door.

MASON REMAINED MOTIONLESS, momentarily stunned from Alex's insinuation.

Billy jumped out of her seat, rolling her eyes. "Perimeter check. You two enjoy your rom-com."

Mason looked down at Billy's plate, amazed to see she had eaten the entirety of her meal. He watched her leave.

"Com check," he heard in his ear.

"Check."

Aurora began eating slowly, her rosy cheeks betraying her embarrassment, but she hadn't brushed of Alex's comment.

She wore her blond hair down loosely, the soft sheen practically begging for his touch. Her cream-colored dress accentuated her tan skin and feminine hips.

"Can you pass the catsup?"

Mason's hand shot out and grabbed the bottle, as though grateful to be assigned a task.

"Thanks." She accepted it and added the condiment to her plate. "That was the fastest catsup draw I've ever seen. You must be pretty quick with a gun."

He shifted uncomfortably, but felt the familiar weight of the gun in his holster.

"I am."

She arched an eyebrow.

He returned the gaze. Protecting someone's life was not the time to be humble and downplay deadly skill.

"You've been playing tremendously well," he commented, wanting to get her mind off guns and his mind off his other skills he wanted to demonstrate for her.

"Thanks. Everything is just clicking out there on the court. I feel like Alex and I can win this."

"And singles?"

Her mouth twitched. "The remaining players are top tier. I'm going to have to unleash the A game—repeatedly—for that to happen."

"You look as strong as any of them."

She looked up at him as though trying to discern if he had meant anything more by his statement.

"Stronger," he emphasized.

Stronger in every way that mattered—and entirely off limits. And sexier and smarter and everything he would want in a woman. But he can't have any of it because Aurora was the client.

They finished eating, and the waiter arrived.

Aurora snatched the bill. "My team, my treat," she replied in answer to his scowl.

They stood, and Mason led her out of the building.

When Aurora's bodyguard placed a hand on the small of her back, heat and electric jolts surged through her. Mason looked so delicious at dinner. He wore his usual pressed suit and starched white shirt, but the sunglasses were out of sight. His clean-shaven jaw was firm, sculpted, and tan. His blond hair coursed in waves away from his face. More attractive than his appearance were the rare moments he let his guard down—a laugh at something Alex said, a genuine encouragement or a question for her.

If his simple touch on her back felt this good . . .

"We're on the move," Mason said to Billy. "Billy?"

Mason slid a protective arm around Aurora and brought her to a halt.

She recognized his posture of sudden alarm. Her heart kicked faster as he simultaneously positioned himself in front of her and drew his weapon.

"Billy?" he repeated, inching toward the door.

Aurora glanced around the restaurant. The few patrons engrossed in conversation and food didn't notice the gun-wielding Norse god.

"Stay behind me no matter what happens. If I say run—"

"—I run. If you say down, I hit the deck. Got it. I read the Rider Client Safety Manual."

Mason gave her a crooked grin.

Now he lightens up.

He was stiff and stoic as a statue ninety percent of the time, but raise the threat alert to orange and he became happy Thor ready to smash something with his hammer.

Was this an orange or red threat level?

They exited the pub to a dimly lit street. Aurora saw nothing moving except a couple, arm in arm, walking on the opposite sidewalk in the distance.

"Follow," he ordered quietly.

Aurora obediently followed him as they turned right and walked down the sidewalk.

Mason produced a flashlight and panned the shadows and dark alleys.

She gasped when she saw a glimpse of Billy's combat boots lying on the ground down one of the alleyways. She saw unmoving legs, but shadows and distance concealed the rest of her body.

Mason passed her the flashlight. He withdrew his phone. "Dorian, we have a situation. I need an ambulance at the alley north of The Old Frizzle pub for Billy and an extraction the next street north of the pub for Aurora."

He slid the phone back in his pocket and resumed his cautious pace toward the next intersection.

"What about Billy?" Aurora's voice sounded coarse and unrecognizable to her own ears.

"Trap."

Aurora sucked in a breath. Was whoever assaulted Billy lying in wait for them to check on her and attack?

Oh, God. Were they just going to leave her on the ground like that? She was obviously injured. Or worse?

Aurora's legs moved her forward even though her body buzzed with fear.

A large figure appeared in front of them.

Mason's arm pulled Aurora tightly up against him. Behind them, two more assailants emerged from the alley where Billy lay. They weren't going to make it to the intersection—the extraction point.

Three guns pointed at them to Mason's one. One of the men sported a broken nose. Aurora stifled a gasp. The train station attacker. She caught herself squeezing too tightly to Mason and gave him a little more space.

The largest man to their right spoke first, his accent unmistakably Russian. "Let's not fight like Wild West, *da*? Let's settle this like Russian *bokser*."

Mason holstered his weapon.

No, no, no. Three against one. What do you have a gun for if not to use it? At least give it to me?

She didn't know how to use a gun, but she'd feel better holding one to deter the attackers.

Was Mason such a fast draw he remained unconcerned about holstering it? Who was faster than three guns? But he didn't have a choice except to lower his gun with the others aiming at him.

Her chest squeezed, and she realized she was hyperventilating as thoughts raced through her mind.

Calm yourself, Aurora.

She fell back on her tennis tactics.

Blue whales are the largest animals in the world.

A common zebra has twenty-six stripes.

Mason turned to her and brought her clenched fists in his hands up to his lips. He kissed each of them and leaned in to her ear.

"When Dorian comes, you fly like a bat out of hell into the car and don't look back."

A sickening feeling wrapped its tentacles around Aurora's stomach and squeezed. Mason planned to sacrifice himself for her. He would take on three tattooed, snarling Russians to give her time to escape.

Before he drew back, he brushed his lips against hers. So brief, yet she tasted him. If his intentions were to distract her from her fear, it worked. If his intentions were to make her wonder what a real kiss would feel like, it also worked.

After he released her hands, she stepped back and pressed herself into the wall. Her heart pounded and her hands shook, dreading the battle to come.

MASON DIDN'T HAVE time to scold himself for kissing Aurora, but he felt supercharged after the look on her face when his lips touched hers. Invincible. Her soft lips, were parted slightly.

Her eyes had conveyed a bottomless well of worry for him. She was convinced he wasn't going to survive this attack. He wasn't concerned for himself, but the kiss was unfair to her.

Later, she would think of the kiss and tell herself he only stole one because he didn't think he would live to take another. Nothing deeper. It was deeper. His feelings had plunged agonizingly deep. How often would he continued to lie to himself about them?

One of the older Russians with a pocked face and gray teeth spoke. "Cute romance. Perhaps I kiss her too when this is done."

"*Cherez moy trup,*" Mason replied.

The leader smirked, but his gray eyes betrayed his surprise at Mason's ability to speak Russian. Perhaps a brief realization flickered in the Russian's eyes that he may have underestimated his opposition, but he was committed now.

Mason was ready for a fight, craved it. His senses sharpened, detecting the smell of their Russian Belomorkanal cigarettes and the trickle of sweat breaking out on their foreheads.

The Russians attacked predictably—street fighters but not military combat trained. The lead man lunged, fists flying.

Mason blocked and landed a series of punches to particularly crippling, weak areas of the human body—the solar plexus at the base of the breastbone among them.

He almost had him down when his comrade flew in with a high kick. Mason caught his foot and wrenched it, spilling the man onto the concrete.

The third man, whom Mason recognized as the train station attacker, stole the opportunity to make a sucker punch.

Mason's vision blurred momentarily from the impact of the man's fist. Mason kicked his right leg out viciously, catching the attacker in the chest before he could make a second punch.

The Russian stumbled back, gasping for air. Before the man on the ground could recover and rejoin the fight, Mason kicked him in the teeth.

By this time, the lead gray-teethed Russian had shaken off his injuries and launched another offensive.

Mason ducked, followed by a fisted uppercut into the man's jaw. He stumbled back, dropping the gun as he tried to pull it from its holster.

Mason shoved him into the wall and retrieved the gun.

The man with the broken nose seemed to think running and leaping onto Mason's back would accomplish something. Mason flipped the man over his shoulder, and the Russian landed with a crunch on the asphalt. By the time he straightened, three pistols lay in a sad little pile at his feet and three Russians were curled around their injuries.

Looking past the bodies, Mason saw Aurora halfway down the block, running like her life depended on it. Golden hair swirled behind her as her sparkling fashion boots echoed on the sidewalk— looking as gorgeous as a shining Mercedes while she ran like hell.

After he finished collecting firearms each of them, he jogged after

Aurora. Dorian had her in the car with the door closed by the time Mason caught up and motioned to him.

"Swap," he said, catching up to them. "Check on Billy down the alley. See if you can get any info out of the attackers. Your Russian is better than mine."

"Russian?"

Mason nodded. "*Mafiya* by the tattoos, Vladimir Pronin's goons if I had to guess."

"Bloody hell," Dorian cursed.

Mason hopped into the driver's seat, dumping the guns carefully onto the passenger's seat.

Peeling away from the curb, he said over his shoulder to Aurora, "Stay down for the next few blocks."

CHAPTER 16

Mason drove to a bed and breakfast on the outskirts of London and checked Aurora and himself into a room under a fake name with cash. After leading her into the dimly lit accommodations, he kept her close as he inspected the room.

She hadn't said anything on the drive, and he started to worry she was in shock. Once he secured the room, noting windows that didn't open and bolting the door, he turned to her.

She trembled, hugging her knees to her chest, as she sat on the bed and stared blankly at the opposite wall.

His heart lurched at seeing her look so fragile. He preferred the rock solid tennis athlete.

"Aurora." His voice cracked.

He sat on the bed and pulled her into his arms, hoping to warm her with his body heat and give her some measure of comfort.

"When I'm faced with something frightening, it's helpful if I dissect it," he said. Maybe this wasn't what she needed emotionally, but it was all he knew how to offer.

"Something frightens you?" she asked in disbelief.

The thought of anything happening to you.

He swallowed. "Yes."

"You dissected those men." She sounded impressed rather than abhorred.

He smiled, tucking her head under his chin and ignoring the throbbing of his swelling knuckles.

"What about them do you remember?"

"Russian. Lots of tattoos. Big guns."

She curled in a tight ball against him. He knew he shouldn't be holding her so close.

"How long are we here for?" she asked.

"I need to know from Dorian things are safe. Maybe a few hours. Maybe all night."

She nodded against his chest.

"I'm sorry if this throws a wrench in your game tomorrow," he said.

"Living is the one thing I prioritize above tennis. But you ... you put your gun away."

"My chances of victory were non-existent in a gun fight. They wanted to hurt us, not kill us, or they would have fired immediately. I had to show them I was willing face hand-to-hand combat." He stroked her hair. He shouldn't do that either, but he couldn't help himself.

"So let's continue our dissection," he said. "Three armed Russians smart enough to try to lure us into an alley to help a friend—"

"Underestimated you, though."

"Yes. So, three Russian *amateur thugs* sent to hurt you before your next Wimbledon match. Someone hired them to intimidate you or keep you from playing."

She shook her head. "There aren't any Russians I would be scheduled to play."

He noted with relief that she'd stopped shaking.

"Exactly. So who would have access to hire armed Russian goons and would want to hurt you and see you fail?"

A long silence settled between them. He felt the warmth of her breath and gentle rise and fall of her chest against him.

"Is there someone who might be threatened by your success? Someone who might be jealous?" he prodded.

"Natasha Bodrov?" Aurora's voice held a mix of skepticism and awe of revelation. "She's psychotic and self-absorbed enough to have written those demonic letters. But her attack would only make sense if she thought my tennis success would bring Jimmy back to me. That's absurd!"

Mason rubbed a hand up and down her arm before stopping himself. "She doesn't know how you feel. She knows you're single. She might even know Jimmy talked to you in Paris. All it would take is one paparazzi or social media photo circulating."

Aurora sat up and looked at him. "How does a Russian supermodel know how to hire Russian thugs?"

"Natasha has access to the Russian mafia." Thanks to Claire's thorough background check, this had been in the Rider File.

"She does?"

"Her uncle is Vladimir Pronin," he said.

"And he is a Russian mobster?"

"*The* Russian mobster. Notorious."

"You know this because ..."

"Because I do my homework when I'm assigned to protect someone, despite orders to not meddle in the FBI's investigation. I'm stubborn like you."

Aurora giggled, an actual girl-giggle with flushed cheeks that made his heart skip a beat. He wanted to pull her back into him, but he didn't want to appear to be offering anything more lasting or more intimate than temporary comfort.

She sobered quickly. "So, Russian mafia. That sounds worse than a crazed killer."

She lay back down, her head resting on his chest. Where it belonged.

No! What's wrong with me!

"It's better actually," Mason said.

She tilted her head up toward him to give him a partly incredulous, partly questioning expression.

"The mafia is a business. Terrorizing and violence need a payoff. The two most valuable assets in organized crime are honor and money, probably in the reverse order. My hunch is when we out Natasha as scheming to keep her boyfriend to herself, the Russian crime lord will be more embarrassed than vengeful, especially if you show mercy toward Natasha."

He avoided the urge to look down at her because her lips would be too close.

"Mercy." Aurora seemed to mull over the word.

Mason suspected the concept would be foreign to most professional athletes.

"You already suspected Natasha?" she guessed.

"Only after meeting the attackers."

He waited silently for her to formulate more questions, but she kept her thoughts to herself. Within a few minutes, the adrenaline crash subsided and Aurora's breathing slowed as she fell asleep in his arms.

He put his phone on silent but watched for text messages.

Dorian updated him: *Billy is scathed with a concussion and overnight observation, which she's grumbling about; the Russians didn't have much to say, but I didn't get rough with them. I let them go with the understanding we would speak with Vladimir about the incident. I encouraged them to come clean before Vladimir heard it from Max.*

Dorian's final text said: *Max knows all. She wants an update from you.*

Mason texted Max: *Asset is safe and sleeping. Think we have the culprit figured out. Will call later.*

Max: *As long as you're not sleeping with her. Keep your **** in your pants, Mason.*

Mason: *Love you too, Max.*

No reply.

Next, he emailed Agent Coble, described the Russian attackers, and asked if the FBI could get its hands on Natasha Bodrov's DNA.

LIGHT STREAMED through the small dining room, dissolving the frightful events of the preceding dark night.

Aurora ate her eggs and sausage ravenously in the dining area of the bed and breakfast where they had stayed.

"Are you going to play today?" Mason asked.

"Damn right I am. I'm not taking this crap lying down."

He smiled at her bravado and exercised enough restraint to avoid commenting on how she was obviously still scared under her tough words.

"Do you think they will try again?" she asked.

He drank his coffee before setting the cup back on the saucer. "They can try. They still can't get to you." He leaned back in his chair. "But I don't think they will. Natasha got in over her head."

"If it's her."

He nodded and appeasingly acknowledged, "If it's her."

Aurora took a sip of her orange juice. "Three against one, Mason. That's pretty amazing." So was the way he held her all night, but couldn't read more into that than it was. Protection not passion.

She remembered waking once while still in his arms. The next time she opened her eyes he'd moved to a chair in the room. He hadn't mentioned any significance in holding her so neither would she.

"I've had training. I think your tennis play is amazing, but you only got this good from years of training to perfect your innate talent."

"Not sure my game is perfected, but I understand your comparison. And your attempt to be humble. Alternatively, you could just accept the compliment."

"Thank you, Miss Meridian."

Her eyes flitted to her plate irritably. Mason's tone instantly reestablished the distance in their business relationship after last night's embrace. A few hours ago, his heartbeat had been steady under her ear. Now was a metronome ticking from behind a stone wall. Fine.

She hadn't been flirting with him. She hadn't even mentioned the kiss—or whatever it had been. So fleetingly brief and a crack in his otherwise professional demeanor. He would pretend it never happened, and she was left never forgetting it.

Miss Meridian.

God, he could make her blood boil when his demeanor turned to ice. She had tennis. She didn't need a relationship, and she had never once made a pass at him. Yet, there he sat, acting as though he must continuously draw a line in the sand to maintain the boundary between them.

She tossed her napkin on the table, dug in her purse, and dumped cash on the table. "Let's go. I need to change and warm up for the match."

***

AURORA LOST.

Although the Russian model's goons hadn't injured her, the intimidation tactics had created a successful distraction. Aurora saw flashes of Billy's unconscious body, guns glinting in the moonlight, and men pounding each other with fists.

The loss happened in a blur of tennis balls and violence. Aurora had felt numb. Disconnected. Someone else had just failed, not her. Perhaps the fatigue kept her from processing the implications of it, but she found herself indifferent.

She sat on a bench in the locker room as Dr. Ruchkin unwrapped and inspected her ankle.

"It feels okay, *da*?"

She stared at the far wall, seeing images of Mason, predatory and domineering. Yet, he had been anything but that when he kissed her. His blue eyes shed their machine-like impermeability and filled with compassion. Passion? Could it even be classified as a kiss? It was so fleeting.

An almost kiss.

The physician rolled her ankle as he palpated her foot with cold, slender fingers.

"Dr. Ruchkin, what does *cherez moy trup* mean?"

He stared at her perplexed, and she wondered how badly she had butchered the Russian words.

"Over my dead body," he replied, a cold edge to his tone.

Cherez moy trup.

The Russians had threatened to kiss her—or worse—when they finished beating Mason into unconsciousness, and he had told them with steely confidence, "Over my dead body."

Just after he almost kissed her.

She rolled her shoulders and shifted in her chair. Mason was an excellent bodyguard, that was all. He had told her exactly what to do and given her the encouragement and strength to do it.

"You are needing anti-inflammatory, *da*? I've got steroid injection for the swelling. Will help you in mixed doubles."

"No needles. No injections. No drugs."

The physician shrugged as he continued to check her ankle's mobility.

The problem was in her head and her heart, not in her ankle.

"You are tense, no?" He frowned. "You need sedative to help you relax or muscle relaxer so you don't cramp like you do sometimes?"

She looked at him and grinned. Was it job security that made him so eager to treat her? Regardless, he seemed so focused compared to her distracted mind.

"No, thank you."

London hadn't been to hot. No doubt, the cramps would come in the weeks to follow. Late July matches brought brutal temperatures.

As far as rest went, she seemed to sleep just fine in Mason's arms, a far better treatment than any tranquilizer Dr. Ruchkin could give her. Of course, the side effect of being close to Mason was craving him more.

Not an option.

Cherez moy trup.

All bodyguards probably said things like, *"over my dead body."*

She clung to the thought. It was safer than believing his words had been meant for her alone.

He did his job.

Kept her safe.

Nothing more.

⁂

MASON WATCHED Aurora exit the locker room dressed in tennis clothes with her hair still pulled back in a ponytail.

He didn't conceal his surprise or confusion. After her match, she usually presented herself clean and back in her jeans with her hair down.

She tossed him her bulky tennis bag. Fury and focus burned in her green eyes.

He caught it reflexively. "Miss Meridian?"

"Change of plans. I need to go to practice courts. Somewhere remote."

"Billy?"

"I'm on it," she said into his earpiece. "I'll have directions by the time you're in the car."

"We'll get you there," he said to Aurora.

She nodded but didn't make eye contact with him.

Was this behavior related to her loss, or was she furious with him? She had turned frigid rapidly at the bed and breakfast. Was it because of the attack or because he altered his demeanor from friend back to bodyguard?

After teetering on the edge of control from holding her all night, he needed to reestablish those boundaries. Although he wanted to ask her if she was angry with him, he couldn't do so with Billy listening.

Twenty minutes of a silent car ride later, they arrived at an abandoned pair of hard courts.

Mason stared at the blades of grass and weeds sprouting through the cracked surface of the tennis court. "That the best you can do, Billy?"

Billy parked the car. "She wants to be alone. This is alone."

"It's perfect." Aurora exited the car before Mason could get out and open her door.

He refrained from snapping at her for breaking protocol, but he still gave her a cautionary look as he came around to her side and shut the door.

Staring past Mason, she walked around him and through the gate of the chain-linked fence.

He grabbed her tennis bag out of the trunk and followed her. After he laid the bag on the ground, she wordlessly pulled out her racquet and a nylon bag with a dozen balls. She walked to the base-line and began practicing her serve.

Her pain, anger, and frustration seemed to explode through her body with every serve—like a tight spring rapidly uncoiling, like the crack of a whip, like the strike of a venomous snake.

Mason understood. Aurora had been made to feel like a victim last night. She had spent years nurturing her strength and independence only to feel vulnerable and dependent on bodyguards. The fear had wrapped its cold tentacles around her, effectively strangling her tennis game. She hated it. Hated her fear. Hated letting it defeat her.

He could empathize with what she felt, and understood the expression on her face. He knew because he had felt that way after his first battle. Despite all of the training he endured, he still felt fear. Fear made him feel weak. He was a Navy SEAL, dammit. By the time the team made it to shore and busied themselves shooting insurgents, the training had conquered the fear. The success of the mission didn't change the fact that he had been afraid.

Each mission had become easier. By the end, he rarely registered butterflies.

He walked the perimeter as she served while Billy and Dorian stayed in the car.

When the first few drops of rain started falling, Aurora made no motion of stopping. Soon a steady London shower poured down, but she continued to practice, oblivious to the world around her. She moved from one side to the other, scooped up the balls, and repeated the process.

When the sky began to darken, she finally quit.

Mason took her bag as she climbed into the backseat. After he put her dripping bag in the trunk, he pulled out a large towel. He sat beside her, both of them soaked in rainwater, and he handed her the towel. He resisted the urge to wrap the towel over her shoulder and pull her into his arms.

She took the towel, still wordlessly and without ever looking at him.

He wanted boundaries; he got boundaries. They just hurt far more than he'd planned.

CHAPTER 17

*B*ack in her hotel room, Aurora stared out the window and waited for the video chat to connect. She had taken a long hot shower to wash away the cold rainwater, but she still felt chilled.

She was alone, but preferred to wallow in her loss without looks of pity from others, however well-meaning they may be. Fury and frustration replaced sulking as she stewed over the Wimbledon loss and the intrusion of the Russian mafia into her life.

"Aurora," her mom greeted her. "We're so happy to see you."

Her dad squeezed onto the image.

"Hi, Mom. Hi, Dad."

"We're so sorry about your loss, sweetie. We wish we could have been there. We promise we will be at the US Open. Things have been so busy with opening the second winery."

Aurora smiled. "Opening" the second winery meant her parents buying out the competition.

"It's better you weren't here." She pulled her cup of tea off the windowsill, savored the orange flavor, and took a sip. "Rider SI earned their keep the other day. Mason saved my life." Or at least, saved her from a Russian maiming.

"Mason?" her mother asked.

"Mr. Stone," Aurora corrected herself. She wrapped her hands around her warm cup of tea.

"What happened?" her father asked.

Aurora thought of Billy lying in the dark alley, then the Russian thugs, then Mason's almost kiss. "Three men ambushed us. Mr. Stone fought them all, and we escaped. Billy got hit, but she's okay."

Her parents gasped, worry etching every line of their faces.

"Are you alright?" her mom asked.

"We're coming to England," her father declared.

"Yes, I'm okay. No, you don't need to come. I think it worked out well. The attack may have given away the person behind the letters."

They stared intently at her through the screen waiting for an explanation.

"Agent Coble is running DNA tests now, so we'll know in a few days."

She desperately hoped everything would come together. If they miscalculated and the attack and letters originated from different villains, then nothing was resolved.

"You're not hurt?" Her dad leaned in closer as though inspecting her for injury.

"I'm not hurt. I'm a little shaken. It would be helpful to keep the Rider team on for a while longer until the threat is gone completely."

Would the threat of the Russian mafia ever be gone completely?

Her mother wrung her hands nervously. "Yes, Aurora, definitely."

Aurora knew continuing to employ bodyguards meant weeks to months of mounting expenses. Her parents paid the sum unquestioningly, but Aurora's many months of around-the-clock security would take its toll on their retirement funds. Would she ever be able to repay their generosity?

A knock sounded at the door. Mason's knock.

Aurora said goodbye to her parents and set her teacup on the counter. As she answered the door, she opened it partially and stood in the gap.

Mason towered over her. Too close and not close enough.

"May I come in?" he asked.

Something in his voice made her spine stiffen. The heavy tone contained unfriendly and business-like tentacles. She didn't feel like dealing with those emotions. She wanted a friend, not an automaton.

"I'm actually beat," she said."

He looked up and down the hallway. "I want to talk to you about the attack."

"Did I break protocol?"

"No. No, you did great." His tone was unexpectedly soft, but she didn't like the edge of regret it held.

She waited expectantly, uncomfortable at the way he seemed to simultaneously have something to say and want reprieve from saying it.

She blocked him and whatever bad news he bore from entering her room.

"I broke protocol. I need to apologize for—"

"No, you don't," she snapped. She didn't care if he planned to apologize for the kiss or for holding her. She didn't want his apology. If no real emotion existed within his actions—which obviously there wasn't or he wouldn't be standing awkwardly outside her room— then they needed to simply never speak of the kiss and the embrace.

"I broke protocol. I need to apologize for crossing a line—"

"It's fine," she lied.

If he apologized, he would downgrade her most terrifying, most intimate night to a lapse in professional judgment. She'd rather pretend it never mattered, and maybe it wouldn't hurt as much.

She added quickly, "You did what you thought was right to control the situation. It worked."

She locked eyes with his, hoping to convey the finality of the situation. She refused to crumble and refused to open the door any further.

He had saved her from Russian thugs. What did her feelings matter in the context of being alive and safe? She didn't need his apology or his pity. He didn't need to flatter himself that his embrace provided her with anything more than an extension of his protection.

His eyes roamed her face, seeming to grow more convinced of her indifference. "Okay. Now that I know you can be cool under that type of threat, it won't happen again."

"I expect it won't," she stated. Hard. Solid. Not an ounce of reluctance.

When Mason walked away, Aurora closed the door. She slid down the wall and sat on the carpeted floor, deflating like a balloon. She'd survived the Russian mafia and Wimbledon. Apparently she could survive killing the only almost-good thing she'd had in months, too.

***

MASON SAT in his hotel room's chair, polishing his black work shoes. Aurora had behaved with supreme maturity when he'd talked to her. She had accepted the comfort when it had been offered, but didn't need it any more. Excellent. He wasn't offering.

So why did his body feel weighted with disappointment?

Her eyes had been steady, voice even, and yet he wasn't ignorant enough to believe the classic 'I'm fine.'

No matter how many times he assured himself a relationship with Aurora wasn't possible, he still wanted her to want him. He wanted some sign she craved him as he craved her.

He'd felt her desire after their brief kiss. He had seen the heat in her eyes. The sensual emotion vanished the next morning at breakfast—her eyes had turned to frigid green icebergs emanating vast cold.

"Are you polishing those or denuding them?"

Mason looked up at Dorian, who had been reading *The Count of Monte Cristo*, then looked down at the shoe in his hand. Mason swore at where he had been too aggressive. He reapplied polish more gently.

"I thought you handled the attack commendably. What are you stewing about?" Dorian asked.

"I hate that Aurora lost because of it."

And that she hates me.

"She'll bounce back. 'Do not be afraid; our fate cannot be taken from us; it is a gift.'"

Mason arched an eyebrow at Dorian. "I'm supposed to know where that quote is from?"

Dorian gave a belabored sigh and set his book down on his chest. "Dante's *Inferno*. But you can appreciate the content without knowing the origin."

"You're saying her fate is to win?" Mason asked.

"I believe it is, yes."

He briefly considered telling Dorian the other reason for his frustration—his feelings for Aurora. The confession sat on his tongue until he swallowed it like glass. He needed to keep those hidden and keep his colleagues from thinking him unprofessional.

Mason dropped the gleaming shoe onto the floor and stood. "I'm taking a walk."

⁂

AURORA AND ALEX positioned their tennis bags and drinks by the bench after warming up for their mixed doubles match.

"You're not with me, Aurora," Alex noted with a frown.

Aurora suspected he worried about her focus after the flaming disaster of her loss in singles. She had also told him all of the events of the post-pub ambush earlier when they had been alone.

Yet, she'd pulled herself together, pushed away negative emotions, and found focus in their games. Day after day, they'd fought through to reach the Wimbledon finals.

"You want to talk about what happened again?" he asked.

"Not really. I might have hero worship," she blurted.

Alex laughed.

She stared at him, incredulous at his insensitive response to confiding in him.

"I'm fairly certain hero worship's where you have feelings for your rescuer."

She blinked at him.

"Aurora, you've been in love with Mason for months now. It didn't happen overnight."

She paled. The word landed with the weight of a match point: inescapable, definitive, and entirely too soon. He was right. She wanted to be in Mason's arms long before she actually had been. The other night likened to dumping gasoline on a fire. The flames already burned, but now they raged.

"What do I do?"

Alex grinned. "Well, he's in your employment, which means you can't do anything until he comes to grips with it. Until he wants to act on his own feelin's, you're stuck. Except, he can't act on his feelings because that would make him unprofessional. It's a lose-lose situation."

She frowned, thinking of how Mason had machine-like control over his every action. He would never do anything unprofessional.

Alex snorted. "He can't move, you can't move, and the two of you are chained together by a contract. Romantic, yeah?"

"Sure. The epitome of romantic." She rolled her eyes.

"So," Alex said, punching her arm as he picked up his tennis racquet, "what you now is channel all your sexual tension into winnin' the Wimbledon championship in mixed doubles."

She glared at him before shifting her eyes to wander the stadium with thousands of onlookers taking their seats and chatting with those beside them.

Alex twirled a ball in his hand, a flicker of worry crossing his expression.

She glanced at the Italian tennis couple dressed in red and black. Sophia and Fabio would be tough opponents.

Alex's concerns were justified, but she had to assure Alex she focused on the game despite the attack and despite her feelings for Mason.

Aurora plucked at the strings on her racquet. "I watched her play singles. I think her shoulder's tweaked, so deep overheads when she's at the net."

Alex nodded. "And his serve is wicked spin."

She looked back at Alex who still fidgeted with the birdie, not making eye contact. She knew how monumental this was. No Irishman had been a runner-up in Wimbledon. No Irishman had ever won Wimbledon.

"Hey," she said to her partner.

Alex stopped twirling the ball but still stared at it.

"Hey," she repeated more firmly.

He brought his eyes up to hers.

"We got this, Alex."

He nodded, face still uncharacteristically drawn.

She narrowed her eyes at him. "We are going to win this. Now, I want to see you flash that carefree smile, or I'm going to have to slap your arse in front of ten thousand people."

He smiled broadly.

"That's more like it. Serve us up."

She turned on her heel and took her position on the court at the net.

For the next nighty-eight minutes, Aurora wasn't sure if she channeled her anger at the Russian attack having successfully distracted her from singles or at her frustration due to unrequited emotions for Mason. Either way they played faster and harder than their opponents.

Aurora and Alex pulled ahead in the second set after winning the first. She fought to quell the rising excitement. Any distraction could tip the tide of success, including counting a win before they secured it.

One point at a time, Aurora.

Their competition played fiercely. Fabio had a powerful forehand. Aurora had to be fast at the net when his yellow bullet came zinging toward her head. Yet, her practice with Alex and Lizzy had honed her reflexes.

The female opponent—Sophia—had been consistent most of the game but her temper flared, and she began making errors. The more mistakes she made, the madder she got, perpetuating further errors.

Alex missed his first serve, but the second kicked wide with spin.

Fabio lunged and managed to push it back over the net, far cross court. Alex adjusted his forward momentum to his left, but took the return of serve off balance and the ball flew high.

Sophia used the opportunity to unleash every ounce of frustration building from their losses to overhead smash the ball. Aurora could only backpedal and hope not to be struck with a hundred-twenty-mile-per- hour birdie. The ball bounced in the court and flew into the crowd.

Aurora walked to Alex at the baseline as he prepared his next serve.

"You trying to get me killed?" She kept her tone light even as she scolded him.

"Keepin' you on your toes, *a stor*." He winked at her. "Besides, you want to show Stone how tough you are. Right?"

She glanced at Mason, standing off court at attention in his suit with his sunglasses on.

"No," she said in a harsh whisper despite the fact no one was hovering close enough to hear their conversation. "Besides, winning shows how tough we are, not taking yellow bullets."

She walked back up to the net.

She had managed at some point to stop thinking about her frustrations toward Mason and had become lost in the game and the moment-by-moment uncertainty of the competition.

Thanks, Alex.

Now she thought only about her tall, broad-shouldered bodyguard—the man who had come to apologize for kissing her, with the implication that it had been a mistake. Perhaps she could refocus with SEAL facts she had stored.

The Navy SEALs make up less than one percent of all of the United States Navy personnel, but strategically impact every mission in which they participate.

Behind her Alex bounced his ball to ready his serve.

The original SEAL Team 6 was given the team number to confuse Soviet Intelligence as to how many teams there were. Only two existed.

Alex's first serve flew by in a blur. Sophia couldn't get a racquet on it.

When he served back to Fabio in the ad court, his first serve landed in the service box. Fabio made the return, a high zinger to Aurora. She volleyed it strategically in the doubles alley at Sophia's feet for a win.

"Last set and we're tied," Alex said.

Aurora nodded. The score was close, too close to feel a resounding confidence that they could maneuver a win out of the finals.

"Prison rules?" she asked.

Alex grinned. "Prison rules."

AFTER CHANGING TACTICS, they won Wimbledon mixed doubles. The crowd burst into enthusiastic applause.

Aurora skipped back to the baseline to give Alex a high five. He dropped his racquet and wrapped two sweaty arms around her. She didn't care even as he squeezed the breath out of her. She felt too elated at this moment, and too grateful for Alex.

He'd taken her doubts in stride, been her partner when she carried the unfavorable black sheep title, and always kept the game light no matter the obstacles and mounting pressure.

"You're a great friend and great tennis player, Alex Rory."

He pulled away and looked into her face. For the first time, his boyish smile faltered. She knew he saw the tears in her eyes.

CHAPTER 18

London. July 10th. As Wimbledon comes to a close, fans delight in the surprise mixed doubles win by the Alex Rory and Aurora Meridian—a victory that arrives under the shadow of a violent attack. This title success came after Meridian lost in the second round singles. What began as speculation of injury, turned out to be an attack on Meridian's life. London police say they apprehended men after an attempted assault on Meridian. Meridian commented that while she "was shaken by the event," her singles opponent "played better and deserved the win." When questioned as to the relationship between this latest attack and the death threats she reportedly received earlier this year, she declined to comment.

Is Meridian a Prime Target?

Aurora had cleaned, changed, and met Alex for a news interview to discuss their Wimbledon win. Alex only had to dab his moist eyes once as the journalist commented on how monumental their win was for Ireland.

After they finished their interview and hugged each other, Aurora and Alex parted ways.

When her phone rang, she recognized her old agent's number on her phone as it rang. "Ralph," she answered as she kept pace with Mason on the walk to the car.

He carried her tennis bag and silently escorted her. As she answered the phone, she saw Mason glance down at her. She imagined him mentally flipping through the Rolodex of names in her file until he came to Ralph Hutch, Aurora's former publicity agent.

"Congratulations! Wonderful win, Aurora." His voice dripped with sticky sweetness, like a rotten apple dipped in caramel.

Now he calls.

"I'm so thrilled for you. This win is huge! I can practically taste your success."

Does it taste like dollar bills, Ralph? A payday for you?

"Thanks." Aurora knew Ralph only called because Aurora became a person of interest again. Unfortunately, as much as she would have liked to tell him where he could stuff his taste buds, she needed Ralph to get sponsors.

"Look, girl. I'm going to see what strings I can pull to get you noticed. We'll get you back in with the big sponsors. I'll be in touch."

Ralph disconnected the call.

Strings?

Aurora had just won a major mixed doubles championship, and Ralph made it sound like a tremendous effort would be require on his part to get a big sponsor for her. *Woe is Ralph*, as Alex would say.

Mason opened the car door for her, and Aurora climbed into the back of the vehicle.

"That's not the happy look of someone who just won Wimbledon." Mason's deep voice carried softly to her ears as he climbed into the car and sat beside her.

She forced a smile at him.

He added, "I know it's not singles, but it's an amazing win."

"I am thrilled. I'm still in shock, I think. I never would have gotten this far without Alex."

—or you.

"He knows that."

Mason took off his glasses and gave her a look of admiration that swelled her soul more than the media interview after the match. He was caring again, which would only lead to hurt when he turned back to stone.

Nodding, she looked out the window and plucked her fingers through a hole in the fabric of her jeans. She shouldn't care if Mason was proud of her, but for some reason, it mattered. Her entire body ached with a ridiculous need to be accepted by him.

Cherez moy trup.

She continued stared out the window on the drive back to the hotel. She thought of how good it felt to sign a plethora of autographs amidst a cheering crowd. She had lingered longest after this match than any other, basking in her and Alex's success. Despite the attacks and the letters, she had won mixed doubles.

"Prison rules?" Mason asked.

She turned to him and grinned. "You heard that? Alex and I were hitting pretty heavy in practice one day during the first season we met. I started taking his balls early—sort of like Federer's SABR—sneak attack by Rodger—technique but on serves and ground strokes. It gives the opponent less reaction time. I won a few points that way, and Alex accused me of playing by prison rules—like playing dirty. Now it's code when we're planning to get uber-aggressive."

"It worked today."

"When we can use it strategically, it can disrupt the other team's rhythm. Sometimes it's effective."

"Sometimes it's not?"

"It's hard to keep up that level of intensity and focus for repetitive games, let alone sets. Overuse can lead to errors, and then it becomes counterproductive."

Mason nodded. "Ever use it in singles?"

"No."

"Why not?"

"I'm a different player in singles. When I'm winning, I'm on. I don't need it. When I'm losing, I don't have the confidence to pull it off."

"I am constantly astounded at the profound strategy in tennis."

She accepted the compliment and turned her attention back out the window. His genuine interest in her life's work made staying mad at him difficult. A few soft words from him could unknot something in her chest.

AURORA PICKED up her phone from the side of the bathtub and answered it.

"I saw your win! I saw your win!" Monique screamed.

Aurora held the phone away from ear. She set it down on the side of the bath and put it on speaker.

"Congratulations!"

"Thanks, Mo."

"Thanks, Mo? You are supposed to be screaming with excitement along with me."

Mo was right. Aurora should be screaming with excitement. She had felt elated on the court, but at no point had she needed to scream. The young girl, whose sole aspiration of victory on the court, had been subtly replaced by a mature woman over the course of years.

As she soaked in Epsom salt in the hotel bath, she struggled to process her feelings. Elation at winning doubles. Depression at losing singles. Worry about the Russian attacks. Self-flagellation for still wanting a relationship with Mason.

"I should," she agreed aloud.

"What's wrong then?" Mo asked.

"I was attacked the night before my singles match. Russian gangsters."

"What?"

"I'm fine, obviously. I'm just . . . jumbled."

"Obviously, you're not fine. They shook you up. Is that why you lost singles? Did you say *gangsters*? What are you going to do about them?"

"My security team is taking care of it. They're good at what they do."

Saved me.

Cherez moy trup.

"What did you say?"

"Nothing." Had she said it aloud? "Mason saved me."

"Good. That's his job."

"It was more than that. He physically saved me, yes, but he also emotionally saved me."

Aurora hesitated, but Monique stayed silent.

"He held me after the attack. Just quietly in his arms. I know it was to help me stay calm, but it felt so good. I felt like I could spend night after night in those arms." She took a deep, steadying breath hoping the lavender scent of the bath salt would help maintain her composure.

"You were just scared," Mo said. Her soft voice held no conviction of belief that the situation could be so simple.

"It's so messed up to want something you can't have, but you keep it close just to feel the warmth even if it hurts."

"Oh, honey."

Aurora sniffed. "Maybe I've just been alone too long. I'm just grasping."

"Don't devalue your emotions," Mo chided her. "You've passed on offers over the years. If you feel something for Mason, it's real."

Her words felt like truth to Aurora.

"What are you going to do?"

"Shelve it."

"Shelve it?"

"I'm going to stop fretting about my feelings. When the season is over and he's no longer my bodyguard, I will ask him on a date. Until then my life is tennis, and he has a job to do."

"And the gangsters?" Mo asked.

"The Rider team and the FBI are working on it." Aurora didn't want to share any details about the speculation of Natasha's involvement until everything was confirmed.

"Hey, girl, all of this is going to work out."

Aurora swallowed. "Since I know your usual dismal outlook on the world, I really value your encouragement."

<hr>

AURORA HAD MOSTLY finished packing for the next day's flight when Mason knocked. After opening the door for him, she returned to her laptop to work on a design.

He peeked into her teacup. Picking it up, he refilled it with water and dropped it in the microwave for a minute twenty seconds.

"Where are we with Natasha?" She continued to type on her computer.

He must have known something because he had brought his laptop with him.

"DNA test on the letters is a match. She'll be arrested by the time she and Jimmy land in the States."

Aurora sucked in a deep breath. "Wow. It really was her." She pushed away from the desk and pulled her legs into her body. "I'm not sure what's worse—Natasha trying to force me to lose or the Russian mafia coming after me because I'm the reason their beloved supermodel is in prison."

Mason opened a tea bag. "I think the latter."

"Swell," she said miserably.

"Maybe, maybe not."

"What are you scheming?"

He leaned on the counter. "Well, I put out a few feelers about the fight incident and Natasha. I think she's more of a spoiled brat and pain in Vladimir's ass. It seems he didn't sanction the soft hit."

Three armed men is a soft hit?

He evidently read her expression. "Soft meaning they weren't his highest professionals, and they weren't instructed to kill."

She nodded.

He pulled the mug of hot water out of the microwave and dropped in the tea bag. "So the question is what would a man like Vladimir Pronin agree to if you didn't press charges against Natasha? And what would you accept in return?"

Aurora considered the question. "I just want to be left alone." She accepted the mug, aware of his proximity and the brush of their hands as the cup exchange hands. The steam curled between them, a spicy chai with a hint of vanilla.

Mason shook his head. "This is a negotiation, Aurora. You are bringing to the table the freedom of his niece. Well, it's still a federal crime to send threats in the mail, but his lawyers will bury those indiscretions. You need to aim high and let him whittle away at your demands."

She sipped her tea in silent contemplation before answering. She thought of what she wanted, trying to dismiss the way her heart picked up pace when Mason called her by her first name.

"I want Natasha to pay the cost of the Rider SI team for the entire season. All expenses. And I want assurances the Russian mafia will leave Rider SI, my family, and me alone."

He smiled. "Now, that's better."

Damn, she hated and loved the way his smile turned her insides to mush.

He opened his laptop and sat beside her at the table. "Let's get Maxine working on negotiations. We'll draft a letter with your requests. She can present it on your behalf." His eyes flickered to the mini-fridge. "And let's do it all over a glass of celebratory wine, keeping the receipt for billing Natasha, of course."

Aurora chuckled.

She uncorked the wine to let it breathe while she watched him work. Excitement stirred in her at the prospect of tying up loose ends with the Russian mafia. For the first time in months, maybe she had some type of control over the next course of events.

But she also was enamored by this version of Mason with his guard down and his eyes twinkling mischievously as they plotted together. He had dropped the annoying "Miss Meridian" and called her Aurora, the same way he had when he protected her from the Russians.

As for the mafia danger, she wanted to believe this marked the end but a celebratory glass of wine felt premature.

Aurora watched Mason type—calm, precise, unshakable. He had kept her safe, was helping with plans to negotiate with the mafia, and warmed her tea.

When this is over... I'll ask him on a real date, she told herself.

If the danger didn't catch up to her first.

Negotiation didn't mean protection.

CHAPTER 19

$\mathcal{M}$axine Rider walked through airport security at Hartsfield International with no intention of boarding plane. As she wound her way to P.F. Chang's, she stuffed her printed plane ticket into her shoulder bag; she didn't need it. She came here to meet a man who ran an empire of fear.

Beyond the airport security checks, neither of them would b armed. She walked to a table in the back where Vladimir Pronin sat, flanked by two standing bodyguards.

She'd arrived early, but the leader of the Russian mafia was already there. The thick, imposing man stood as she approached. He adjusted his Italian suit. She did nothing to adjust her cargo pants and crimson sweater. She knew the man's reputation as a lethal crime boss, and the Italian suit didn't add to his intimidation or disguise the blood on his hands.

Without his bodyguards, she believed herself fully capable of killing the mobster. The silverware on the table would suffice; she didn't need a gun or hunting knife. Perhaps she had been faster in her younger, leaner days, but so had he.

His full wavy, peppered gray hair was immaculately pushed back and handsomely framed his trimly bearded face. His pale blue-green eyes seemed to pierce through her. She met his gaze, undaunted by his polished appearance, his lethal confidence, and his ruthless reputation.

He smiled wolfishly, approving her lack of fear. Maxine looked down at his extended hand, half expecting to see a red shadow of blood from the lives he had extinguished. Instead, his coarse hand was carefully manicured. She shook it.

"Maxine Rider, it is an honor." His deep Russian accent sounded smooth as silk.

"*Spasibo*, Mr. Pronin, for rearranging your travel schedule to meet with me."

"*Pozhaluysta, menya zovut* Vladimir."

She nodded. "Call me Max."

"Max," he smiled. "I like that very much."

They sat at the small table across from each other while his bodyguards remained standing. She didn't acknowledge the hired help. They were a foolish display of force. If he'd wanted to impress her, he would have met her alone.

A waiter brought hot sake. With a wave of his left hand, Vladimir dismissed his bodyguards.

Well, color my big, white butt impressed.

Sipping her sake, she savored high-octane liquor—even if it tasted like jet engine fuel. What did she care if it put hair on her chest? No one looked at her chest these days anyway.

Vladimir tasted the beverage before carefully setting the cup back down. "I am troubled by the news of my niece. The least I can do is hear of your offer in person."

Maxine tilted her head in a slight bow.

"Tell me, Max, what happened?"

Maxine suspected Vladimir already knew. A man as intelligent as he was did not arrive to a meeting without first knowing all of the facts. He likely already had his niece cowering in the corner of a room somewhere, awaiting his judgment.

"My client has been receiving anonymous death threats for several months. The threats culminated in an attack in London. Three Russians in your employment—"

"—previously in my employment."

She made a small surrendering gesture with her hands. She meant no offense. "Previously in your employment, attacked my client and the team protecting her. The FBI has since run DNA tests on the letters. The DNA test is positive for Natasha Bodrov's saliva. I suspect she hired the hit."

"You can prove this?" He raised his eyebrows.

"I cannot ... yet."

Maxine could have Claire dig. The tech savvy woman searched like a bloodhound on the computer. Claire would scour Natasha's electronic correspondence—every email, text, and social media post—and find the connection between the supermodel and the Russian thugs.

Maxine's hesitation lay in the risk of exposing Claire. If Claire's hacking turned up other Russian mafia hairballs, she might inadvertently become a target.

Maxine wanted to try this meeting first. She was far more willing to paint a target on her own back than risk one of her employees, one of her Rider SI family members. Especially with a man like Vladimir Pronin.

"I would prefer to not have to prove it. I would prefer to settle this without unearthing that information. I start turning over rocks and I may find more than the usual *chervi*."

She hoped she had pronounced "worms" correctly or her rusty Russian would show.

Vladimir sipped his sake. The glint of enjoyment in those faded aqua eyes never wavered. "David does not want to face Goliath."

Maxine smirked. "Catholic school is almost five decades behind me, but I'm pretty sure that scenario worked out well for David."

Vladimir chuckled. "Love is such a fickle thing, is it not?"

You bet your ass it is.

Maxine nodded. "It can make one behave irrationally."

She doubted Natasha had been motivated by love.

Love of self perhaps.

"It can make you see threats where none exist," Vladimir said.

Maxine turned the tiny porcelain sake glass in a circle as she took the opening he was giving her. "It would be a waste to punish someone harshly for misguided actions under the influence of love."

"How would Maxine Rider punish such actions?"

Her eyes locked with Vladimir's. "Financial penalties combined with motivation to not disappoint her uncle again."

"Go on."

"My client is willing to not pursue charges in exchange for Natasha paying the full expenses of my protective services retroactive from the start of the threats, and in exchange for assurances my client will not be targeted by anyone in your organization going forward."

Silence blanketed the conversation as he finished Vladimir sake. "I like you, Max."

She wasn't interested in his friendship, but liking her was better than not. She didn't feel compelled to share his sentiment.

Vladimir was the first criminal opponent she had encountered who claimed to like her. Most criminals initially betrayed annoyance or boredom, underestimating her until it was too late to realize their mistake. This worked in her favor. Vladimir did not strike her as one to underestimate his antagonists.

He gave her a crooked grin, which she most certainly did not find attractive.

"You and I, Max, understand a different, darker world than many of our clients and our families. We both have certain people we wish to protect from the horrors and violence we have known and perhaps even perpetrated."

Maxine frowned at his comparison of herself to him, though she couldn't argue. She thought of her son. He lived in his secluded world of emergency medicine, not exposed to the same hazardous living that brought patients through his doors. She liked to think her work protected him and people like him—even if he wasn't on speaking terms with her.

Vladimir added, "Obviously we execute our protective strategies differently."

"Yes, my executions do not involve actual executions."

His eyes crinkled with amusement. "*Segodnya, da.* In the past, I think you could not have made such a statement."

Can't argue with that crappy truth.

She forced a smile, feeling the bulge of her cheeks. "Guess that's the beauty of self-improvement. I recommend *How To Win Friends and Influence People.* You won't find mention of death and destruction."

"Different strategies," he reiterated, as though they were football coaches with different offensive plays—pass the ball versus pound the field. "But I find your client's terms acceptable."

Maxine felt one corset loosen from around her chest as another tightened. She had just cut a deal with one of the most ruthless crime lords of the ages. His network of drug trafficking, gambling, and money laundering was international in both its breadth and body count.

While the arrangement fared better for all parties involved, a deal with the devil could still pave her way to hell.

"Good. Let's shake on it," Max said.

Russian men rarely shook hands with women. Was he willing to respectfully acknowledge her as an equal?

Vladimir didn't hesitate to accept her challenge. He not only accepted her hand, standing as she stood, but he embraced it with both of his.

She knew her face betrayed her surprise, but she quickly recovered.

"Again. I am honored to meet you, Max."

How could that be? Yet, his voice seemed sincere.

"*Spasibo.* I won't detain you any longer, Vladimir."

He released her hand and watched her with an amused quirk of his lips.

Picking up her bag, she turned to leave.

"Max," he called.

She stopped but did not turn back to face him.

"I do hope our paths cross again someday."

I don't.

Turning halfway to meet his gaze, she replied, "If we are David and Goliath as you suggested, I expect we might." Her tone held no malice or threat, only dismal observation.

Her business comprised of helping people. His business comprised of helping himself at the expense of others. She felt certain there would be an inevitable time when her job would be to protect someone from his wrath. They would come to blows, and she wasn't sure who would be left standing.

"*Dosvidaniya*," she bid him farewell.

"*Uvidimsya*, Max." *See you,* Max.

VLADIMIR WATCHED Maxine Rider as she left the airport restaurant. He admired the formidable woman. He enjoyed the moment when he eked past her defenses and made her squirm, just a little. Her steel exterior concealed a passionate woman—passionate about people, her work, her team.

Zamechatel'nyy. Krasivaya.

Admirable. Beautiful.

Her beauty lay in her conviction.

He drummed his fingers lightly on the table, contemplating the former Marine. Before this meeting, he had endeavored to learn all he could about her both from internet sources and word of mouth. She'd been divorced for many years and estranged from her son. She personally met every client they served. On occasion, she helped people who couldn't afford her company's services despite a tight operating margin. Bad business.

He shook his head. However, her behavior had earned her a fair reputation, which in turn brought in better paying customers. He supposed the situation was not unlike some of his distributors who gave discounted drugs to establish a rapport (and addiction) before increasing the cost.

In any case, Max possessed savvy and deadly calculation, despite the appearance of neither. She had earned the Medal of Honor for bravery during the Gulf War. She was credited with having saved the lives of half her team. She understood loyalty and honor, qualities he respected.

She reminded him of some of the paintings of Catherine the Great in the Tretyakov gallery. Her oval face held similar rosy cheeks, and a delicate neck led to a full bosom.

She pretended not to understand him. She operated under the misguided American pretense that all criminals and their activities should be lumped together as purely evil. There was a reason his endeavors fell into the *organized* crime heading. Without strong and honorable men, or women (he did not discriminate), there would be only crime. Disorganization bred chaos—bloodbaths, low-level power plays, and more collateral damage than necessary.

He brought organization, standardization, and structure. Perhaps with time, Max would see the value he brought.

Maxine the Great, he mused.

Tough little lisichka.

"Who is a fox, sir?"

Boris appeared at his side. Vladimir realized he had been mumbling some of his thoughts.

"*Khorosho*, Boris. I have made an agreement with Mrs. Rider. Spread the word that tennis players are off limits."

"Very good, sir. All tennis players?"

"*Da.*"

"For how long?"

Vladimir continued to tap his fingers. It didn't have to be all tennis players and he didn't feel obliged beyond the season, but he felt inexplicably generous after his meeting. "Indefinitely."

"Very good, sir. It will be done."

"I will need to talk to Natasha when we land. She must make amends for her mistake."

"Yes, sir."

Natasha Bodrov was a soft, spoiled little *krolik*. He could not relate to her foolishness and would not indulge it.

Vladimir had been battle-hardened during the depression in Russia before the turn of the century. Russia's financial transformation erupted as a frenzied privatization, creating a chaotic competitive environment and the rise of Russian tycoons and bloated expansion of criminal mafias.

Vladimir had been on the right side of wrong in the FSB (the KGB's post-Soviet successor), fighting criminals instead of being catalogued as one. After his brutal and harsh stint in border patrol, he'd seen enough violence and killed enough men for a lifetime.

He also learned he could lose his entire family to the chaos from which he fought to protect Russia. What use was combating threats from abroad when domestic threats rampaged the country? While he protected Russia, no one protected his family.

The solution was simple: the best way to protect his family was not to fight crime but to control it. Little by little he gained control. Some immediately recognized the value he brought. Others required convincing. Now he had control—his kingdom, free of chaos.

Yet, here he stood, still doing border patrol, keeping their group tightly cohered, guarding against threats, and cleaning up other people's messes.

THE LONG FLIGHT from London to Washington, D.C. cramped Aurora's legs. Several times she stood, and Mason moved out of her way so she could walk the aisle. She tried to ignore the way their bodies brushed against each other.

Someday I won't be piling up credit card debt with plane rides. Someday I'll own my own graphic design company and fly first class.

She sat back down with a sigh. When he retook his seat beside her, their knees bumped.

"Anything I can do?" he asked.

The thought of him massaging her sore legs just made her want to leave and walk the aisle again. With last night's memory of sipping wine as they worked closely over his laptop, Aurora suddenly felt claustrophobic sitting beside Mason on the plane. Every time he listened or refilled her tea, she had to remind herself: his contract demanded courtesy, not affection.

She could feign disinterest a few more months. After that, he'd no longer be paid to sit beside her. If he chose to—*then* she'd know.

She shook her head and opened her novel. Instead of reading, she wondered what news would await them when they landed. Would the Russian mafia really accept that one of their own had acted out of line and allow a truce?

"I'm a good listener," Mason said, interrupting her thoughts. and there were those blue eyes once again gazing at her with genuine ... something. Affection? Concern? Maybe it was her imagination.

When I no longer need a protection team, I'll ask you out ... I want to know if you'll say yes or no. She couldn't say any of that but had to bide her time.

Instead, she said, "You are a very good listener. Are you as good a listener when you aren't on duty?"

He cocked his head to one side. "I'd like to think so. I'd like to think I listen because I care and not because I'm paid to."

Warmth slipped into her chest—dangerous warmth.

"I'm worried about what Max will say. No, it's not over because the mafia stands behind their own. Yes, it's over and we're pulling your security team ... and what if that shakes my confidence in my game?" She picked at a tear in her jeans.

"We won't yank the rug out from under you. If Max brokered a deal with Pronin, implementation will take time."

"And only then I lose ... my team?" She glanced at him, wondering if you knew she almost said *you.*

His gaze darted away. "You won't need us any more."

Right. Of course.

Repacking the novel she hadn't read, she pulled out her earphones and turned on music. Closing her eyes, she listened to Aerosmith's "Dream On."

CHAPTER 20

Natasha paced the floor of her apartment, biting her nails and swearing in Russian.

Vladimir had summoned her.

Dyadya Pronin.

She groaned. Could she flee? No. Vladimir had the resources to find anyone. She had to face the consequences for upsetting him. She'd used his goons for her petty vendetta. She had only wanted to scare Aurora, make her leave tennis so there was no danger of Aurora luring Jimmy back to her.

She knew the ramifications for those who disobeyed or embarrassed her uncle. The spectrum varied, but any penalty would devastate her future. He could cut her off from the family. She was as good as dead from her enemies without his protection. He could send her to Siberia. Yes, he had done that to others. Some had chosen death over Siberia. Lastly, he could have her assassinated.

She ran to the toilet and vomited her breakfast—black coffee and a single rice cake. Sitting down on the cold floor as the room spun around her, she buried her head in her arms.

Vladimir's decision would be based on the current state of his business. If his syndicate was orderly, her punishment would be less severe. If, however, he needed to set an example, hers would be a death sentence.

She hated feeling weak.

She'd dismissed Jimmy from the room when he asked what bothered her and tried to comfort her. What did the soft American know of the Russian mafia? What did he know of her hardships as the niece of the Russian crime lord?

Nichego.

She stood, walked to the sink, and washed her face. She knew with sudden clarity she and Jimmy were finished. He possessed good looks and charm, but these traits were not what she needed from a lover. She needed someone strong, someone deadly. She needed protection—protection both from her own selfish, foolish acts, and from other threats, both within the family and external to it.

She no longer wanted a playboy. She wanted a warrior.

***

Aurora enjoyed a relaxing day off between matches of the Citi Open.

She worked on a graphic design for a veterinarian sign with a feline logo as she waited for her company to join her at the coffee shop a few blocks from her hotel.

Her phone buzzed with an incoming call.

She put the phone to her ear. "Hi, Mom."

"Max called me. Natasha Bodrov was behind the letters? All to keep you away from Jimmy Fisk? Are you still interested in him? I thought it was over?"

"Mom. Mom, yes it's long over."

"Why would she think—?"

"—because she's an unstable, insecure woman."

"So, it's over?"

Only the stalker drama, Aurora thought. Not the part that actually hurt—the proximity to a man who was off limits.

"It's over," Aurora repeated.

"She's going to prison?"

"Probably not." Aurora fiddled with the tilt of the cat's head so it gazed inquisitively at the letter V of the "Veterinarian Clinic."

"That doesn't sound over."

"I agreed not to press charges. In exchange, she'll pay for the security detail for the entire season."

A long silence stretched between them as her mom seemed to consider the large amount of money she would suddenly not have to pay.

"That's sizable."

It doesn't cover the cost of a broken heart.

If Aurora had never had death threats, there would have been no need for Maxine Rider's services. If Aurora had never met Mason, she wouldn't have these impossible-to-squelch feelings for him. Soon, he would have to leave and she would have to reassemble the pieces of her heart.

"Will she agree to leave you alone?" her mom asked.

"Yes."

Because her crime lord uncle was cleaning up her mess, yes, Natasha was finished terrorizing her.

Aurora thought it best to leave out the Russian mob details. She knew how much it frightened her and could only imagine her parents' response would be magnified. Aurora felt relieved Vladimir had agreed to a bargain—no charges in exchange for full payment of the Rider SI fees regarding the Meridian family.

"You dropped your elbow a few times during serves."

My mom—a ball of encouragement.

"Yeah, Mom."

"You're losing momentum when you do that."

"Yes." She wanted to remind her she did win the game but kept mute.

Mason watched from a table away as Aurora's former agent entered the coffee shop. Aurora cut the conversation with her mother short and closed her computer.

"Ralph," she greeted the bobbly-headed man.

She stood as Ralph Hutch gave her a hug.

"Aurora Meridian! How is my shining Borealis?" Ralph sounded like a zealous cheerleader. He straightened his shimmering suit after the embrace.

At least he knew better than to call her Prime, Mason thought.

"Fine, Ralph. How are you?" She didn't match the other man's enthusiasm.

"You haven't been returning my calls. I'm glad you finally agreed to meet with me."

Aurora only smiled, a polished, white-toothed smile and nothing like the warmer smiles she reserved for family and friends.

"It's been busy since Wimbledon."

Good. She didn't apologize.

Mason had dug into Ralph's past as part of his investigation through Claire. He had apparently dropped Aurora quickly after her injury and hadn't shown any interest in her until this season. Now that she continued to climb the ranks, she seemed to be worth the agent's time. The man was a leech—quick to latch on and take his fill, but quick to leave when the blood and fame had drained. He didn't make lasting relationships, except with his ferret.

"I got a call from Accents. They have a clothing line. It's a new exercise line they are going to roll out, and they want athlete models."

Exercise clothing. Mason breathed a sigh of relief. For a moment Mason had worried Ralph would say lingerie, which would have been none of Mason's business either way.

"Models?" Aurora asked.

"You and Alex," Ralph said.

"Alex."

Mason saw Aurora's shoulders drop ever so slightly. Her mixed doubles blessing and curse. Mixed doubles had given her the points she needed to get back in bigger competitions, but it didn't grant sustainable prize money or fame. Now, she would have to consider sharing a sponsor.

"I'll talk to Alex. I don't know if he has any prohibitive clauses with his watch sponsor."

Mason knew it would take some measure of swallowing her pride to ask Alex to share a sponsor with her. He watched Aurora's nose wrinkle as she sipped her tea. He wondered if the expression originated from cold tea or distasteful conversation.

"You're doing great, girl," Ralph cooed.

"I didn't last long at Roland-Garros or Wimbledon." She bobbed her tea bag up and down with irritation in the cup.

Ralph patted her hand. "You've always done well in the US Open. This year you'll see Arthur Ashe Stadium. I've got a feeling. This is going to make a great comeback story."

In his earpiece, Mason heard Billy ask, "Did you just growl?"

He swallowed but didn't answer. He sat too close to Ralph and Aurora to reply to Billy; they would overhear him. Maybe he had growled. Aurora didn't need other pressures; she had enough going on without her former agent putting pressure on her to turn herself into a news media sensation.

He kept silent for the rest of the conversation, happy Aurora wasn't vying for this man's affections.

⁕

THE NEXT DAY Mason watched as Aurora hugged her parents and then sat down at the restaurant table with them.

Mason and Billy had discussed the restaurant layout the day prior and decided one of them needed to be directly at the table because the restaurant would be crowded for lunch. Billy argued that Mason could feign congeniality better than she; and, therefore, he should be the one at the table. He pursed his lips, but couldn't disagree. Part of him didn't want to disagree. What were the mother and father of this remarkable woman like?

He shook hands with her parents, and they exchanged introductions. They had met Maxine in the early stages of discussing the security detail, but he was the first team member they were meeting. Rider SI had been protecting their only daughter for months now.

Her parents had placed their trust in Maxine's organization. Now, they would put a face to the active team. Mason wanted to ensure he conveyed confidence and security. He played the part of the rook.

As they sat, her father seemed to appraise Mason's size and appearance. Mason wore a sleek navy suit and omitted the sunglasses Aurora claimed made him look unapproachable, which was usually the appearance he sought. Today he needed to portray strong but friendly.

Aurora's mother was an older, equally attractive version of her daughter dressed in style with a loose blouse and slacks. Her father wore pressed jeans and a blue dress shirt. His peppered hair lay in steep recession.

As Aurora adjusted her chair, ringlets of loose blond hair tumbled forward. Mason had an irrational urge to brush the strands off her shoulder. He forced his attention back to her parents.

"We are grateful to you for saving Aurora in London. Twice," her mother said.

"Yes, ma'am. It was a team effort."

"Suck up," Billy said in Mason's ear.

"Seems a dangerous thing for an unstable young woman to have access to hit men," her father commented.

"Yes, sir."

Mostly it was dangerous for anyone to have access to hit men. But Mason didn't mention that.

Mrs. Meridian adjusted the placement of her silverware. "I know we have a contained source now, but I feel better knowing the security team will be with her for the rest of the tennis season. I want everything to be settled and behind her before the team leaves."

Mason felt tempted to list all of the reasons Aurora needed security for even longer, but he didn't want to alarm any of them. Her wealthy parents made her a target. Her growing competitive tennis career made her a target. An attractive woman traveling internationally made her a target.

"We'll continue to keep her safe as long as needed," he said.

She at least needed some basic self-defense training, including handling a gun. She could learn other techniques on traveling safely in disreputable areas. Why hadn't he started any of this? He needed to train her in the few months before their time together concluded.

Aurora's father ordered a bottle of wine—a Meridian Vineyards Pinot Noir. "Agent Coble tells me you fought three Russian criminals single-handedly and won. Is that normal in your line of work?"

The waiter poured water for everyone and left to retrieve the wine.

"It's variable. Threats range from ignorant panicking bystanders, to ex-lovers with rage and no experience, to unarmed or armed criminals, to hardened hit men."

The entire Meridian family looked at him with fascination.

He placed his napkin in his lap.

"It seems your Navy SEAL training has served you well," Mrs. Meridian said.

"Yes, ma'am. SEAL motto is 'The only easy day was yesterday.'"

She smiled. "Your parents must be proud."

The waiter returned with wine. Mason politely declined.

"I like to think so. My father died when I was in high school— lung cancer. My mom had a stroke a few years ago that stole her memory of our family."

Aurora looked stricken. "You never mentioned them before."

"It's all in the past."

He was surprised at her reaction. His emotions on the matter concluded long ago. His father had been the glue of the family, and the loss had been difficult, but those events transpired over fifteen years ago. His mother battled depression after his death, but had never been a doting mother. The divide that rifted between them was neither troubling nor surprising. It was what it was—she was trapped in her own emotional turmoil and unable to give any of herself to anyone who might need her attention, including a teenage son. He escaped to the military. In the Navy, he made a new family.

"I'm sorry," she said, taking a sip of her wine.

Perhaps he shouldn't have divulged information about his past. He wasn't usually so forthcoming. The conversation had turned dismal rapidly. "The turns in my life led me to the military and then the SEALs followed by Rider SI. I've enlarged my family. I see only that things have unfolded as they should."

"Well, we are the better for the man you've become whether it was because of unfortunate events in your life or despite them." Mr. Meridian raised his wine glass, and they all toasted to Mason.

"Here, here," Billy said in a soft, genuine voice.

Mason swallowed back his discomfort at the attention. He looked at Aurora who seemed to be absorbing and contemplating his words —events have unfolded as they should. Events had led him to Aurora.

She smiled weakly at him, the swirling emotions in her emerald eyes deep enough to drown him. He feared his momentary expression may have betrayed his feelings.

The waiter returned, and the Meridians ordered salmon salads. Mason followed their lead.

"Congratulations, Mr. and Mrs. Meridian, on your latest conquest. I heard you acquired another vineyard," Mason said.

"Expand or die," Aurora's father said.

"Thrive to survive," her mother added in a light tone. She winked at her husband who pursed his lips at her playful mocking of him. The gold bangles on her wrist jingled as she took a sip of her water.

Aurora's mother turned the wine bottle label toward Mason. "Did you know Aurora does graphic design? She did this label for us."

"Yes, ma'am. She's talented." He inspected the decorative label.

Pinot Me!

Meridian Vineyards

Two crimson cherries connected by their stems were animated with happy faces. Lips puckered, they looked as though they would kiss at any moment.

Relief eased into him as the conversation finally veered away from him.

"It's clever and eye-catching," he said.

He amused himself imagining Aurora forming her own puckered lips as she drew them.

"Thank you," Aurora said.

He looked at her parents. "Your daughter seems to apply herself with full effort to everything she does. I think her graphic design business will do well."

"Suck up," Billy said again into his ear.

Mr. Meridian set down his wine glass. "Yes, well. Sometimes her intensity knows no bounds. Did she tell you about the time she was ten and threw her racquet?"

"No, Dad. Why would I—"

"She was losing in the second set and missed a forehand just deep. She threw her racquet into the court."

Mason glanced at Aurora who fidgeted with her napkin.

"I took her out of the game," her father said.

"Forced her to forfeit," her mother added.

Mason remembered Aurora telling him how fiercely competitive she had been—craving the win.

Her father continued, "After that, we had a long talk about how a missed point is never the fault of the racquet—occasionally the ball, occasionally the net, most often the tennis player, but never the racquet."

"She's never thrown her racquet since." Her mother smiled as she adjusted one of her necklaces.

Aurora gave a slight uncomfortable roll of her shoulders.

Mason thought about the many times he'd watched Aurora play. Never once had she been rough on her racquet. She didn't slam it, throw it, bang it, or curse it. Now, the ball—the birdie—she abused terribly, but never the racquet.

CHAPTER 21

Mason lay awake on a couch in a Washington DC apartment. A friend of Aurora's parents allowed her to stay in their apartment while they traveled in Australia. The free room meant Aurora didn't have a hotel bill to foot, but also put all of them under one roof.

In the three-bedroom apartment, Aurora, Billy, and Dorian each got their own room. Mason got the couch. He'd assured everyone that the dispersal was acceptable; he could sleep anywhere. And he had—boats, planes, deserts, caves, and jungles.

As he stared out the window while everyone slept quietly, he was surprised to discover the one place he couldn't sleep was under the same roof as a beautiful woman while only two inches of wood composite separated them.

He lay awake thinking of the night he'd held her in his arms. How many times on this job had he suppressed the urge to share her victory or defeat after a match by sweeping her into his arms?

She'd won today, though it looked as though she was wilting in the July heat. Despite diligent efforts to stay hydrated, she seemed utterly exhausted after the match. She'd stretched dutifully and drank one of her protein shakes, but her energy was spent and she was in bed by eight o'clock. No celebratory dinner occurred.

A scream of agony tore from Aurora's room.

In a heartbeat, Mason was off the couch, through her door, and at her bedside. She lay in bed, her arms and legs bent at odd angles, her face in anguish. Her body appeared contorted as though possessed by a demon.

"Aurora, what's happening?" He was afraid to touch her for fear he would aggravate the source of her pain.

Her eyes snapped open and focused on Mason. Tears streamed from the corners of her eyes. For one gut-tightening second, he thought she'd been poisoned.

"Cramps," she gasped.

"What can I do?"

"Ice bath. Pickle juice."

She groaned and crescendoed in a cry, the sound tearing a painful wound somewhere in his chest.

He saw the shadows of Billy and Dorian behind him.

"I'm on the ice," Dorian replied.

"I'll get the pickle juice," Billy said groggily as she lowered her gun. "I hope they have pickles here."

In a few seconds, Mason got the bathwater running. Dorian added the ice and left.

Aurora was whimpering now. It seemed when she tried to adjust positions to relieve one cramp, others formed in different muscle groups. An extension of one muscle was a flexion of another. Both arms and legs seemed to be taking part in the agonizing rigidity.

Mason clenched his jaw and scooped her into his arms as gently as he could and carried her to the bathroom. She wore a white T-shirt and short pajama shorts. Touching her caused her pain, but there was no avoiding it if he was to get her to the tub. Her fingers dug into his shoulder, not in fear but in reflexive pain.

He looked down at the ice water grimly. "This is gonna hurt."

"Always does," she replied through gritted teeth.

He set her gently into the bathtub. As the cold water engulfed her, she gasped and arched her back from the shock.

Billy entered the bathroom with green liquid in a cup, making a face. Mason took the pickle juice and knelt by Aurora.

After she had caught her breath and the pain eased, she took the juice and drank. When she was finished, Mason took the glass and passed it to Billy.

"Are we good here?"

"Yes, thank you, Billy," Aurora replied in a weak voice.

Billy left with a wave and a mumble.

A coil in Mason's chest loosened as Aurora's distress subsided. She closed her eyes momentarily, and Mason's gaze wandered over her body. Her chest rose and fell with each deep breath. Her soaked shirt clung to her body, wrapping around her perfect breasts, and the chill had made her—

Mason averted his eyes.

When he looked back at her face, she stared back at him. Her eyes stayed wide and still, though her teeth chattered slightly.

She knows.

He swallowed and forced himself to turn away, leaving in search of a towel. He found one and set it down on the hook by the tub.

"Are you okay?"

"Yeah," she said, tinted blue lips protruding as she trembled. "Not the ... first time.... Just heat and a long ... singles match." She gave him a weak smile. "Relax, Stone ... I'm not going to break."

On command and by the sound of her voice he did manage to relax a little.

"Pickles are an interesting choice," he said.

The corners of her mouth turned up as she closed her eyes. "Quick way to get ten times the FDA recommended daily sodium allowance ... and it works every time."

Mason caught his eyes wandering again, and he snapped himself straight. He'd never carried someone while trying so hard not to feel the shape of their body against him.

"Can I get you anything else, Miss Meridian?"

She looked at him through slits in her eyes before waving him a dismissal.

THE NEXT MORNING, Aurora sat at the kitchen counter watching Mason cook omelets. Billy took her omelet to the terrace along with her black coffee as she mumbled something about too many people to be around this early. Dorian lingered in the shower.

Aurora enjoyed the company of everyone sharing the apartment. The bustle was a soothing contrast to the silent hotel rooms she'd been inhabiting.

Aurora ate as Mason cleaned the pan in the sink.

"Wow. This tastes great. If you ever wanted to quit security—"

He looked up at her, and she had the sense not to finish the observation aloud.

She suppressed a grin and sipped her orange juice. "Just a compliment."

"How are you feeling?" he asked.

"Like someone took my major muscle groups and wrung them dry."

"You can play singles tomorrow?"

"Yes. Hydrate. Stretch."

"And more pickle juice?" Mason's eyes sparkled.

"Don't make fun. It worked." She jabbed an empty fork in his direction.

He grinned. "I saw a documentary one time on terrible diseases that are now eradicated or easily treated. An artist's sketch of someone with botulism looked all contorted with muscle contractions like you did."

"Swell." And not at all flattering. Ah, well, she could console herself knowing he'd found her attractive in the ice bath. The true tell-tale sign? He'd reverted back to the formality of calling her Miss Meridian. She understood now his poker face and that he implemented it when his true caring nature slipped to the surface.

"You scared us. I'm glad we were all here to help."

She swallowed another bite of food. "Me, too. The times I'm

alone, it takes a lot longer for all of those steps. I would be infinitely more sore if not for your team."

Mason finished washing the pan and began eating Dorian's omelet.

"You managed to win in that heat," he said, watching her eat.

She nodded. "The points are good. After Montreal is the US Open. Last major."

Last chance.

"You and Alex already took Wimbledon mixed doubles. Now you know you can do it again."

She looked at him briefly and then focused intently on her omelet.

He drank a sip of coffee. "You want the singles win. I get it. You can do it, Aurora."

Her heart leaped at the degree of confidence in his voice. She forced herself to stare at her half-eaten omelet.

She arched her back in a stretch. "I think I need to splurge on a massage. Of course, cramping would happen when we're not at a hotel with a spa."

With her budget, she seldom resided at a hotel with a spa.

"And of course, you won't take medications that might ease the pain," Mason said.

"Nope." She bared her teeth at him. "Back when I had lucrative sponsors, I got a massage once a week," she reminisced. "I think there is one down the street."

Mason shook his head as he finished the last bite of omelet.

Her hope deflated. Of course he would turn a massage into a security threat.

He swallowed and chased it down with coffee. "We'll call a service and have them come to the apartment," he said. "It'll be more controlled here, and Billy can stay in the room."

Looking around the brightly lit apartment with its many windows, she surmised she wouldn't get the complete relaxing ambience of a massage in a spa, but a massage in any room could still ease her aching muscles.

"How about late morning?" Mason asked.

"Yes."

"We'll have them here and ready when you get finished stretching."

She blinked, surprised at the softness beneath his tactical precision. "Thanks."

SEVERAL HOURS LATER, the masseuse arrived. Mason could tell Aurora's muscles held the tension of the previous night's cramps even after an hour of stretching.

The masseuse had set up a table in the main room. He had a short stature beneath his cotton yoga outfit. He had large hands, curly, sandy brown hair, and a generous sized nose. Mason squelched a prickle of jealousy that this man's hands were about to be all over Aurora's body.

After Mason poured her a glass of water and hot cup of tea, he left her in Billy's care.

He and Dorian moved down to the lobby where he sat in an uncomfortably small chair and batted a fake fern out of his face.

"Com check," Mason said.

"Check," returned Billy.

"We're in the lobby."

"Copy."

The sounds of shuffling filled his earpiece followed by the squeaking of metal.

"I can't believe you ate my omelet."

Mason looked at Dorian. His short, dark, peppered hair extended down sideburns of equally short length.

"Shorter showers, man."

Dorian opened *Don Quixote* and turned his attention to his book.

"Is Mason okay?" Aurora asked Billy. Mason could hear her voice through Billy's earpiece. "I mean, he's usually not cheerful but he seemed especially tense today."

He hated seeing her in pain. He'd been scowling and clenching his jaw throughout the morning but couldn't seem to stop.

"Probably brooding because he didn't get all of his beauty sleep," Billy replied.

He heard Aurora's silky laugh. "Guess that's my fault."

"You want the truth?" Billy asked.

"Careful, Billy," he warned in a whisper to her.

Dorian shot him a questioning look. He wasn't wearing his earpiece. Mason shook his head dismissively.

"The truth," Billy began, "is under that steely gaze, rigid jaw, and prickly exterior there is a man who deeply cares about good people and his job."

Mason shifted his weight in the lobby chair. Where was she going with this?

He heard a muffled noise like sheets being adjusted.

Billy continued to speak to Aurora, "You are both a good person and his job, ergo he is affected when you're suffering. Every time you are afflicted and he can't remedy the situation, he feels bad."

Mason grunted.

Billy continued more sharply. "Rather than just acknowledge his limitations and accept that it sucks you're hurting, he gets grumpy."

"But he did fix it," Aurora said. "He got me an in-room masseuse."

"Well, if he sees you're better after it, perhaps he'll be less grumpy... until he invents the next thing to be grumpy about."

"Not helpful, Billy." Mason stood and walked to one window, watching pedestrian traffic outside the hotel.

He heard her cough, which he suspected was her covering a chuckle.

"What about you, Billy?" Aurora asked. "You're always unflappable."

"Pain, struggles, suffering, asshole boyfriends—they're all part of life. No sense getting upset about them."

"What then?"

"Bees."

"Bees?"

"I'm allergic. Anaphylactic. So I have this recurring dream I'm in a park protecting a client when forces of darkness descend to kill her. I get stung as I'm drawing my gun and running toward her. Next, I reach for my EpiPen, but it's gone. I go down, suffocating, and the last thing flashing before my eyes is my client, my asset, being assassinated."

"God, Billy, that's awful," Aurora said.

Mason remained silent. He hadn't known Billy's fear. He knew of her allergy; everyone at Rider SI did and was made aware of her epinephrine injection if she needed it—one in her pocket and one in her travel bag. Her fear that her allergy might result in the death of someone under her protection surprised him.

Billy asked Aurora, "What about you? Pain doesn't stop you. You know how to pick yourself up after defeat. What rattles the great Prime Meridian?"

Mason knew. He'd seen the way the FBI files had rattled her. She had paled like the moon, and her face stretched with worry.

"Jimmy did. Sometimes when I saw pictures of his Russian girlfriend I would get rattled. Not because I wanted him back, just because it was a reminder that I'm not in a relationship. Then I remembered a relationship would just be another distraction. It's better this way."

Her last sentence was meager and unconvincing.

She was rattled by death threats and loneliness, the former of which magnified the latter.

He'd silenced the threats, but her loneliness echoed in him like his own. He ached to be the one she reached for.

But she was the client—and desire was the one danger he was never allowed to fight for.

CHAPTER 22

$\mathcal{A}$urora felt positively giddy the next day. She did her five-mile run, ignoring the dull aching of her ankle. After showering and dressing, she paced the hotel room anxiously.

Monique drove to D.C. for a medical conference, and they planned to meet at Lincoln Park between her sessions.

"It's not a secure location." Mason leaned against the wall.

Aurora rolled her eyes. "My deranged stalker is finished. *Konets.*" She smiled sweetly at him, proud of her Russian.

He narrowed his eyes at her, and she ignored the way his smoldering look made her weak in the knees.

"What? Max said that's Russian for *the end*."

The corners of his mouth lifted in pleasant surprise.

"There will be a crowd." His voice remained calm, but his body held tension as his implication that predators hid among crowds sent a skitter of uncertainty along her spine.

"Not like the train station," she countered. "We'll park our butts on a bench, and you and Billy and Dorian can keep close. Honestly, Mason, you act like there's a sniper after me."

His jaw ticked. He took her mug, put it in the microwave, and warmed up her tea.

"Okay, it's your job to think that way, but I can't live like that. Ask

Billy. I wilt without social contact. I need to get out with Mo and feel like a human being."

Of course, Mason wouldn't understand such a notion. The man didn't seem to need human contact.

Infuriating cyborg.

After handing her mug to her, he stared at her.

"Mason?"

"Miss Meridian."

She sipped her tea. Perfect. Of course it was. He always knew exactly how she liked things. Exactly how to steady her. Exactly how to undo her.

She smiled sweetly at him. "May I please see my friend at Lincoln Park?"

An hour later, Aurora's wish was granted. She squealed with delight as she hugged her friend. Nearby, children shrieked as they ran around a playground.

Monique's brown curls danced around her head. "Girl, you look fabulous."

Aurora waved a hand at her friend as they pulled away from the embrace. Her bangles jingled from the motion. "I'm so glad you could come visit me."

Mo gave a tsk. "Of course."

They sat down on a nearby bench under the shade of leafy maple trees. Walkers, runners, and parents pushing strollers passed them.

"How are things?"

Aurora smiled. "I'm playing well. Competitive. This is definitely my last singles season, though."

Mo frowned.

"I physically can't do it anymore. My ankle protests nearly every match. The constant travel is hell on my sleep cycle. I can't keep this pace anymore. Ten years of this, Mo. And fifteen years of tennis before the circuit."

She left out the isolation of living from hotel room to hotel room.

Her friend sat sideways on the bench and leaned back to assess Aurora. She recognized Mo's narrow-eyed, critical appraisal.

"This doesn't have anything to do with Eye Candy?"

"Mason and the team are on until the end of the season. That is all. Stop looking at me like that. I like him, but I wouldn't change my life for any man. Definitely not one that isn't interested in me."

Mo blinked at her. "A man who holds you in his arms is not *uninterested*."

Aurora pursed her lips, regretting having shared that detail with her friend. "It doesn't count. I was shaken up, and he was trying to make me feel safe."

"In his arms?"

Aurora fidgeted with her bracelets.

"Detached and safe is guarding a door with a gun," Mo continued. "Compassionate and safe is holding you in his arms until you fall asleep. The stem of the word compassion is passion. Eye Candy cares about you."

Aurora refused her friend's words. "He cares about keeping me safe. Beyond that there is a professional code—"

—a rock solid, ice-cold boundary—

"—that he will not cross. I'm not going to put him in a position to break his code."

"In what position are you going to put yourself?" Mo wriggled her eyebrows.

"Funny." Aurora sat back and crossed her legs. "Not in a position to pressure him into something he will regret later."

And then try to apologize for.

Mo bit her bottom lip. "So you won't make a move because you're afraid even if he does act on it, he won't mean it or will regret it. And he can't make a move because of some foolish professional code. But until one of you makes a move, the other is blindly operating under the assumption the feeling isn't mutual. This is like a screwed-up stalemate."

Aurora scowled. She didn't want to spend her time with Mo talking about unattainable fantasies. "I've spent months with Mason.

If romantic thoughts remotely crossed his mind, I would have seen some signs." Except, sometimes she did see signs. Signs that were easier on her heart to brush aside than believe.

"Love is blind."

"First of all, love? Really? You just jump straight to that? Secondly, that phrase applies to seeing another person's faults, not feelings."

Mo responded with a tsk of disagreement.

Desperate to change the subject, Aurora's mind searched for other topics. Before Mo could dredge this annoying conversation further, Aurora changed the subject. "I have someone for you to meet."

Mo grinned and elbowed Aurora. "You've been thinking of me amidst your drama."

Aurora smiled. She wasn't going to admit that the thought of setting up a blind date with Mo and Marco Gold only just occurred to her on the walk to Lincoln Park.

"He's a reporter," Aurora began cheerfully.

———————

MAXINE RIDER STARED at the message on her phone: an invitation to play chess via the internet with Vladimir Pronin. Shock and curiosity roused her.

She'd ignored the request at first. She'd left her phone in the house and went outside to pull weeds in her garden. The cilantro wilted in the July heat, but gave off a pleasant aroma, making her crave a margarita with a side of guacamole and chips.

After an hour in the heat, she came back inside and washed the dirt off her hands before glancing at her phone on the kitchen counter. She sighed.

She unlocked the phone and downloaded the application to play chess. After setting up a username, she joined the game she had been invited to with the Russian mobster.

Tentatively, she moved a pawn.

He instantly messengered her through the app, *Welcome, Max.*

She sent him back, *This is an unusual request.*

Ours is an unusual relationship, he replied.

She snorted. She could not dispute his statement.

He moved a knight.

That night, she played against the world's most infamous Russian mobster from the safety of her home in Alpharetta, Georgia. She examined the board play-by-play in between cooking dinner, washing dishes, and preparing for bed.

They moved their pieces thoughtfully, ever mindful of protecting the king. She could practically envision her players—Mason, Billy, Barry, Dorian, Ryan, Reece, and Claire—as well as Vladimir's known employees based on Claire's research—Boris, Ruslan, Sonya, and Mikhail.

The only faceless player on her side was the king. Who was Rider SI protecting? No single person. Perhaps she guarded an ideal—the ideal that good people deserved to feel safe.

It was more than that. Members of her team—her family—had the ambition of being the ones to keep people safe. Often what began with good intentions in their early military career was corrupted by the horrors of war.

Her men and women had the chance to use their skills to help individuals on a smaller, more manageable scale. Through Rider SI, they could fulfill the youthful idealism they had embraced when they first joined the military. Perhaps her king represented both the safety of individuals and the redemption of her team members.

By midnight, the game ended in a stalemate.

"Fitting," Max muttered. "Perfectly fitting."

<hr>

MASON TRIED to shake images of Aurora in pain. She was since fully recovered, exercising and in good spirits, but the cramping incident had scared him more than he wanted to admit. She was tough as steel, but he started to wonder if he was. His chest had squeezed when he'd seen her physical suffering from the muscle contractions.

This morning, he'd left her in her room after their morning exercise routine and rested on the couch after a shower, staring at the ceiling.

Dorian sat in the lounge chair reading *War and Peace*.

"Do you miss your family?" Mason asked. He knew Dorian's daughter had visited him in Paris. They'd spent a day together sightseeing.

Dorian closed his book. "Every single day."

"How do you manage a family and this work?"

Dorian's expression grew sad. "I'm exceedingly fortunate to have an understanding family. Katie has her own interests, her own life. I think that stemmed from marrying a little later. But I am by no means a family man to emulate."

"What do you mean by that?" Mason turned to look at him.

"Katie and I had a brief, wonderful week together when I travelled between missions and she took a holiday in Rome. She didn't know my identity."

Which was what, exactly? Mason refrained from asking.

Dorian rubbed his chin in thought. "Six years later, I couldn't shake images of this amazing woman who had such a profound impact on me in just a few days. I tracked her down. She was unmarried, a writer, and with a nearly six-year-old child."

"Oh."

"Yes, oh. Quite right. I arrived at her doorstep prepared to grovel for putting her through a brief relationship and giving her a child to raise without help. She accepted me. Eventually, so did Dia."

"She let you return to a traveling job?"

"She lets me do what I'm good at and passionate about as I do her. She jokingly says she put up with me being gone for six years, what's a few months here and there. Besides, I made up for the six years gone by being exclusively around for six years after that. Then we decided it would be okay if I took Max's security job for a while."

Mason worked out the math in his head. Dorian had been some type of covert agent until about age forty-five, followed by stay-at-home dad until fifty, and then back to work again.

"What's after Rider SI for you?"

"I'm hoping when Max gets her company in the green, she'll trade my fieldwork for consultation work. Then I'll have more time to travel with Katie."

Mason felt a pang of guilt. If not for his rock star debacle, Max might be sooner in the green. Instead, she had lawyers to pay.

"Is there someone with whom you are thinking of planning a future?" Dorian asked.

"No," Mason lied.

"Lamenting someone with whom you should have planned a future?"

Mason chuckled. "No."

He had always been frank with women about his career goals and never promised anyone a future. He maintained distance romantically because he believed a relationship couldn't work with his type of employment. Thoughts of Aurora made him wonder if perhaps he could have a functional relationship. Maybe he just hadn't found someone with whom he was willing to expend the effort.

Dorian gave him a skeptical look.

Mason stared back at the ceiling. "I don't mind imagining I could have what you have someday."

Dorian reopened his book. "Well, don't wait as I did. When you decide you have genuine feelings for her, let her know sooner than later."

Glancing over at Dorian, Mason tried to discern if he suspected Mason had feelings for Aurora. His British nose stuck back in his book before Mason could scrutinize his expression.

Mason could fight six men in an alley without blinking.

But the one thing he couldn't fight was this ache to be the one she reached for.

CHAPTER 23

*A*urora was working in her hotel room on a graphic design when Mo texted her.

You're winning more.

Despite the odds and despite the threats, Aurora clawed her way higher in the ranks. She shucked off the wounded bird she'd been when Monique had first met her. The days of licking her wounds and sulking in self-pity were over. Nor was she the egocentric star Mo had seen on TV before meeting her in person.

Aurora caught herself smiling at nothing. Winning used to feel like relief; now it felt like momentum.

Instead of texting her friend back, Aurora called. "Are you working?"

"Yeah," Mo said. "Somebody's out sick, so I'm taking the shift. I'm stuck with Dr. Green."

"Dr. Green?"

"Well, that's not his real name, but he's wet behind his ears. When they're fresh out of residency, sometimes they're too new to even appreciate how much they don't know. And they don't always appreciate that I'm a valuable resource to them—not their lackey."

"How do you deal with that?" Aurora stood and stretched from side to side.

"Usually, over time, we earn each other's mutual respect. Still, I prefer the nightshift when I have fewer newbies to deal with."

"Have you ever had problems with new doctors?"

"One got mad at me for stopping his RSI—rapid sequence intubation. I spoke up because the patient had a history of malignant hyperthermia which is a contraindication to paralytics."

"Wow. I did not even understand half of what you just said."

Mo laughed. "Enough about medicine. How is Eye Candy?"

Aurora groaned. "Don't start," Aurora said too fast—too defensive. *God, was she that transparent?*

Pivoting, she asked, "Did Marco call you?"

"We have date number two on Saturday night," Mo boasted.

"That's fantastic! I was hoping the two of you would hit it off."

"Okay. Okay. We're only at our second date. Much has still to be explored. Maybe when your season is over, the four of us will double date."

"Four of us?"

"You, me, Marco, and Eye Candy."

"Sure, Mo. And pigs will fly and pots of gold will spawn at the end of rainbows."

But the tiny, traitorous part of her that kept replaying the feel of his arms wasn't laughing ... it was hoping he would say yes when she asked him out after the season.

MAXINE WATCHED from the doorway as Claire took an offensive stance and prepared to fight. A dark city street rose up around them with graffiti-laden buildings shimmering liquid black from the glaze of moisture clinging to them. Dim, watery streetlights of yellow, red, and purple glowed around them.

On the large, wall-mounted screen, Claire's character gave her opponent a long, lingering gaze of steel and ice. The Amazonian woman across from her stood a foot taller than Claire. She wore a red leather outfit and defied the laws of physics by being able to move in it as snug as it was.

Claire had spent endless hours on the Meridian File honing algorithms to mine through social media and emails in search of a would-be killer. She deserved some recreational fun even if Maxine didn't understand her choice of recreation.

Interesting how crazy Natasha sent the letters but discreetly avoided sharing her dirty deeds in any electronic format. Smart crazy. A dangerous combination. Fortunately, she was no longer their problem.

Claire bounced lightly on the balls of her feet. "I'm going to smack that smug look off your face." She adjusted her virtual reality headgear.

Maxine put her hands on her hips as she watched the two women fight on screen where the program was casting. Apparently in the virtual reality game, Claire was some type of black belt in taekwondo.

"I guess that's one way to practice fighting," Maxine said.

Claire yanked off her headgear as she cursed. "No sneaking up, Max!" She blinked as her eyes adjusted to the bright room. "And yes, virtual martial arts is the ideal way to fight. No real injuries. No real blood. Unlike the rest of the testosterone-laden macho team at Rider SI, I prefer my violence to be a holographic."

"Shouldn't you be at home enjoying a day off since the tennis star crisis had concluded?" Maxine asked.

From the room across the hall, Claire's computer chirped. She laughed nervously.

"You're still doing work for Mason, aren't you?" Maxine narrowed her eyes at her.

Claire blew blue strands out of her eyes. "After the Russians attacked and before Natasha was discovered as the instigator, I'd already programmed another algorithm to run. This one analyzes Russian mafia connections with people in and around the tennis circuit."

Maxine pursed her lips. She had warned Claire not to till the field too deeply in a Russian mafia landmine or it could blow up in their faces.

"I think the algorithm is done running. I'll comb through it and see if anything turns up."

"Be careful," Maxine warned. "The Russians bury people who get curious."

"I'm always careful," she said cheerfully.

She pulled the goggles back over her head. "First, a warrior clad in red is waiting to eat pavement. Well, virtual warrior eating virtual pavement."

As entertaining as Claire's VR violence was, Max's mind drifted back to their real threat landscape. She hoped Claire's search declared the tennis player free from threats.

THE TRIP FROM WASHINGTON, D.C. to Montreal had been uneventful. The weather was the only noteworthy thing. The heat surprised Aurora. The normally pleasant Canadian temperatures had been replaced by a heat wave. Temperatures were expected to peak in the nineties, rivaling the heat wave of 1957.

While those temperatures were not astronomical, heat radiating off the court raised the ambient temperature. Combined with the humidity, court play was sweltering.

The July heat rose in waves off of the tennis court like solar flares from the sun. Half-filled bleachers held spectators milling about or fanning themselves in an attempt to combat the warmth.

Singles midday match. Lucky me.

To survive, she did more than stay hydrated. She added special tablets to her water bottle containing salt and electrolytes. She hoped that would be enough to counteract the depletion during sweating.

Deep into the match, she realized enhanced hydration wasn't enough. Aurora recognized the signs of heat exhaustion even as she felt them. Her parched mouth felt like cardboard, but she didn't feel thirsty anymore. Under the scorching sun, she no longer felt hot. Cold chills spread over her body.

One more game.

If she won the next game, the match would be over and a cool room awaited her.

She wiped her face with a towel and took a drink from her water bottle. Tucking a ball under her skirt, she walked to the service line with her racquet and first-service ball in hand.

She couldn't pull any fast facts from her arsenal. Her brain felt like a sizzling piece of bacon shriveling under the sun. Glancing at the exit of the courts, she saw Mason. He was probably sweating buckets under his suit. At least he avoided direct sunlight.

They hadn't worked out a signal for "I'm having heat stroke," but a furrow above his sunglasses indicated he knew something was wrong.

Reaching the service line, she scanned the crowd. Her eyes couldn't focus. She saw nothing but a blur of colors.

When she looked at the ball in her hand, her concentration finally narrowed.

Hey there, chicky.

The largest bird, the ostrich, hatches eggs as big as cantaloupe.

Sync.

Aurora floated through the air.

She opened her eyes to see Mason's face surrounded by short, disheveled blond hair. With his sunglasses removed, she could see his blue eyes maintaining a fixed gaze ahead of him. She lifted a hand and touched his face. They were so close, touching.

"Is this a dream?" She ran a hand up into his thick hair.

This close, she could see the details of his blue eyes—rich sky blue encircled by a navy ring with flecks of silver in his iris. He looked down at her and smiled, melting her heart into a puddle.

Why couldn't he always look at her this way? Was it so difficult?

But behind his smile lurked fear. No. Worry.

Why would he worry in a dream?

"No, Aurora, you're not dreaming. But you're going to be okay."

Blinking, she noticed he carried her through a corridor lit with fluorescent lighting.

She already felt okay. Was she injured? Nothing hurt. Was she in shock?

Mason gingerly set her down on a small bed. Aurora's eyes took in the supply cabinets, shelves, and general sterility of the room.

Infirmary. She bolted upright. "The match! I have to play!"

Warm hands cupped her face and eased her back down to lie on the bed. Mason leaned over, blue eyes devouring her—a tropical ocean in which she could lose herself.

"You won, Aurora. Just rest now."

A thumb brushed across her lips, and she sank into the bed. A pair of lips gently pressed to her cheek.

MASON WATCHED as Aurora closed her eyes. His face and scalp still tingled where she had caressed him.

What's wrong with me?

He had nearly kissed her poor swollen sunburnt lips but turned at the last second and kissed her cheek.

Maybe she wouldn't remember.

He'd never forget. He needed to just tell her how he felt.

As he held her hand, Dr. Ruchkin started an intravenous line. She didn't flinch.

"Lots of players getting heat stroke this tournament," the physician commented.

Mason nodded.

"How's Aurora?" Billy said through his earpiece, alarm and worry in her voice.

He'd told Billy he was taking Aurora to the infirmary the instant she'd fallen into his arms. Billy would monitor their exit point.

Aurora had won and weakly waved to the crowd before packing

up her bag. As she left the court, she'd signed a few autographs but looked pale and disoriented.

Mason had emerged to escort her indoors, but when they had just reached the inside of the doors, she'd collapsed.

"She's okay," he told Billy through the mike. "She needs to cool off and hydrate."

He recalled the sidelong look in her eyes when she had glanced at him from the court before serving the last game of the match. She had wanted or needed to convey something. Perhaps she'd known she wasn't going to last much longer in the heat. Regardless of the specific intent, her eye contact, or lack thereof, had served the purpose of placing him on high alert.

Mason watched Dr. Ruchkin connect a bag of saline. He turned and started to draw up something from the cabinet with a syringe.

"Just saline, Doc."

Aurora would be furious with Mason if he let her receive medication to which she had not consented.

Dr. Ruchkin looked surprised. "It's just sedative."

Mason shook his head. "No. You know she's particular about what goes into her body."

The physician shrugged and set down the medication on the table. He busied himself taking her blood pressure.

Mason removed his suit coat and laid it on the back of a nearby chair. Looking down at Aurora again, he ran a hand through his hair. Already some of her color slowly returned. By the time she finished the bag of saline, he should be able to get her away from the facility and back to the safety of the hotel.

His phone rang. He pulled it out of his back pocket and looked at the screen.

"Claire," he said, answering the phone.

Claire didn't make casual phone calls, and she usually texted less important details. A phone call meant she had something important to say.

Mason walked just outside the infirmary and partially closed the door, standing guard outside. He wasn't sure if Aurora should or shouldn't overhear Claire's news.

"I kept digging on all the names you gave me to investigate. I told you Dr. Sasha Ruchkin is a horse gambler. Turns out he owes a lot of debt to a Russian mobster—none other than our new friend, Vladimir Pronin—through a low-level bookie, Sergei Bazin. I combed Ruchkin's correspondence. Nothing sketchy, just a lot of tennis players' names. So I cross-checked the players' names and their performance after their name appeared in Dr. Ruchkin's email or phone messages. Mason, they all lost. Some by illness, some by injury, some unknown. All of the losses were lopsided—games they were favored to win. They can't all be coincidences."

Mason's stomach lurched and hit rock bottom.

Claire said something about different players, but Mason couldn't hear her through the roaring heartbeat in his ears. As he spun back toward the infirmary door, he heard a sickening click.

His hand reached the doorknob two seconds too late. He yanked the knob.

Locked.

"Aurora!" he bellowed.

Not just his client—his heart—and she was trapped on the other side of that door.

CHAPTER 24

"*A*urora!" The shout stabbed through the fog in her mind.

Mason!

Her eyes flew open. She still lay in the infirmary, but instead of seeing Mason's ocean blue eyes, she saw the obsidian, shifty eyes of Dr. Ruchkin. Dark, greasy strands of black and white hair fell into his pale face.

The doctor's hand hovered over her IV line—plunger dropping, liquid sliding into the tubing.

Panic surged through her. Gasping, she frantically yanked the intravenous catheter out of her arm. She rolled off the bed and landed catlike on the floor. Her aching muscles protested the sudden movement, but the cold marble floor helped drive her to full awareness.

"Miss Meridian," Sasha reprimanded calmly.

"Aurora!" Mason cried again from the hallway.

He kicked at the door with a thunderous blow. It wouldn't take his massive quadriceps many strikes to break down the door, but Aurora wasn't going to wait to be rescued.

Dr. Ruchkin and the gurney stood between her and the door to Mason. The physician drew something into a fresh syringe. The sight of the long needle drove her heart rate into a wild frenzy. The yellow-capped bottle said ROCU something. The rest of the words she couldn't see.

Her eyes blurred, and her head spun momentarily. When the brief disorientation cleared, Aurora dashed for the other door behind her and tugged it open, relieved to find it unlocked. She sprinted down a corridor and into the women's locker room.

Blinking under the bright lights, her eyes searched the room. Because the evening matches weren't launching for another hour, no women players were present. Shoes, racquets, and tennis bags lay scattered throughout the room.

Something wet ran down her forearm, over her palm and off her finger.

Blood.

The puncture wound where her intravenous line had been bled in a streak down her arm. She bent her arm up to stop the flow, but looked at the drips on the floor in annoyance. She had undoubtedly left a trail all the way here.

Very stealthy, Aurora.

She grabbed a racquet and hastily circled the room, cutting off all of the lights. A dim illumination came from under the closed bathroom door emitted enough light for her to avoid tripping over benches and equipment. She hoped if Sasha entered he would be temporarily blind until his eyes adjusted.

Hearing the door creak, she hid behind a row of lockers twenty feet from the door. She tried to slow her fast, panicked breathing. She combed her brain for fast facts.

Chris Evert and Serena Williams are tied for the most US Open wins —six each.

Why Dr. Ruchkin? She knew he was macabre and had avoided him on principle, but what did he gain by harming her? Was he working for Natasha?

A dark form slinked into the room.

Not Mason. Mason would have called to her. Mason didn't slink.

She tried to steady the racquet in her shaking hand. The locker room seemed to constrict around her, every shadow sharpening.

"Miss Meridian, please, you're injured. Let me help you." Ruckin's voice projected away from her, so she felt some relief he didn't know precisely where she was.

Ruchkin stilled.

Aurora heard footsteps in the hallway outside the locker room.

"Aurora!" Mason called from the hallway.

She dared a look around the corner of lockers. Sasha, his back to her, moved closer to the door and out of her line of sight.

Good luck with ambushing a former SEAL.

Mason had military combat training and a gun.

The glint of the physician's needle winked at her, sending a jolt of alarm along her spine. If he caught Mason by surprise, he might get close enough to inject whatever poison he held into Mason.

Aurora gritted her teeth.

Cherez moy trup.

She tiptoed quietly down the length of the lockers, closer to the door.

Mason, if you shoot me, I'm finding a new bodyguard.

Mason's footsteps grew closer to the door.

"Aurora?" he called as he entered the women's locker room, gun raised.

"Look out!" Aurora cried, but she knew she was too late.

Ruchkin, like a rabid animal, leaped from the shadows onto Mason.

Mason released a roar. He fell to one knee as Sasha buried his needle into Mason's shoulder. Despite the agony he must have felt, he managed to fling the lanky Russian halfway across the room. Ruchkin skidded along the floor past Aurora.

She unleashed a forehand swing. The racquet frame cracked into the physician's knee. He bellowed a high-pitched scream and clawed at the pain. Aurora took the racquet back for another swing.

Sync.

She brought the racquet face down in an overhead swing on top of his head. The strings snapped like twigs as they struck, and Sasha quieted into unconsciousness.

Aurora stared at the remnants of the racquet—only the second time in her life she had hit anything other than a tennis ball with a racquet. He sagged instantly, unconscious but breathing.

She left the racquet encircling his neck and ran to Mason. He remained on one knee and couldn't seem to stand despite looking like he tried to push himself upright. His face flushed with the effort.

"Mason."

"Something's wrong," he struggled to say.

She helped ease him to the floor. He seemed to grow heavier and more rigidly immobile, but he still stared up at her. His breaths came in ragged, labored gasps.

Frantically, she felt for his phone and dug it out of his back pocket. She pressed his thumb to the pad to unlock it and dialed Monique's mobile number.

"Hello?"

"Mo!"

"Aurora? What's wrong?"

"Mason's been injected with something by the tennis physician. I don't know what to do." Panic and fear had her throat tightened.

"Okay, honey. Is he awake?" Mo asked.

"His eyes are open, but it's like he can't move or speak."

"Does he have a pulse? Is he breathing?"

Aurora felt his chest.

"Yes, pulse. Oh, God, I think he stopped breathing."

"What was he injected with?"

"Oh, God."

Mo's voice snapped. "Aurora, what medication was injected?"

Aurora thought about the vial in the infirmary. "Reca ... no, rocu-something."

"Rocuronium," Mo replied in a grave voice.

Aurora put her on speaker and set down the phone.

"What does that mean? What do I do?"

"You have to start giving him rescue breaths."

As Mo gave directions, Aurora hastily knelt over Mason and put her mouth to his. She followed Mo's instructions, pinching his nose and lifting his jaw with each breath.

Slow. Deep. One breath every five seconds. Her shaking hands and trembling lips obeyed her brain's command.

Billy appeared at some point and restrained the unconscious, traitorous Russian.

Aurora kept breathing as Mo talked in the background. "Rocuronium is a paralytic. All of his muscles are paralyzed including the muscles that breathe. It doesn't work on the heart muscle so his heart will keep beating. You just need to keep breathing for him until the medication wears off."

Faintly, Aurora heard Billy on her phone calling for an ambulance.

"Mason, please don't die," Aurora said.

She breathed again.

Mo encouraged her, "You're his lungs now, Aurora. Don't stop."

"I just found you," she said, voice shaking. "You can't leave me."

Breathe.

"Who's going to make fun of my sponsor's sunglasses? Who'll run and train with me?"

She was rambling again, but she didn't care.

Breathe.

She wiped tears out of her eyes. She went to wipe a tear of hers that had fallen on his face when she realized the tear belonged to Mason. Several more fell from his eyes.

Breathe.

"I love you, Mason. Don't you leave me," she said softly, kissing his forehead and running a hand through his hair.

Breathe.

An eternity seemed to pass before medics arrived. They checked and inspected Mason. The medication was wearing off, and he must have started breathing some on his own because they only slipped an oxygen mask over his face and seemed to think that sufficed.

Aurora huddled in a corner watching as Mason was loaded onto a stretcher and disappeared.

She wondered if she would ever see him again. There would likely be some type of recovery time. What if Maxine reassigned him?

Another stretcher came for Dr. Ruchkin. Police quarantined the area, but Aurora didn't move. Billy never left the locker room. She spent time either talking to the police or on the phone—presumably with Maxine Rider—but always kept an eye on Aurora.

A few minutes—hours?—later, she heard Billy's voice.

"Aurora?"

She jumped slightly. Looking up through blurry eyes, she saw Billy, her big brown eyes framed by short, bobbed hair.

She should be with her partner. Instead she's here with me, still on the clock.

Aurora sniffed. With Billy's help, she stood. Her legs shook, partly from the heat exhaustion and partly from the terror of everything that had happened since the game.

Billy stood by her side while Aurora gave a statement to the police. She recited the events in a numb, detached monotone. Her voice didn't even sound like hers.

After the statement, she declined Billy's offer to take her to an urgent care clinic, requesting instead to go to the hotel. On the ride home, Billy explained she would check on Mason later.

Once alone in her room, Aurora went through the motions of showering and drinking fluids, including a protein shake. She wasn't hungry, but if she didn't replace at least some of the calories she had burned during the tennis match, her body would be useless the next day.

She spent sixty seconds after her head hit the pillow wondering how Mason fared before exhaustion conquered her.

MASON WOKE to a foreign buzzing and a vibration on his arm. He looked down to see a young woman taking his blood pressure.

His eyes roamed the hospital room. He took in the tiny wall-mounted screen, a narrow window with a streak of light pouring through, a hospital bed with rails, and a pole where intravenous fluids hung.

His head pounded like he'd had a night of binge drinking.

After the blood pressure cuff finished cycling and the nurse assistant left, he sat up in bed and scrubbed his face with his hands. He noticed in place of his clothes, a patient gown draped haphazardly over him.

On the nightstand beside him, his phone lay charging.

Bless you, Billy.

He snatched it off the table and pulled out the cord as he called Maxine.

"Morning, sunshine. Are you done taking a siesta and ready to get back to work?"

"Max, I—" He stared at the ceiling, feeling like a failure. How did he apologize for fucking things up . . . again?

"Is Aurora okay?"

"She is."

A measure of relief washed over him, but he'd still failed his role. "I'm sorry, Max. I know I screwed up."

He touched a finger to his lips, remembering Aurora's frantic mouth-to-mouth resuscitation. Her life-preserving breaths. He had a sudden sinking feeling he'd be pulled off the case and never see her again. He'd left her alone in a room with a dangerous madman. She could have been killed. Maybe he needed to be replaced. Maybe she needed someone more competent.

"Mason," Maxine began, her voice was uncharacteristically soft, "you saved Aurora. You stopped the Russian doctor."

He didn't respond.

"What I see is you did your job—all three times. The train station, the street thugs, and the doctor. And nobody got dead, especially not you or the asset. So it's a win-win."

He exhaled long and slow. "Thanks, Max."

Her voice returned to its usual state of irritable gravel. "Now, stop sleeping on the job. You need to wrap this case up with a bow so we can move on to the next one, assuming, that is, that Dr. Ruchkin was the final threat to Miss Meridian."

Mason scratched at the stubble on his chin.

"I don't know. I think we should finish the season. Keep the protection on through the US Open."

With everything she'd been through, she needed to feel safe until the end.

"Okay," Maxine agreed, skepticism unconcealed in her voice.

"Good pep talk, Max. I'll call you with updates."

"Keep your—"

Mason hung up the phone before Maxine could say something crude, unprofessional, and entirely necessary under the circumstances.

The wall he'd erected between his feelings and Aurora crumbled before his eyes. While saving his life, she'd confessed she loved him.

Although he couldn't move or breathe thanks to the paralytic, he remained fully cognizant of her looming over him, breathing for him, and caressing him. He could smell the vanilla soap she used and taste the salt from her tears. If she hadn't breathed for him, he would have died. If she hadn't done it in a soothing manner, he might have lost his mind with panic and fear.

Perhaps confessing love was something people did in moments of hysteria. Perhaps she hadn't meant it. With all of his being, he hoped she meant it. If she didn't love him, he was lost.

He'd also seen her clobber Sasha with the tennis racquet. The woman possessed so much coiled power. The Russian would never walk the same again with his new knee injury.

The lunatic had, however, gotten the jump on Mason, which never should have happened. He'd been too afraid he wouldn't get to Aurora in time. He lost his focus and rushed his entry. It wouldn't happen again.

Like Maxine said, he needed to get back to work. He couldn't protect Aurora from the confines of a hospital room.

He dug into his plastic hospital belongings bag for his clothes, rummaging through what was left of yesterday's attire. His shirt and underwear had apparently been cut off of him and were balled into shreds.

What possible purpose did cutting off his underwear serve?

His pants were intact, so he slipped into them.

He texted Billy. *Status?*

Billy: *En route to you.*

Good. Billy could pick him up, and he would make it back to the hotel to see Aurora after her morning routine.

CHAPTER 25

 $\mathcal{M}$ ason paced the floor in nothing but his suit pants. He had showered and let the nurse know he needed to be discharged. No one had returned.

Finally, a physician entered, her long white coat gleaming.

She introduced herself as Dr. Vastan. Short, dark brown hair framed amber toned skin. Pakistani heritage, Mason suspected.

"I need to be discharged."

"Mr. Stone, you received a frightening drug intended for use by experienced physicians for anesthesia. I need to watch you for at least twenty-four hours. Preferably forty-eight." Her English had a faint Canadian accent.

"I need to get back to my job."

"I'm sure your job will understand given the circumstances of your paralysis."

"The woman I'm protecting might still be in danger."

If Aurora was unlucky enough to have a third party planning her demise.

Impatience broiled within him. He continued to pace the floor, trying not to loom over the short woman. His size could easily make her feel threatened, and that wasn't his intent. Making the gatekeeper uncomfortable would not work in his favor of being released.

He also knew from experience if he left AMA—against medical advice—his health insurance wouldn't cover a dime. Maxine had included that information in the employee orientation. She explained that she paid out of her ass for health insurance so her employees damn well better use it when they needed it and not pretend to be impervious to danger only to later rack up a larger bill for delaying their need for medical attention.

The doctor stood her ground calmly. "It is not safe. We need to monitor your heart function."

"Look at me. I'm a picture of health."

The woman blushed at his shirtless glory.

"I—" Mason stopped as motion in the doorway caught his eye.

Aurora stood before him in jeans and an "I Love NY" T-shirt. Her long, blond hair fell in waves behind her. Her normal radiant glow had been reinstated after a night's rest, though her face was still pale and her lips stretched with worry.

She stepped into his room, closer to him.

He swallowed.

"You do look like a picture of health," Aurora said. "You're okay?"

"Yes. And you?" He stood motionless, surprised by her presence, and caught by the overwhelming desire to pull her into his arms—a desire so strong it froze him in place.

"I'm okay."

"Thanks for saving me."

"Guess we're even." She shrugged.

Her gaze roamed over his bare chest. Judging by the relief in her eyes and the heat in them, the words she had spoken to him yesterday were not fictitious conjuring from fear and anxiety.

She loves me?

How was that possible? He'd been such a jerk to her. How had his behavior successfully kept her physically at arm's length while entwining them in emotions?

She was lonely, he reasoned. This feeling for him was just a phase that would pass. He couldn't quit his job even though he desired her with his whole being and body. He was not a quitter. He loved Rider SI, and he knew that love was real. He didn't want another incident.

But Aurora wasn't a hormonal, twenty-something, drug-using rock star. She was a mature, athletic woman just a few years younger than he. It also sounded like she'd had her heart ripped out by Jimmy, so she wasn't likely to make any hasty moves without knowing the other party held interest.

He just needed to maintain the status quo until the tennis season was over. He would keep her safe until he completed the job. Until then, he would have to fight his desire. Until then, he would have to focus on the job. Just a job.

Aurora smiled at him, and he had to place his belongings bag in front of him so no one would know what that smile had just done to him.

Just a job.

Billy slipped into the room. "Doc, if we keep a twenty-four watch on him, will he be okay to leave?"

Dr. Vastan tapped a pen against her lips as she looked at the women. "Okay. Okay. But give me time to get your discharge paperwork."

Mason watched the physician leave.

Billy tossed him a bag. He peered inside to see a change of clothes.

When he looked up, Aurora had disappeared. Gone. Disappointment crushed him.

Billy must have interpreted his expression. "Dorian is taking her back to the hotel. She kept pestering me until I agreed to let her see for herself you were okay."

"Get dressed," she ordered. "I'll take you to lunch."

⁂

MASON STARED out of the window as he and Billy sat at a noodle cafe. By the time the food arrived, they still hadn't spoken much.

"You all right?" she asked.

"No," he admitted.

"I can't imagine being paralyzed—not being able to move or breathe like that. It's the kinda shit nightmares are made of." She twirled noodles onto her fork.

Turning to look at Billy, Mason thought of her anaphylaxis and fear of bees.

Maybe there would be consequences to telling her, but he needed to talk to somebody levelheaded.

He took a deep breath. "When I think of it, I only see Aurora, haloed like an angel from the ceiling lights, saving me."

Averting his eyes, he chewed and swallowed a mouthful of noodles.

He felt Billy's gaze bore into him. "What are you telling me, Mason? That you're in love with Aurora?"

He stared at his noodles, poking them with his fork.

"'Cause I already know that," she said, shoving a mound of noodles into her mouth.

His eyes shot up to her. "What?"

She chewed and swallowed. "You've been in love with her for months now."

"Well—"

"You look at her like she's the sun and you're starving for warmth."

"But—"

"What I can't figure out is why she loves you." She jabbed an empty fork in the air in his direction.

"She does?" He stared at her.

Billy looked at him blandly. "Yeah, she does. Despite the fact you've mostly been a jackass to her."

"Maybe."

"You've basically been putting her through slow agony as you awkwardly suppress your own feelings."

Mason ran his fingers through his hair. "I tried to prevent all of this."

Billy snorted. "Yeah, because you can flip a switch and prevent two people from falling in love."

"I thought—"

"No, Mason. What you did was compare this scenario with your last one. Your last asset was a child and a junkie. The woman before you is a mature, willing adult who loves you for you ... mood swings and all."

She took a gulp of her soda as Mason ruminated on her observations.

"How do I make it work?"

Billy shrugged. "Hell if I know."

"Maxine won't like it."

"Nonsense. She'll ride you about it, but you know she likes a good love story."

Mason chewed his lip, thinking of Maxine's affinity for romance novels. "Okay. I've got to talk to Aurora." He started to stand.

"Cool it, Stone," Billy snapped. "You waited this long. You can wait until I finish the noodles that *I* paid for."

⁂

AURORA CALLED Monique to let her know everyone survived. Aurora had agreed to stay in the hotel room under Dorian's surveillance until Billy got Mason back to the hotel. She used the time to make calls and pack clothes.

"Honey, you scared the hell out of me," Mo said.

"I thought he was going to die."

"And he would have if you hadn't saved his stony butt."

Aurora thought of his pale face, flaccid body and shuddered. She'd never been so terrified in her life.

"I withdrew from the rest of the Rogers Cup. I can't play after this."

"Understandable."

"I have some time before the US Open to pull myself together."

A long silence stretched between them.

"So, you love him," Mo said.

"Ugh . . . you heard that."

"So did he."

"What?" When the room seemed to tilt, Aurora gripped the back of the chair.

"Paralytics paralyze muscle. They don't make you deaf."

"Well, crap."Aurora had promised to keep it professional. She'd screwed that up.

"You think he'll leave?" Mo asked.

"Yes."

"Well if he's got as much honor and integrity as you've implied in our many conversations, he won't run from love. He'll run toward it."

Aurora frowned. "Unless he doesn't feel the same way. Oh, Mo, why is this so hard?"

"Love ain't easy. But you saved the life of the man you love, Aurora. That will be a comfort, even if doesn't stay."

When they finished talking, Aurora stood in her hotel room staring at the silent, bland furniture. She needed to busy herself with something, anything. She jerked out her suitcase and started packing, unpacking, and repacking again.

⁂

AT RIDER SI HEADQUARTERS, Maxine walked down the hall to Claire's office. The mostly vacant floor housed only her and Claire at the moment. The rest of Rider SI worked their assignments, growing the business and spreading a good reputation.

The company's reputation was now more secure thanks to the singer's lawyers talking sense into their celebrity. After the documented time line and video footage supported Mason's innocence, she dropped the accusations. No lawsuit to fend off. No tarnish of Rider SI's integrity.

Max had believed Mason's innocence. She handpicked and vetted her team. None of them would impose themselves on a client. Fortunately, Mason had recognized the danger of the situation and had left the room immediately, knowing he needed to make himself visible on the time-stamped hotel surveillance videos. If he'd stayed to talk to the girl and try to smooth things over without a witness, it would've been his word against the pop star.

Now, with the tennis ordeal also concluded, Maxine could focus her attention on new hires and new clients. Her tennis team trio—Dorian, Mason, and Billy—had just proven themselves worth their weight in gold. They had protected a soon-to-be high-profile celebrity.

Max had faith in Aurora's tennis game. She genuinely liked the tough athlete. Aurora was close to her son in age and was single like him. Not for long. Billy and Dorian indicated a consensual relationship brewing between Mason and Aurora.

Now that Aurora's danger abated (because surely after three attacks there could be no more), Max was unconcerned if Mason wanted a relationship. He deserved happiness—if such a thing was achievable with another person. She'd heard of it happening for some people—this happy relationship enigma—though she couldn't claim to have experienced such a thing herself.

Except for David. Her son had been the one relationship that brought a wealth of happiness ... until she let him slip away from her.

She needed a stiff drink. Well, first she needed to talk to Claire.

At the end of the dark hallway, she knocked on Claire's door before entering.

"Yo, Max," Claire greeted her while pulling headphones off her ears.

Maxine scanned the computer programmer's office. The overhead fluorescent lights were turned off as usual. In the center of her desk glowed three monitors with various online searches and open files. Off to one side stood a neatly trimmed bonsai tree illuminated by glowing LED lights. Claire called them her fairy lights, claiming the ambiance enhanced productivity. As long as the woman continued to be their eyes and ears on the internet, she could have a disco ball in her office.

"I want to thank you for finding out about Sasha Ruchkin," Maxine told Claire.

"Sorry I didn't call you first. I thought Mason needed the info ASAP."

Max nodded. "You did the right thing."

"I wish I'd figured it out a day sooner."

"It worked out. Everyone's okay."

Claire gave a weak smile.

Maxine regarded her fair skin and blue-haired bob. "Better to know about a threat sixty seconds in advance than anytime after the attack. You did good."

The young woman beamed at the compliment. With a bright smile, she said, "Congratulations on burying the diva's accusations."

Max cocked her head. "How do you know that already? No. Never mind. I have a bottle of Jack and a chess game waiting on me. You wrapping up here soon?"

Claire nodded.

Maxine left, closing the door and leaving the blue-haired fairy in her twinkling office.

***

"Boris."

"Mr. Pronin?"

"Someone has broken my agreement with Mrs. Rider. A Dr. Sasha Ruchkin assaulted a women's tennis professional."

Boris scowled faintly and gave a slight swallow. He'd been charged with disseminating the word about Vladimir's proclamation that tennis players were off limits. Vladimir sensed Boris's fear that the blame fell to him. The Russian mobster didn't need to blame his assistant. Boris's personality was such he would recognize his level of responsibility in the matter. Vladimir knew that as large and secretive as his organization was, spreading orders was not as simple as sending a mafia-wide memo. Nor had he taken to tweeting such messages.

Nevertheless, an example was needed to ensure compliance to the rules, especially knowing and adhering to them when they changed.

"Send Ruslan. The doctor can be relocated to a Russian prison, Yakutia perhaps. His bookie, Sergei Bazin is an American citizen. Acquire his assets and ..." his voice trailed.

He could not exile Sergei, and life in an American prison would hardly suffice as a message of deterrence to the rest of the organization. Vladimir's tentacles could reach within the prison system and make life exceedingly difficult for Sergei, but it seemed like such a tiresome way to toy with a man before his untimely death. A simple, clean death would prove definitive and not belabor the inevitable. It also did more to convey a clear message about not breaking the rules.

Max would not approve.

He smiled at his sentimental thought, surprised that side of him had resurfaced after so long. Max represented a world he could never inhabit—but one he admired from afar.

"Mr. Pronin?" Boris prodded tentatively.

"A swift execution," Vladimir concluded.

Max would probably not see his mercy in ending Sergei's life quickly. She would be appalled at murder regardless. Nevertheless, a merciful death was all he had to offer. Anything less and he could not be sure his orders to keep the tennis players safe would be obeyed.

He would keep his promise to Max and fulfill his own hope of seeing her again.

⁂

Maxine stared at her phone as Vladimir moved a bishop.

He sent her a message. *My apologies for Dr. Ruchkin's untoward behavior. He and his bookie will be dealt with.*

She pursed her lips. She'd sent him a message about the attack because it violated their accord, even knowing what the consequences were likely to be. Death or exile. She would find out later from Claire which verdict had been dealt. Maxine knew her role of passive acceptance in it left her soul stained.

Not much more than it already was.

Yet, she couldn't protect Aurora indefinitely. She had secured her safety from one group of predators even though it likely came at the cost of life.

I trust our agreement is still in effect, Vladimir wrote.

Letting out a laborious sigh, she replied, *Yes.*

She would not covertly investigate his niece, and he would leave Aurora alone. The bleak fate of those with a hand in attacking her would send a message that would keep her safe. Vladimir didn't have to go to extremes, but he may have felt his honor was threatened. He had declared Aurora off limits, and either Ruchkin's bookie didn't receive the message or didn't heed it. Either way, Vladimir's legions would abide his word more carefully once his message permeated the ranks.

Maxine felt both relieved and appalled. She wanted to believe the justice system remained the only route to ever be taken, but Vladimir's version of justice may have been more effective at ensuring the safety of her client than jail time for a bookie.

She would never confess those feelings to Vladimir.

But she could play chess. A battlefield where no real lives were loss.

Sure ... internet chess against a Russian mobster was completely innocuous.

CHAPTER 26

*A*urora finished packing when a knock came at her door.

She put one hand on the knob. "Who is it?" she asked, though she recognized Mason's three quick knocks.

"Mason."

Her heartbeat kicked a little faster at the sound of his voice. She grew annoyed by the giddy bubbling in her stomach.

Why did I tell him I love him?

She had to keep their interaction professional. She hoped he wouldn't remember the confession despite what Mo had said.

When she opened the door, Mason loomed over her, fully dressed now, unfortunately. His face portrayed the same mask of irritating calm.

Stone wall Mason.

She turned and walked over to her suitcase.

"Feeling better?" She resumed packing. "You look better. Breathing definitely suits you. I like you breathing better than not." She could feel him standing in the doorway, as stoic as ever, as she rambled. She continued, "Maxine told me the team will stay on to finish out the season. I appreciate that. I understand, too, if you can't stay or need a break after what happened." She wasn't sure if she referred to the paralysis or her declaration of love, but he could sort out for himself which one was cause for leave.

She ground her teeth with her back to him as she stuffed tennis outfits into her suitcase—far too aggressively. She would lose him because of her crisis-induced confession. She'd confessed her love, and they hadn't had so much as a first date.

It already hurt, and he hadn't even left yet. An ache spread across her chest as she contemplated losing what she never had. Another fantasy relationship.

Jimmy had turned out to be a fake. Hans was gay. Mason was off-limits.

Finally, she threw her blow dryer in the suitcase and spun around to meet Mason's eyes.

"Will you say something?" she demanded. She breathed hard, anxiety and frustration driving up her heart rate and burning her cheeks.

His usual blank expression of calm was replaced by lips curled in a small smile and eyes sparkling with delight. He stepped toward her as he extended a hand and lifted a blonde curl.

"I love the way your hair shimmers in the sunlight like liquid gold." His voice was deep and tranquil.

Aurora stood frozen, mouth slightly agape.

He continued, "I love to watch the amazing combination of grace and speed you display on the tennis court."

She swallowed as he moved closer, barely a wisp of space between their bodies.

"And I have wanted to kiss you since the first moment we met." He tucked a strand of loose hair behind her ear. "I know you've gotten a lot of mixed signals from me. I tried to ignore how I felt. I thought distance was safer—for you and for the job—but I only succeeded in acting like a jerk. I'm sorry.

"I don't want to start anything that promises an us when I don't know if there can be an us. And I don't want you to do anything because you feel like I will protect you any differently."

She bit her lip. "If it's possible, you are even more attractive when you're nervous."

As he leaned down, she met him halfway for a soft kiss. Their lips met in tentative contact at first as it took her a moment to process all of his words.

As his confession of feelings for her sank through her layers of disbelief and self-doubt, the kiss deepened. Soon, her entire body tingled with desire. When he wrapped her in his arms, the kiss grew hungrier.

They pulled away simultaneously, and she could tell from Mason's expression he was as awestruck as her by the electricity flying between them. He leaned forward and placed his forehead against hers as though needing to steady himself. His breath mingled with hers—warm, unsteady, wanting.

She laid one hand on his chest, smiling. "You mean we could have been kissing like this the entire time? You *are* a jerk."

She felt the rumble of a chuckle in his chest.

"Did you even hear what I said?" he asked softly, brushing a thumb across her lips.

Heat radiated through her body. "That you're not a fortune teller? Yes. I understand that. Admittedly it was drowned out by the part where you said you wanted to kiss me."

He pressed his lips against hers again, a lusciously exploratory kiss in which she lost all concept of time and space.

When they finished, she felt his heart pounding against her hand on his chest.

In a breathless whisper, he said, "I love you, too, Aurora."

With his words, a hard barrier in her chest, like coal around a diamond, shattered. Warmth and relief enveloped her. She fervently wrapped her arms around Mason, absorbing his heat and strength and solidarity. She stifled the urge to cry tears of joy.

Aurora Mercedes Meridian does not cry in the arms of a man.

Perhaps one drop fell, but Mason didn't need to know of the rogue tear's escape. She took a deep breath, smelling his sandalwood scent.

She pulled away abruptly, but Mason kept his arms around her, arms in which she would be content to spend a lifetime. She stared up at him.

"Your job!" she said with alarm.

He caressed a hand across her cheek.

"It's okay. I'll still be employed despite falling in love with you. I'll be with you every match to the end."

She smiled as relief percolated through her.

"Can I kiss you again?" he said, voice filled with intoxicating desire.

"I wish you would."

⁂

THE NEXT AFTERNOON, Aurora sat on the plane to California watching passengers board.

Home. It seemed like ages since she had been home.

Aurora and Mason weren't seated together. She'd booked this flight months ago, and their relationship had just become something more.

Everything she'd been feeling, he'd been feeling too. He'd been trying to suppress it under a facade of disinterest. He'd been so good at his disguise she thought she only imagined or projected during the times he seemed to care.

He did care.

He loves me.

Her doubts had been sizzled away by his kisses. She could have kissed him into the night, but he'd had to go. He had to make a statement to the Montreal Police about what happened. He had to document everything for Maxine Rider's files.

Aurora had been busy packing, followed by pacing, hoping he would return. She busied herself on a graphic design project.

When the dark sky descended, she thought she would just close her eyes for a moment. Resting transformed quickly into sleeping. Mason hadn't returned for the night, but his morning kiss before they drove to the airport reinforced the prior day's confession of love.

Now, the distance from him on the plane felt agonizing. She tried to distract herself by working on designing a car wrap on her laptop before she had to stow electronics. Mostly, she stared at the screen.

Her phone buzzed.

"Maxine?" Aurora lifted the phone to her ear.

"How are you, Aurora?"

"I'm okay. I'm once again grateful I had your team."

"Well, thanks to you Natasha is footing the bill now."

"Yeah, I'm glad that worked out, too." She closed her laptop.

"Billy tells me your overhead swings are as wicked off the court as they are on the court."

Aurora grinned. "I've never struck someone before, and he got every ounce of fear and anger in me."

"Well, he won't be bothering you again. And Natasha won't bother you again. And the Russian mob won't bother you again."

"Are you sure? I'm twice bitten now. Makes me a little skittish."

"I'm sure." Maxine's voice held solid conviction.

She wanted to ask how Maxine could be so sure, but maybe she didn't want to know. She sensed there were wheels spinning in the periphery—a dark, sinister periphery running in parallel to the brighter world she knew.

After a moment of silence, Maxine said, "Thank you for the business cards."

"Oh, good, you got them."

"I got them. Gold, huh? The rook's a nice touch."

"Your team has been my golden protection. Might as well convey to the rest of the world the level of confidence your company inspires."

After a brief pause, Aurora bit her lip. "I owe you truth in another matter, Maxine. I have been in love with Mason, even before he saved me. I'm sorry if I broke any rules."

She had partly read and partly skimmed the ten-page company-client agreement she had signed. There had been a clause on relationships, though she didn't recall the specifics.

"Did he in any way coerce you?"

Aurora snorted. "God, no. He mostly pushed me away for months."

"And you love him after that?"

"Sometimes, when he let his guard down, I would see the real Mason, and that's who I love."

She heard the sound of Maxine taking a large deep breath. She didn't want to anger a woman like Maxine, but the former Marine didn't sound angry over the phone. She also didn't want Maxine to think they tried to sneak a relationship by her.

"It won't be easy," Maxine warned.

"It hasn't been so far."

"He'll travel a lot with work."

"Me too," Aurora said.

"The best I can do is try to give him shorter assignments, but I can't show favoritism to different employees."

"I'm happy with anything you consider to be fair."

The flight attendant closed the door and announced the cease and desist of mobile phone use.

"Alright, then. You have my blessing."

Aurora chuckled. "I guess that is why I told you—for your blessing. Thank you, Maxine."

⁂

Aurora felt the small jolt of the plane's wheels contacting the runway. She looked out the window at the familiar sight of the San Francisco airport. After the plane taxied and parked, she grabbed her carry-on bag and joined the mad rush to deboard the plane.

The plan was the same as every other flight: as Aurora, Mason, and Dorian made their way to baggage claim, Billy would pick up the reserved rental car.

"I told Max," Aurora confessed to Mason.

He placed a hand on her shoulder. "So did I."

"She's not angry?"

"No."

"There she is!" A woman cried.

Aurora jerked her head to her left to see a throng of reporters. She had passed the threshold beyond which a boarding pass was needed to cross and entered public territory.

Her heart raced. There were so many of them—eagerly snapping photos. She had forgotten how intimidating the attention could be. They called out questions, but none of them were tennis related.

"Aurora, tell us about the attack!"

"Were you injured?"

"Are you still in danger?"

"Do you plan to play the US Open after the attack?"

Mason walked between Aurora and the crowd, shielding her. His glasses were on, and he had stretched to his full intimidating height.

Unspoken communication seemed to have flowed between him and Dorian. Dorian broke off toward the luggage conveyor belts, while Mason steered her toward sliding glass doors. He barreled through the crowd as they hurled questions at her, snapping photos relentlessly.

He slipped cash to an airport attendant and cut in the line waiting on taxis. He jerked the door open and ushered Aurora inside to the protest of waiting passengers. "Start north on 101, and I'll give you more directions in a minute."

The cab driver obliged.

Aurora pulled her seatbelt over her chest and clicked it, taking a steadying breath as the voices, pressing bodies, and flash photography stopped assaulting her senses.

As they pulled away, the paparazzi's shouts faded into silence.

Mason pulled out his phone. "Billy, we had a media swarm." He eased his free hand into hers. "Pick up Dorian. We can meet you in Brisbane." He frowned into the phone. "You're right."

He turned to Aurora and dropped his voice to a whisper. "Your apartment will be just as bad. Any objections to the winery?"

Aurora shook her head as she glanced at the cab driver. If he knew they were going to her parents' winery, would he sell that information to the media? Would they figure it out regardless?

Aurora leaned into Mason. She felt grateful to still have her team—her amazing trio. They belonged to her through the US Open.

She had her team. And Mason. Woe to anyone who tried to take either away.

CHAPTER 27

Mason watched as Aurora embraced her mother. "Aurora!"

She hugged her in return, then smiled sheepishly. "We hit some unexpected paparazzi. Sorry to crash your home."

"We wouldn't have it any other way," Mr. Meridian assured her.

She hugged her father.

Aurora introduced Billy and Dorian to her parents, after which Mason commented, "Nice to see you again."

"Truly stunning estate you have. It inspires me to reread James Conaway," Dorian said with a smile as he shook hands with her father.

Aurora's father beamed.

He extended a hand to Billy next, then Mason, "Good to see you again. Thank you for keeping our girl safe."

"Sir." He shook hands before taking a step back, gaze roaming the grand foyer with its high, vaulted ceiling, dazzling light, and marble floors. Paintings of wine and vineyards decorated the walls.

Had Aurora grown up in this luxury? He swallowed. How could he keep her sustained in the lifestyle she knew?

He switched off those thoughts and shifted his mind back to

awareness of his surroundings. Three entry points, not counting ground floor windows. At least one camera was stationed at the front door. Judging by the panel by the door, the alarm system was good quality.

"You've had a long flight. Why don't you get settled in your room? We'll show your security team to their beds," her mother suggested.

Mr. Meridian led Dorian up the stairs, and Billy followed. They carried their luggage, careful not to bump bags into the gleaming mahogany wood railing.

Mason hoisted his luggage and started to follow, but Aurora slipped her hand into his free hand and squeezed.

"Mom, Mason and I started dating after the incident in Montreal. With your permission, I'd like him to stay in my room." Her voice was solid and determined. Only the firm grip in his betrayed her nervousness.

They hadn't talked about letting her parents know, but the decision was hers to make. As far as he was concerned, Aurora and Maxine accepted him. The rest of the world would have to answer to these women if they had objections to his feelings for her.

"Oh?" Her mother looked back and forth between Mason and Aurora before her gaze dropped down to their entwined fingers. "Oh." Her eyebrows lifted. "Sure, honey. That's fine." She forced an uncertain smile.

Mason felt Aurora's grip ease, followed by releasing him. He adjusted his luggage and picked up her bags. He followed Aurora up the stairs and down the opposite hall from where Billy and Dorian had gone.

"Don't do that, please," she said in a soft voice.

He looked over at her quizzically.

"I saw the way you looked at my parents' place. It started as we drove down the vineyard, then the outside view of the house, then the foyer. It's impressive and expensive and worth millions of dollars. But it isn't me. I don't need this kind of luxury. I don't want it unless I earn it. I've lived without it for years now."

"Okay."

"Don't infer that my parents' lifestyle is mine."

"Okay."

"Or that I have financial expectations from the person I'm dating."

"Okay."

"Why are you grinning?"

He set down the luggage in the bedroom and pulled Aurora into his arms. "Can I still buy you dinner once in a while?"

"Yes. I just meant—"

He kissed her. "I know what you meant. I've seen how carefully frugal you are. I promise no inferences."

He kissed her again.

"Good."

ALONE INSIDE HER BEDROOM, Aurora waited for Mason to drop the luggage before she slid her hands around his torso and under his jacket.

He released a light groan as he eased the door shut with one hand while keeping her close with the other. "Am I allowed to infer your desires based on your current actions?"

She smiled enticingly up at him. "Yes, you are."

She pushed away from him, kicked off her shoes, and pulled a water bottle from her carry on bag. She took long gulps as she gathered her nerve. "Stay with me."

He stared at her.

"All night," she added.

He took out his earpiece.

He moved close to her, looking down into her eyes with playful hunger. "Yes, ma'am."

He wrapped his arms around her, lighting her body on fire. The feel of his lips on hers sent a rush of heat to her core. His hands moved around her, delicately lifting her shirt over her head.

When let it fall to the floor, his eyes danced over her bare skin in approval and anticipation.

She gasped as he lifted her into the air and set her down on the bed. In moments he removed his gun, holster, and clothes and lay beside her in the bed.

She slid off her jeans, hands shaking with delighted anticipation.

His pressed his warm body against her.

She ran her fingers along the muscles of his chest and abdomen. It had been too long since she reveled in a man's embrace. For the first time, she felt as though she curled in the right man's arms, and she clung to the moment.

He wrapped his large arms around her and kissed her senseless again as his hand trailed along her torso and around her breaths. His sublime touch had her aching and arching for more.

Heat scored her body everywhere his fingers skimmed. Soon, his hand was lower, stroking deliciously as he kissed down her moans. With only a few sensual thrusts, her body quaked with delight.

When he hovered over her, his eyes gleamed with content and passion. "We can take it slow," he offered.

She'd waited for this level of intimacy with him for far too long. "Please, tell me you have a condom."

He chuckled as he eased back. "Yes, ma'am."

His absence left her cold, but he was back in an instant with protection in place. When he slid inside her, she shifted to take all of him. Bodies locked, they held the position a long moment as if both savoring it.

"I love you," he said as he began to move.

Her mind went incandescent with the flood of physical bliss pouring from his body in her and around her. They moved in unison, adjusting with each tantalizing thrust as they built toward an unseen peak.

His fervent kisses drove her wild as his lips glided along her neck, jaw line, and lips, even as he murmured her name.

Deeper he drove, deeper she willingly took, until they crested and the world burst in color and glory.

She cried out his name, and his body made its final tremors before collapsing onto her. Reveling in the moment, she kept her body locked around his and cherished his panting body pressed against hers.

⁂

AURORA WOKE the next morning comfortably in Mason's arms. Her world was tennis and Mason, and was no longer complicated by threats and worry and self-doubt.

She ran a delicate finger down his bare chest. "You have scars." She'd barely noticed them during their rounds of intense love-making last night.

His abdominal muscles tightened beneath her fingertips. "I do." On his lower right abdomen a small, dense scar paled against the skin around it.

"What's this one from?"

"Eight millimeter steel-cased full metal jacket from an AK-47."

She swallowed. "Oh."

He brought her hand up to his lips. "I'm kidding. That was where my appendix was removed."

She laughed as she playfully smacked her palm against his chest. "Jerk."

He chuckled. "Not my fault you picked the most uninteresting scar to ask me about." His voice sobered. "The bullet wound is on my thigh."

"Seriously?"

He nodded.

She glanced down were the covers lay over his legs. "Can I see it?"

The thought of Mason—her Mason—shot and suffering made her feel claustrophobic. Her gut clenched as her imagination regurgitated visions of him on the floor of the locker room. Frozen. Vulnerable. She had been terrified, though he seemed fully recovered from the event.

She tried to fathom how Mason might respond to a bullet wound: "Well, damn, that stings a bit," or "I just dry-cleaned this suit," or "At least it wasn't three inches higher."

Her fingers crept toward the edge of the sheet. "Did it hurt?"

"Yes, it hurt. Still does sometimes. Yes, you can see it. But there's a toll for crossing certain territory."

She bit her lip. "Is there now?"

He gave her a boyish grin with sparkling blue eyes that weakened her knees. She had a feeling she'd be willing to pay any price he demanded knowing the sensational return on investment—the ecstasy of his kisses, the sublime safety of his embrace.

She eased her fingertips to the edge of the fabric and slid it down as he unleashed a low hiss. Emboldened, she kissed the skin over his hip bone.

"I think I might enjoy the toll," she said with a purr.

⁘

AROUND THE DINNER TABLE, everyone filled their plates with lasagna and broccoli. Aurora's parents had fixed her favorite dish for the group dinner. The scent of garlic-infused tomato sauce filled the air. Aurora sipped her wine—a Meridian Vineyards' 1978 cabernet. The full-bodied dark fruit flavor danced on her pallet.

Her father conversed with Dorian as the lean British man rapturously inquired about the process of pruning vines and picking grapes. Meanwhile, her mother asked Billy about her days in the Marines and how she met Maxine.

Maxine was the only person missing, Aurora thought. The Rider SI CEO seemed like family even though Aurora had never met her in person. She'd spoken with Maxine this week, and she'd promised to come to the US Open so they could finally meet.

The US Open. The gap was closing as the tournament approached. Aurora had spent ten days in Napa Valley. Ten days of domesticity with Mason—discussing world news over breakfast eggs and toast, learning favorite meals and holidays, and exercising together.

She had bought some of Coach Jareh's time and took his professional pointers to heart. She trained every other day with Lizzy who continued to play well on the ITF. Mercifully, her friend didn't probe into events that transpired in Montreal. Aurora had even asked her if she wanted to play women's doubles together next year, and Lizzy had accepted.

Either the media hadn't deduced where Aurora was staying or hadn't bothered to drive all the way into wine country. She hoped their quest for sensational journalism would subside before she went to New York for the US Open.

Regardless, Mason would be with her. He continued to run when she ran and lift weights and stretch alongside her. They talked about favorite foods and favorite travel spots. He had confided to her that he had wanted to walk along the river walk in Strasbourg holding her hand when they'd toured the city. She'd assured him she would never ask or expect him to leave his work. Rider SI felt like her family. He'd smiled at that.

"Penny for your thoughts?" Mason's whisper was only a breath away from her ear.

Her eyes focused back on the dinner. She turned to smile at him. "I love big, bustling dinners like this. When the US Open is over, we should have a big Rider SI company dinner. Most of you live in Atlanta? We could plan to have it there."

Mason's blue eyes sparkled mischievously. "We'll crash Maxine's place and have a cookout. There will be too many of us for her to fend off, and she can't fail to show up because it's her place."

"Perfect."

◆◆◆

After landing at LaGuardia and driving to the hotel in New York, Mason and Dorian secured Aurora's room as she waited at the doorway. Billy had taken the team's luggage to their other rooms.

When Mason glanced out the window to see New York pulsing below he saw only a city of lights, crowds, and unknown threats. While the mafia threat was over, she was a celebrity now—with all of the usual danger that entailed.

Mason's gaze trailed over Aurora as she arranged her tea bag container and protein shake mix on the kitchenette counter. When they finished their sweep, Dorian left and Mason lingered.

As the door clicked shut, he spun around and grabbed Aurora by the waist. She released a gasp of delight. He turned her in his arms and pulled her to him. Her eagerness in meeting him for a kiss made him swell with desire. The kiss lengthened and deepened, leaving them both feeling intoxicated.

Mason cupped her face in his hands. "I don't deserve you."

"I'll be the judge of that."

He pulled her to him for a hug.

He could sense something was on Aurora's mind. US Open, maybe? She had trained mercilessly in California. Now, the tournament would start in a few days. Aurora was ready.

He smoothed a curl around her ear. As sexy as she looked in her tennis skirt and exercise clothes, he loved the casual travel days when she wore jeans and her hair loose. He looked into her green eyes.

"What's on your mind?" he asked.

"There's a fund raiser I go to annually. It's tomorrow night."

"Yes. I have your full itinerary for the next three months."

"Will you be my date?" she asked. "I mean, I know you will be there as my protection, but can you also be my date? Can you do both, or am I asking too much? Why are you grinning at me?"

"You're asking me as Aurora, not as the client."

"Yes."

"Then yes. Always."

He leaned down and kissed her again. He liked that she seemed always willing to meet him for a kiss.

"I would be honored to go as your date."

And her nervous rambling was adorable.

***

MASON STOOD tall in his tuxedo as he knocked at Aurora's hotel room.

She opened the door wearing a stunning emerald and silver gown. The colors accentuated her green eyes.

"Be still my heart," he said, a little breathless.

She smiled, completely sweeping him off his feet.

"You look stunning." He entered the room as she stepped aside from the door.

Ravishing.

It would take all of his effort to keep his hands off of her so they could make it to the fundraiser. Her green dress hugged every curve while making her look like royalty. She was his queen, and he could have bowed down and sworn allegiance to her in exchange for nothing more than the look of adoration she bestowed upon him.

"You look amazing in a tux." Her gaze roamed hungrily over him. She seemed to notice his tidy haircut, and her twinkling eyes suggested approval.

He wanted to run his hands along every inch of her amazing body, but refrained touching anything he might inadvertently tussle. He leaned down and kissed her softly, thankful she hadn't yet put on lipstick. She reciprocated the kiss as something like a purr spiraled up from her throat.

She stepped away from him. "Keep kissing me like that and we'll never make it to the gala."

Is that an invitation? A promise of something more to come?

He straightened, wrapping restraint around his desires. He wanted to give her an escape—a night of fun and romance. Later, he could entertain other activities with her.

Maxine stared down at the dancing couple on the floor. Mission accomplished. Aurora's safety was secured, and the accusations against Mason vanquished. Rider SI completed their contract with the singing diva and received more lucrative offers worthy of the team's talents.

She adjusted the string of pearls around her neck, and felt

someone walk to stand beside her. The fluid and subtle motion barely rustled her black, silk pant leg against her skin.

"Maxine Rider," a man's voice purred.

She turned to meet the dark gaze of Lucius Titan. "Lucy," she replied with genuine surprise.

"You're the only one who dares call me that." His whisper oozed irritation.

Mission accomplished.

Lucius Wallenius Titan, owner and CEO of Titan Enterprises, orchestrated one of the most lucrative security companies on the rise. Like Maxine, he hired ex-military. Unlike Maxine, he had pliable morals.

In fact, did he have morals? Perhaps not.

Maxine had crossed paths with him when he'd been part of a private security team employed to intervene in Afghanistan—Americans paying Americans to incorporate unconventional methods to end the war sooner while keeping the military's hands clean in a strictly conventional role.

US soldiers had no part in the atrocities committed, but the fact that her country paid a private company still soured Maxine's stomach. That a man like Lucius Titan could look at himself every morning, slap on his smug smile, and consider himself a jolly good fellow made her want to pistol whip him with the SIG from her shoulder harness.

Lucius had taken remnants of his former employer's company and built his own dark legacy through Titan Enterprises.

"Cold in here, Max, or is that your Marine standard issue?"

"I'm surprised to see you here, Lucy. Didn't your house go up in flames?"

Claire's secret spying had revealed that a psychotic employee from Titan Enterprises blew up their base of operations.

"I always rise from the ashes."

Max fell silent. She remembered the bodies of women and children found after Lucius's team attacked long ago. She hadn't known who was responsible at the time, other than a private security force.

After some digging, she later learned it was his team—code name Phoenix—who completed the assignment. Did he know she knew his code name? How could he?

"Which one is yours?" he asked.

"Aurora Meridian," she answered. Lying would accomplish nothing. Lucy had the resources to discover her clients.

"Cute. Marine bulldog helping the underdog."

Only someone as pompous as he would consider that an insult.

"Yours?" she asked.

"Those two men." He jutted his chin toward the bar at two of the top twenty men's tennis professionals.

Lucius guarded two celebrities.

Pretentious prick.

His company was three times the size of hers with twice the health and other benefits—she was reminded of this when she interviewed some of the young punks who applied practically straight out of boot camp and tried to negotiate their terms. They would cite the competition's income and benefits, and she would promptly show them the door.

Everybody needed a solid paycheck, but if applicants hadn't done their homework to know the different moral character of each company, they weren't worth her time.

Besides, Lucius may offer better retirement, but money proved little use to his employees if they weren't alive to spend it. Titan ex-military had truncated life expectancies, though recruits wouldn't learn that in the brochure.

Maxine took a deep breath and another swig of her watered-down whiskey. She reminded herself she wasn't in competition with Lucius Titan. Her clients were good people genuinely needing help, not billionaires wanting discreet escort services and access to illegal drugs.

"See you around, Lucy." She walked away from him.

"You betcha, Max."

She didn't know when, but Titan would cross a line one day—and she'd be waiting.

· · ·

AURORA FELT LIGHTER than air as Mason held her close on the dance floor. The last several months had been an unbelievable storm of fear, pain, agony, and mounting anticipation culminating in love.

He looked delectable, his blond hair trim and his blue eyes sparkling with desire—*for her.*

He leaned in close and whispered in her ear. "It's killing me being so close and not kissing you."

She smiled. Perhaps they could leave. She had mingled with everyone she intended to see. She had her media photo taken and made her donation.

"When the song ends, we'll leave," she said.

Her eyes trailed from his mouth to his neck to his crisp tuxedo.

"I'm glad I finally got to meet Maxine. It was nice of her to come to the gala."

Mason's mouth quirked. "I've never seen her hug someone before. I know you initiated it, but there was no hesitation on her part."

"I was surprised to feel the handle of a gun poke me." Aurora giggled.

"You're still a client we're protecting."

"True."

The song ended.

"Exiting," Mason said to Billy.

She remembered Billy could hear their conversation.

As they walked toward the exit, Mason paused at a rolling display screen of the evening's top donors. Aurora followed Mason's gaze.

"Vladimir Pronin." She gaped at the name third highest on the list.

Mason shook his head. "Max said his honor had been violated when Dr. Ruchkin attacked you. Perhaps this is his way of making amends."

"I was satisfied with his word that it was finished. Do you think he has a hidden agenda?"

"With a crime boss, it's always possible, but Max thinks he's sincere on this one."

She gripped Mason's hand a little tighter. "I'm not sure about trusting the Russian mafia, but I do trust Maxine."

Mason lifted her hand to his lips and kissed the back of it. He led her out of the conference center. Billy had pulled the car around, and they climbed inside the vehicle. As she pulled away from the curb, Aurora laced her fingers in Mason's.

CHAPTER 28

Mason woke for the second time the next morning. The first time he woke he caressed Aurora's back and found her suddenly willing for another round of intimacy. The second time he woke to the sound of a knock at the door.

He looked over at his phone, which lit with a text from Billy. *Ralph, Aurora's agent, approaching.*

What a nuisance of a man. He scrubbed his hands over his face to wake himself.

He rolled out of bed and looked down at his sleeping beauty as he pulled on his pants and shirt. He didn't deserve her, but that didn't seem to stop her from giving herself to him. He would make sure she knew every day she had done the right thing. He would earn the love she so freely gave.

He reached the door, but didn't open it. "Hello?"

"Hi, Ralph Hutch here to see Aurora Meridian."

"How did you get this location?" Mason asked.

They never stayed anywhere under Aurora's name.

Ralph's tone turned sassy. "She's famous now. People recognize her, and people talk."

Mason's jaw tensed. If Ralph found them, others could too. They would have to move hotels. The options were either somewhere more obscure or one of the pricey ones where visitors couldn't reach any floor without a keycard.

"Tell him I'll meet him in the dining room in fifteen minutes," Aurora said.

Mason turned to see her awake in the bed. Her long blonde hair cascaded around her bronze shoulders. He would never tire of staring at this woman.

He relayed the message through the closed door to Ralph.

"Fine."

The sound of footsteps leaving clicked against as he pressed his ear against the door.

Mason looked back at Aurora. She sat up with the sheets pulled around her.

Darn it.

She sent him a quizzical look and smiled. "Don't worry. I've got plans for you later."

He felt his mouth go dry. He approached, leaned down, and enjoyed a succulent kiss.

He leaned back from her. "Let me clean up quickly, and I'll be out of your way."

She bit her lip as she stared at his partially buttoned shirt.

Aurora sat before Ralph as her eggs grew cold and plasticized. She dipped her tea bag up and down in her cup absentmindedly as the agent prattled on about all the labor-intensive sponsor hunting he'd been doing.

"So, I thought we would do exclusive interviews about the whole stalking, death threat incident. The public is dying—no pun intended — to hear your story from your perspective. I mean, this stuff could make you a media sensation—how you fought through the ranks despite what you endured with the letters. Then, there was an attack on your life." Ralph clutched his chest dramatically. "You haven't even given me the specifics. We can sensationalize this just a touch and you'll go from interviews to book deals."

Sensationalize.

Sen-sa-tion-al-ize. The syllables rolled around in her mind.

Sensationalize?

Aurora scowled. "I don't want to relive any part of the death threats or the attack."

"Oh, sweetie. That's okay. If you are worried about a public performance, we'll just do one-on-one interviews. Very private."

A private interview? That was an oxymoron.

"I don't want to talk about what happened ... at all."

"Just with me then, Aurora." Ralph gave a sickening sweet, disingenuous smile.

"I want to be known as Aurora the tennis sensation, not Aurora the victim."

"But you're not a victim. You're a *survivor*. You survived an attack — a mysterious attack. Do you know how difficult it is to be your agent and tell reporters I don't have any details about the attack?"

Aurora looked down and momentarily squeezed her eyes shut.

A dark hallway.

Blood dripping on the linoleum.

Black, demonic eyes hunting for her.

"No one needs those details," Aurora said.

"But they will *love* you for it."

She opened her eyes and stared at the agent. "I'm not profiting off my personal life."

Ralph leaned back in his chair. His expression grew calculating. "This is your chance to secure your future. After the US Open, no one will remember you unless you take this opportunity to grasp public interest while you can."

"You're assuming I won't win the US Open."

Ralph shot her an incredulous look, which he instantly smoothed over with a polished smile. "I want you to win, sweetie, but you need this contingency plan."

Aurora sipped her tea, set it down, and pushed it aside. Lukewarm.

"If I don't win, I don't deserve the spotlight. I'm not going to use the attack to engage the public. This is about tennis only."

Ralph gave her a dismally resigned pout. He crossed his arms. "Fine. I'll keep working on the sponsors."

They sat for a moment in silence.

Ralph seemed to come to a decision as he leaned forward. "Okay. I can respect your decision."

Aurora glanced across the room and saw Mason seated in a corner, unobtrusively watching. Her heart stuttered momentarily.

As she looked back to Ralph, she pulled her face into a neutral mask the way Mason did.

Ralph raised his arms in surrender. "It's my job to maximize your media coverage."

Except when she'd floundered in obscurity.

"Now you have established what parameters you want me to work within, I will do my best."

How magnanimous of you.

"Thank you, Ralph."

Aurora pushed her plate of uneaten food away from her. She would never let anyone profit off her pain

---

Aurora's alarm clock chimed at 5:00 a.m. She pressed snooze and cuddled back into Mason's arms. His bare, warm wall of muscle made her feel safe. The rhythmic rise and fall of his chest with each breath was comforting.

What seemed like two minutes later, it went off again.

"Nooo," she complained.

"Come on, sunshine. You've got training. I'm not going to be the reason you lose the US Open."

You might be the reason I win it.

She felt safer, more relaxed, and settled around Mason.

Protesting, she rolled out of bed and slipped into her exercise clothes. Looking back, she saw Mason watching her with intense blue eyes. How was that possible? She must look a wreck at 5:00 a.m. with unruly hair and without makeup.

Turning away, she found socks and shoes and slipped them on her feet. When she finished knotting her shoes, she looked up to see Mason dressed and slipping his earpiece off the charging dock and into his ear.

"Com check," he said, presumably to Billy or Dorian.

He put his running shoes on as she pulled her hair into a ponytail. They both slipped on their sunglasses and smiled at each other's appearance. They each dropped a keycard into their pocket. Lastly, they carried their phones as they exited the room to go for a run.

They kept a steady pace.

Aurora felt smooth focus as she breathed. Her feet carried her swiftly across the pavement. The sounds of early morning traffic surrounded her, rumbling engines and tires on asphalt.

Shops still slumbered with their storefront metal covers locked tight. Traffic lights changed into bright colors in stark contrast to the dimly lit gray sky before sunrise.

She loved New York—the bustling city with the constant reverberation of jackhammers, honking horns, and distant sirens echoing off surrounding buildings. The strange mix of wafting food scents and street garbage welcomed her. The gargantuan city somehow made her feel both minuscule and vibrantly alive.

She glanced at Mason. Her world turned in blissful harmony, even if just for one moment in time.

⁂

Aurora embraced her friend.

"I'm so proud of you," Monique said.

As they separated, Mo took a turn about the hotel room. "This room is bigger than my apartment."

The Hyatt suite had a kitchenette and lounge. The hotel was also a far cry from the motels Aurora had stayed in when she lost more than won.

Mo walked to the window.

"You can see the dome of Arthur Ashe Stadium at the USTA Billie Jean National Tennis Center," Aurora said.

"I'm gonna be watching you from center court." Mo turned back to her friend who was grinning from ear to ear. "I'm so happy for you—both tennis and Eye Candy. You've come along way from the crushed spirit I met. I knew you could do it. You learned to thrive under adversity."

"Thanks. It means a lot."

Aurora fixed a cup of tea. "Can I get you anything?"

"Pass. I'm not a tea drinker. In fact, it's kind of weird how obsessed you are with tea."

Aurora chuckled. "How's work?"

Monique circled the hotel room, still absorbing the grandeur. "The usual. Junkies, drunks, car wrecks."

Aurora walked toward the kitchen. "That's terrible."

Mo shrugged.

Aurora picked up her teacup. "You are too jaded. You need a new job."

Monique snorted. "Maybe I should join the tennis tour. I hear you created a vacancy."

Aurora laughed.

"Did you actually hit Dr. Ruchkin over the head with a racquet?"

Aurora nodded.

"I have treated some unusual traumas, but struck by a professional women's tennis player is not one of them. I looked it up. There is actually a billable medical code for struck by tennis racquet. What happened to the demonic physician by the way?"

Aurora curled up on the couch with her tea, pulling her long legs into her body. "My security team tells me he has been deported."

"Back to Russia?"

Aurora pursed her lips. "Siberia, I think."

"Siberia? People still get exiled to Siberia?"

"Apparently." Aurora's stomach flipped. Siberia wasn't a punishment—it was a disappearance.

Monique let out a tsk. She joined Aurora on the couch.

"Speaking of your security detail, where is Eye Candy?"

"His name is Mason."

"Well, I helped save his stony butt, so I deserve to meet the man you've been pining over."

Aurora narrowed her eyes at her friend. "Thank you for making me sound like a hormonal teenager with a crush."

"Girl, when we're in love, we all act like teenagers with a crush."

"Mason thought he would give you and I time to chat and then join us for dinner."

Monique leaned back and crossed her legs. "So, he's handsome, protective, and thoughtful."

"And Marco is joining us for dinner?"

Mo smiled broadly. "You picked a good one for me, Aurora. We might go places."

CHAPTER 29

New York. August. The US Open has been an emotional roller-coaster this year with both stunning wins and heartbreaking losses. One of the greatest tales of triumph is Aurora Meridian's conquest to the women's singles finals. She has had a solid performance this year, steadily rising in the ranks. This is the first of the major four tournaments in which she has advanced this far. Amazingly, her success has been as one of the oldest female players on the singles circuit and while facing death threats. Aurora has not commented on the source of the threats, but states it has been resolved and she credits her survival to 'an incredible security team' and the steadfast support of her fans.

***

*A*urora sat next to Alex on the bench as they took a break. "Thanks for practicing with me."

He nodded. "Especially since we lost the Open."

They had been defeated in the US Open mixed doubles quarterfinals.

"We'll always have Wimbledon," he said.

She took a long gulp of water. Setting the bottle down, she wrung her hands through her towel. "We could always try again next season."

Alex blinked at her. "Are you asking me to be your partner?"

She bit back a smile. "Yes, I am." Her future plans to continue mixed doubles as she built her graphic design business would keep her life in a steady balance for the next few years.

He gave her a crooked smile. "I don't know, *a stor*. I'm told my quick Irish accent's a wee challenge to decipher. And I smile incessantly, which doesn't portray fearsome on the tennis court."

"I think I can manage. That is, if you can tolerate my mood swings."

He tilted his head. "I suppose I can."

He stuffed their practice balls into his bag. "Do I have to keep putting up with the Norse bodyguard?"

"His name is Mason. And he is officially more than just a bodyguard."

"So I suspected."

"How so?"

"Well, despite a crazed lunatic coming after you with a—what did you call it?"

"A paralyzing drug."

"Yeah, that. Despite that, you're calm and glowing. You're obviously happily in a relationship with him."

"Yes, I am."

Alex used his towel to ruffle and dry the sweat in his hair, making his short hair stand on end. He looked at her with soft brown eyes.

"Good. You deserve a happy relationship."

"Thanks, Alex."

"Aye, but don't imagine I'm going to take it easy on you." He stood and thumbed the strings of his racquet.

She followed him back onto the court. "You better not."

Aurora's pulse heated as Mason traced a finger along her breastbone while they lay in bed. She'd spent the entire month of August training for the US Open and getting to know Mason better. She had no regrets that their relationship was progressing.

The US Open women's singles final competition would take place tomorrow.

"I need to tell you something, and it needs to be said before the finals," he said.

She looked at him quizzically, his serious tone piquing her interest.

He took a deep inhalation and exhalation. "I love you, Aurora. I want to marry you. And you need to know I want to marry you no matter what happens on the court tomorrow. And I'm not specifying a time frame."

She smiled.

"I believe you can win this," he continued. "I don't want to propose after the finals and have you think it had to do with the outcome."

"You're going to propose?" Her heart skipped a few beats.

"Yes."

"You're letting me know in advance you're planning to ask me to marry you?"

"Yes."

"But you're not asking me now?" she bit back an amused smile.

"No." He tensed. "I'm not prepared right now. You deserve a dinner date and a diamond ring. You deserve more time to get to know me." He lifted her hand and kissed the back of it. "I want to give you everything you deserve, but you have to know now."

She considered his words but wanted to clarify. "So, if I win, I know your proposal isn't about the money?"

A few million could tempt anyone.

"Yes."

"And if I lose, I know your proposal isn't a consolation prize?" She didn't think a man as phenomenal as Mason could be anyone's consolation prize.

"Yes."

"But, right now, you're not actually proposing?" She arched an eyebrow.

His blue eyes clouded with concern. "I'm sorry. I've never done this before. I'm doing it all wrong." He flopped back in bed, staring at the ceiling. "You don't need this type of distraction before your match. I'm a jerk."

She leaned over him, skin against skin, her hair falling onto his shoulder. Staring down at him, she was even more enamored by his emotional struggle. Her heart already belonged to him permanently. She knew his mannerisms, his career, and his convictions. The rest she could learn on their journey together.

"What if I don't want you to wait to ask me?"

His eyes snapped to hers. "Aurora, you deserve—"

"What? A ring? A ring can wait. Like you said, it's not about the money, or lack thereof. You're saying you want to ask me to marry you. I'm saying I want to say yes." As she spoke, she maneuvered over him completely and slid down against him.

He sucked in a sharp breath.

"So, why are we waiting for me to play a tennis match and you to buy a—"

He grabbed her shoulders and pulled her closer. "Marry me, Aurora Mercedes Meridian."

His voice resonated with such an aching desire she stilled in his arms. She stared into his intoxicating blue eyes.

"Yes." She melted into him, pressing kisses along his bare chest while feeling his arousal press against her.

Pushing up, she retrieved a condom from the nightstand, opened it, and rolled it on to him as his eyes glazed with desire.

When she slid back over him, taking him inside, he murmured her name. He let her move her hips and set the pace as his hands roamed, caressed, and heightened the pleasure.

His mouth found her breasts and she gasped her approval. Fused and moving in unison, she let the friction build until pleasure exploded through her body. His arms crushed her down to him as his last few delicious thrusts took him over the edge.

Liquid and languid, she melted into him.

AURORA HAD ENTERED the last major tournament of the season. The culmination of years of hard work had climaxed in reaching the US Open women's singles finals. Her opponent was ranked fifth in the world—Slavica Stefanovic.

She marveled at the packed seats at Arthur Ashe Stadium. The roof was retracted, allowing the September sun to fill the arena. Once these grounds were a natural wetland turned coal ash depository. Now, F. Scott Fitzgerald's Valley of Ashes held the largest tennis stadium in the world. Over twenty thousand people looked down at the blue and green court.

The hardcourt would be slower play compared to slick grass, but faster than clay. The US Open and other professional courts added sand to the paint composition to slow the ball and thus slow the pace of play.

Aurora had made it to the finals. Her body zinged with excitement, anticipation, and adrenaline.

After her semifinal win two days ago, she'd trouble sorting through her feelings. She had been ecstatic just to make it that far. Did she need the grand slam win? How important was victory at tennis when she had achieved victory at life? She'd survived the last attack, she'd won Mason, and she'd progressed further on the tennis circuit than she had done in a long time. What did the US Open title achieve?

How could she win with this mentality? If she wasn't craving the win—demanding it with every ounce of her being—how could she expect to win? Where was her kill or be killed ambition?

She stood on center court as her eyes panned the crowd. Fear and worry had so long been her dark companions that she basked in the warmth of their absence. She looked at Mason, dutifully by the entrance. He gave her a smile and a nod.

My fiancé.

She felt ready to spend a lifetime loving him. Win or lose.

In that instant, she found her resolve. Every sound on the court became crisp—the peeling metal of a new can of balls opening, the yellow chick bouncing on the smooth court surface, the squeak of her shoes and swish of her skirt.

She wanted to win. The familiar craving rose within her. She envisioned it happening from her first service game to her last down-the-line slice backhand.

Her motions flowed flawlessly as her legs swiftly covered the court, her wrist snapping at the serve, and her knees bending at the net.

Wheels up, Aurora.

She took the first set by storm, disrupting the predictions she would be defeated in straight sets.

The second set proved more of a struggle. She was down three games. Her service game had been broken. Her opponent kept the ball to her less powerful backhand. Slavica strategically ran her side to side, back and forth, and up and down the court, working to wear down Aurora. Now, the third set would come easier to Slavica.

Aurora sat on the bench and drank water.

I'm down three games.

She wouldn't come back. She never came back. A losing game was a lost game.

She stood. Her eyes panned the crowd as she walked to the base-line ready to be on serve. Alex sat in the crowd giving her a strained smile. Mason remained impassive. Mo leaned so far on the edge of her seat she looked like she might fall out of it. Her parents clasped hands in a white knuckled grip. Maxine squinted in an expression that appeared painful. Coach Jareh gave a determined gaze as he did when he was pleased with one of her serves. Even Lizzy had made it to the finals, traveling from Europe after her last ITF tournament.

She sat with one fist clenched as if ready to launch it into the air in victory for her friend.

The rest of the crowd pulsated with fear and hope, pressing in on her, willing her to win. There were claps and fans calling her name.

She didn't want to lose. Not today. Not here.

She remembered telling Mason, "When I'm losing, I don't have the confidence to pull it off."

In singles she wasn't able to make a comeback; paradoxically, she had managed it in doubles.

It was time to break the cycle and turn her singles game to her favor.

Prison rules.

Aurora shook out her limbs. For the next twenty minutes she would have to be fast and aggressive. Hurt as it may, this was her only path to victory.

She embraced the aggression, serving and volleying. She forced pressured points on her opponent. When her opponent served, she took the serve early, returning the ball before Slavica had reset her stance.

She'd noticed the player's backhand had lost pace. Aurora wondered if Slavica had tweaked her left wrist. The next game entailed rapid serve and volley again, keeping shots to her opponent's backhand.

She was tied three to three in the second set. She had fought her way back to even the score.

Aurora didn't break Slavica's serve in the next game—three to four as they switched sides.

After several long rallies and key aces, Aurora tied the game. Four to four.

Point by steady point, Aurora kept her focus. She finally broke Slavica's powerful serve.

A few harrowing points later and Aurora was up forty-thirty and on serve. She didn't dare pan her eyes around the stadium.

There is no crowd.

No sun. No heat. She envisioned herself on the cracked, worn court outside London, rain pouring down around her. Only her and the yellow chick. No one else. She would strategically place the serve down the line. As she had that day. As she had a thousand times before this moment.

Sync.

Aurora took a second to register the ace. The crowd unleashed a defining roar. She clutched her racket to her chest as she basked in the glory of her win.

The women's singles US Open championship belonged to her.

STANDING in Arthur Ashe Stadium and accepting the US Open trophy felt surreal. The cool metal gleamed in the sunlight. She hardly heard the announcer's words.

Abruptly, the microphone appeared in front of her. Damn, she should have rehearsed something. Winning had been so unexpected. She thanked her family, her sponsor, her friends, and her security team. Lastly, she thanked her fans and all tennis fans for supporting the sport.

The interviewer flashed a pristine smile at her and the camera. "Congratulations again, Aurora. You fought your way to the top this season and demonstrated an amazing turnaround. How does it feel to transition from unlikely victor to US Open champion?"

She smiled. "I am awed and exhilarated to be here."

He nodded at the camera. "What's next for the great Prime Meridian?"

Aurora kept her smile firmly in place. She wasn't going to let old titles ruin her happiness.

"I'll finish out the season and hope to finish strong, but this is my last singles season."

Primordial soup. She was finished. Her body screamed in agony after three sets of singles. Tennis had been her life, her everything. Now her body and mind were ready for the next phase.

Her graphic design business.

Her relationship with Mason.

Competitive doubles with good friends.

"You want to expound on your retirement?"

"Yes, stay tuned later this week for the full interview I'll be doing with Marco Gold." She had to give Marco his due. Through her highs and lows he continued to report on her while honoring her requests of what would and would not be printed.

"Will we still have mixed doubles to watch you in? With Alex Rory?"

"Yes. Alex is a phenomenal doubles partner, and I wouldn't have made it this far without him. We hope to be in more majors together next year."

"Wonderful. We look forward to more great tennis. Congratulations, again."

"Thank you."

She continued to stand and smile as the announcer addressed the audience and remarked on all of the amazing outcomes and upsets in this year's US Open.

Aurora tuned him out and looked toward the exit of the court. She set her eyes on Mason standing at attention, smiling and waiting.

Her fiancé. Win or lose. But she had won. She won her freedom from threats, she won Mason, and she won the US Open.

<<<~~~>>>

****QUICK NOTE FROM THE AUTHOR****

Are you ready to embark on a new adventure with the next Rider Files couple? Do you want to learn more about Maxine and Vladimir?

She's running from the mob. He's running from his past.
Sparks and bullets fly in this romantic suspense
adventure.

Find out more in **Masters File,** The Rider Files Book 2.

———·—

KEEP READING the series to watch Billy get in over her head—and heart—when she's assign to protect rockstar Ethan Storm (*Storm File, Book 5*).

Keep reading the series to find out what secrets Dorian's daughter is keeping from him (*Sizani File, Book 8*).

———·—

DO you want Rider File story from me?

In the bustling streets of a sprawling Atlanta metropolis, where shadows dance and danger lurks around every corner, an unlikely love story unfolds amidst the web of a gripping romantic suspense thriller.

When the notorious Chinese mafia sets its sights on tightening its grip over the city's underworld, chaos ensues. As the danger escalates, a resilient female cop, Diz Ocana, finds herself thrust into the heart of her friend's kidnapping.

Meanwhile, skilled and compassionate paramedic Rico Cabrera, has dedicated his life to saving others. Growing up in the same neighborhood as Diz, he knows firsthand the darkness that plagues their city. Fate reunites them, kindling a connection that defies the boundaries of their respective roles.

*~~~***<<<GRAB CABRERA FILE HERE>>>***~~~*

THE RIDER FILES SERIES

Meridian File / Masters File / Box Set 1

McMillan File / Maltisse File /Box Set 2

Storm File / Sullivan File / Box Set 3

Sharp File / Sizani File / Box Set 4

Rivera File / Rucker File / Box Set 5

Richmond File / Redwood File / Box Set 6

Atlas File / Angel File / Box Set 7

Buy 4book box sets direct from author and save 10%

Payhip. Use code E152M0GZG4

DEAR READER

Want to keep in touch?

If you enjoyed this book and want to know about future releases by CB Samet you can CLICK HERE to sign up for my mailing list! I promise I won't spam you. I only send an email when I have a new book released, giveaways, or special discounts. You can also unsubscribe at any time.

If you loved this book, kindly let others know by posing a brief comment on social media or leave a review where you purchased it so readers can find their next favorite romantic suspense series.

Even more ways to follow me below!

Thank you for reading,
    CB Samet

OTHER BOOKS BY CB SAMET

Looking for more romantic suspense? How about with an urban fantasy twist? Check out my supernatural adventures...

The Shadow Guardians Trilogy

Urban fantasy Norse Mythology Adventure

Get *Raven's Flight, a prequel novella* for FREE. In my newsletter, you'll learn about me, special discounts, and new releases.

Raven's Flight, prequel novella

Raine Down, Book 1

Rosalyn's Run, novella

Storm Surge, Book 2

Anka's Orb, novella

Sky Fall, Book 3

Olympian Awakenings Trilogy

Urban fantasy Greek Mythology Adventure

Grab the prequel exclusively HERE.

Stone Hearts

Winds of Destiny

Flame and Shadow

The Dr. Whyte Adventure Novels

Thriller Series

Black Gold

Whyte Knight

Gray Horizon

Sweet Romantic Suspense

"Well-written... tales of love and ghosts."

— KIRKUS REVIEW

IN BOXED SETS

Romancing the Spirit Series #1

Sadie's Spirit / Willow's Windfall

Cassie's Chase / Phoebe's Pharaoh

Vanessa's Valentine / Autumn's Angel

Romancing the Spirit Series #2

Carol's Christmas / Allison's Alibi

Gracelynn's Genie / Michelle's Miracle

Heather's Hero / Chloe's Cupid

Follow Me

BOOKBUB

FACEBOOK

YOUTUBE

PINTEREST

INSTAGRAM

GOODREADS

CHIRP

TIKTOK